MA

15 Lovely Loci

A NOVEL

CreateSpace Independent Publishing Platform
ISBN 9781726421331

For Angie, my rising star.

"We fight it down, and we live it down,
Or we bear it bravely well,
But the best men die of a broken heart
For the things they cannot tell."

- *Henry Lawson*

Stars in the Sky

Stars in the sky, like two bright eyes,
Are shining down at me.
As their bright light gleams, once again it seems
You're with me in my memories.

I am waiting once more
watching stars in the sky
Longing for you
and another June night.
Still the soft breezes sigh
as when we said goodbye,
Long ago…
'neathe the stars in the sky.

Wondering if you are lonely too,
Hoping the stars will tell
That I love you still 'neath their silvery hue
And hope you have memories, too.

\- *Nellie Raymond*

CHAPTER 1

GRACE
FRIDAY, AUGUST 31, 2018

It was in the twilight of summer—before the dawn—when Grace McKenzie Clark finally pulled onto the notoriously bumpy, unlit road leading to her family's summer home. Blue lights illuminated the dashboard: 5:57. *Good. Still very early*, she thought, as she drove the well-known, yet seldomly used dirt road. *Still a few more hours before Jack and Matthew are due to arrive.* Plenty of time to re-rehearse what she was planning to ask them, given the chance. How, exactly, she would form the questions for her two older brothers she had no idea, but decided she'd figure it all out later. She usually did.

Unable to sleep the night before, Grace had been driving in the dark, white knuckled, from her home in Philadelphia to central New York state for the better part of five hours. Her family's small cottage, located a few miles northwest of Ithaca, in Trumansburg, was now is sight. It had provided 250 feet of lake shore rest and relaxation for the McKenzies for more than forty summers. Something Grace really needed now. *A little R&R*, she thought. She welcomed the sight as she parked her late model Land Rover in the familiar gravel driveway and finally exhaled.

Feeling confident she was doing the right thing by coming home for the long Labor Day weekend, Grace turned off the car's ignition and lowered the window. Her thoughts began to drift, peacefully, listening to the familiar sounds of dawn over the lake: small waves rolling gently to the shore, a half dozen or so squirrels scurrying over dry, crumbled leaves, ripe acorns dropping to the ground from century-old trees, one by one, and several birds chirping all around her; the species of each easily identifiable thanks to her dad's excellent tutelage.

As the sun began to rise, Grace thought more about her dad. It was here at the cottage, as she had hoped, that her fondest memories of him would come back to her. Although the memories would surely spark the fire within her heart, reigniting her recently-acquired depressed emotional state, she was willing to endure a little more pain in order to accomplish her goal of learning the truth.

With a heavy sigh, she opened the car door and stepped outside into the brisk, autumn-like air. Trails of smoke from the neighbors' nightly bonfires lingered in the air, mimicking the fog over the lake. She opened the back door for Bailey, her four-year-old chocolate lab, who jumped from the bench seat and took off running straight towards the lake.

"Okay, boy, but just a quick..." The sound of Grace's voice faded into oblivion as Bailey jumped into the chilly water with a loud and hardy *plop*.

"Crazy dog," Grace mumbled as she watched him swim towards the little island of trees a hundred feet out from the shore. Shaking her head with a chuckle, she gathered her two overnight bags from the back, flung one over each shoulder and followed the slate stepping stones leading to the front of the cottage. As she walked, bright yellow, orange, and red leaves scuttled along the path and swirled around her ankles.

The cottage wasn't much; simply a modest, three-bedroom bungalow approximately 1,500 square feet in total, but it was paid off and one-third hers. Hardie board siding, once painted a handsome, inky blue—a custom color that she and her dad had selected after staring at dozens of tiny paint chips for weeks—was badly weathered and beginning to chip underneath the eaves. Grace made a mental note to remind Matthew it was time to repaint again. But the wrap around porch, she soon discovered, was as strong as ever and something else that reminded her of her dad. She paused near the front door and dropped her bags.

They had built the porch in 1999, she and her brothers, with their dad's help. It'd been the year after their mother had mercifully died, following a sixteen-year stint battling early-onset Alzheimer's disease. Upon receiving the news of her mother's death, then twenty-nine-year-old Grace reported for work the very next morning—much to everyone's surprise—to explain that although her mother had indeed just passed away, she actually died in her mind when she was sixteen; when her mother could no longer remember her name.

"Oh, Grace, I never knew," her boss, Dr. Margaret Liu, had replied. Grace shrugged her shoulders and returned to her desk. A few tense moments later, after Dr. Liu had formed a story in her head, she added, "This must mean you never really knew your mom? As an adult, I mean."

"Yeah," Grace said, grinding her back teeth. She had a hard and fast rule: never share too much of yourself at work. "The funeral is on Saturday, so I won't need any time off." With that, their brief conversation regarding her mother and her recent death was concluded, never to be spoken between the two women again. When Grace returned home the following summer in order to help build the enormous porch, she was anxious to get away from the hustle and bustle of big-city life for a little while, too. Although Upstate New York never really felt like home to her, at least not the small town of Cincinnatus where she and her brothers were raised, it was always nice to return home for a visit. Especially to the cottage.

This year was no exception.

Grace followed the porch around to the back of the cottage to check on Bailey. The days were turning very chilly here. *Much earlier than in Philadelphia.* She wrapped her wool sweater a little tighter around herself. The porch, she recalled with each additional step, was originally designed so that all four Adirondack chairs that their dad had built to adorn it could easily be moved from front to back. The front of the cottage faced west where one could sit and watch the sun set over the distant hills, something Dad especially enjoyed. The back of the cottage, Grace's favorite, was where the sun rose each morning and sparkled brightly on cloudless days over the lake.

Eventually, however, it seemed silly to everyone involved to keep moving the heavy chairs from front to back and vice versa. Therefore, and for the last six years since their father's death, all four sturdy chairs rest permanently on the front of the porch as Dad would have preferred. Their back-porch-replacements: four new, but cheap, vinyl white knock-offs that Matthew's wife purchased two months earlier, were now scattered haphazardly around the back yard.

Strong wind, Grace surmised as she stepped down off of the porch and began to collect them. Once all four chairs where back where they belonged, she pressed her finger and thumb into the corners of her mouth and let out a loud whistle. "Bailey, come."

Duty-bound, Bailey quickly swam to the shore, pausing only to shake himself, vigorously, before returning to her side. Grace couldn't imagine her life, at the age of forty-eight, without her constant companion, Bailey. After she and her ex-husband, Paul Clark, had finally divorced last year, after fifteen years of marriage, Grace decided she needed someone loyal in her life. A good dog, perhaps. Bailey fulfilled her requirements perfectly. Ever since she first laid eyes on him sitting at the front of his cage in the local shelter waiting patiently to be adored, she knew he was the one for her. It was truly love at first sight.

"Good boy," Grace said, wiping him down with an old towel she found hanging on a hook near the back door. Once he was sufficiently dried, she walked around to the front of the cottage. Bailey followed.

Inside, the stagnant, dank smell of the friendless cottage—it had been far too long since anyone had vacationed here—mixed with the undeniable smell of kerosene and accosted her senses. She spotted two offending oil lamps—something else her sister-in-law had probably purchased—on top of the mantel and took them outside to rest on the front porch. Back inside the cottage, the air, thick with dust, was illuminated by shafts of light streaming through the cloudy windows. Old cobwebs on the ceiling and walls billowed from the draft coming through the opened door. But the absolute silence, not even the hum of the refrigerator, was the worst of all. *God awful silence.* Nothing like the bygone summer days she remembered well.

After closing the front door, Grace opened all of the sooty windows as far as they would go, plugged in the refrigerator, and got to work. Dusty white sheets covered the sparse furniture in the main room: four comfortable chairs, an ottoman, and a beat-up old love seat. Grace pulled the sheets off and threw them in the washing machine. Next, she made her way to each of the three bedrooms, stripping the beds to air out the mattresses. Fresh linens were then collected from the hall closet and left in each bedroom. Finally, with clean sheets tumbling in the dryer, the lemon-fresh smell of furniture polish lingering in the air, dry wood crackling in the fireplace and one lit jasmine-scented candle later, the cottage was once again acceptable. Smells and all.

Checking the time once more, Grace was surprised to see that more than two hours had already passed. Jack and Matthew were expected any minute, and she hadn't spent any additional time figuring out what or how she would ask the questions she had for them. Her heart began to race. She spread a blanket out on the floor in front of the fireplace and took a seat, trying to calm herself. Bailey rested his head in her lap—that helped.

She watched the yellow flames dance blissfully beyond the hearth, envying their carefree waltz. *It can't be true!* Grace choked back tears for a moment before she decided she'd allow her heart to take the lead. All her mind knew for sure was that she wanted answers. Answers she hoped Jack and Matthew would be able to provide. Matthew, more cantankerous than ever, would probably remain tight-lipped and glare at her the entire time she spoke, or simply storm out of the cottage and go back home. Especially if what she suspected was true. *Family is too important to him. He'd probably take a beating before admitting to any of it.*

But Jack, her oldest and more level-headed brother, might crack under pressure. Open up and spill his guts; tell her everything he knew, if anything at all. *That was the plan.* "What do you think Bailey, will it work?"

Bailey licked her face. She rubbed the top of his head and turned around to face the fire again just as a thick log popped, relinquishing bright yellow sparks of amber into the air. Startled, she backed away from the hearth.

Bailey backed away too, but it wasn't the sparks that caused him to move so quickly. With a steady gait, he crossed the living room, pushed open the front screen door with his nose and began to bark.

Matthew, Grace saw upon standing, had just arrived. She ran her fingers over the top of her head, combing her long hair away from her face.

Outside, Bailey by her side, they both watched as Matthew stepped out of his pick-up and shot Grace a quick wave. "Howdy, Sis."

She smiled.

In the morning light, Matthew wore his sixty-one years well. His once blonde hair, now completely gray, remained thick with disobedience. The unruly mane had always suited him well. Untamed yet attractive, but as far removed from anything consider typical GQ male good looks. *Exactly Matthew.*

Grace stepped down off the porch and greeted her brother with a customary peck on the cheek and brief embrace. "You look good, Matthew. And you're right on time."

"You said nine, right?" Grace smiled and nodded her head. "Coffee on?"

"Of course. Come on in, I'll pour us each a cup."

"Right behind you," he said, retrieving a large, camouflage-print duffel bag and two fishing poles from the bed of the truck. Once he stepped onto the porch, Bailey approached him and let out another loud bark.

"Your dog doesn't like me."

"Nobody likes you," Grace teased. "Bailey, come."

Bailey let out a small gruff in Matthew's direction, followed by a long sniff before returning to Grace's side.

Matthew gingerly followed his sister—five steps behind Bailey—and set his bag down on the floor. "Fuckin' dogs."

"I see you're still afraid of them," Grace said as selected two large coffee mugs from the hooks where a mix-matched set of six hung above the stove.

"I'm telling you, Sis, they don't like me. None of them do," Matthew said, keeping both eyes squarely fixed on the dog.

"That's because they sense your fear, dummy."

"Who, me?" He let out a nervous laugh, but Grace could tell he was still afraid. *And of Bailey? How foolish.* Although she'd heard the story many times of how Matthew had been attacked by a neighbor's dog when he was only six, she couldn't quite understand the strength of his fear now. Like most of her older brothers' stories, it happened way before she was born so she wasn't there to witness the attack.

"Still take yours black?" She asked, pouring coffee into each mug.

"Affirmative."

Grace smiled again, crossed the living room and handed him a cup. "Let's sit out on the front porch and wait for Jack."

"The dog, too?" Matthew asked, leading the way.

"Yes, Matthew, the dog too."

The pair settled into two of the Adirondack chairs and began sipping their coffee. Bailey rested comfortably besides Grace and soon fell asleep—much to Matthew's delight.

"So, what's this all about Sis? Why'd you summon us both up here for the entire weekend?"

A lump rose in Grace's throat. Trying to buy some additional time to think, she took another sip—a large one this time—and swallowed hard before responding. "I'll explain everything after Jack gets here," she said, somewhat abruptly, before burying her face into the giant mug again.

Matthew furrowed his brow but said nothing more on the subject. He clearly knew he'd get his answers soon enough. After pondering a few seconds longer what his sister could possibly be up to this time, he finally abandoned the thought entirely and changed the subject. "I love it up here in the fall."

"Yeah, why's that?" Grace was relieved that the subject of their conversation had indeed changed.

"Summers are too damn hot and humid, and spring is just so goddamn unpredictable. Winters up here are long, cold, and depressing; there are no other words to describe them. But fall is perfect. Sometimes I walk outside on days like today and think to myself, this weather couldn't possibly be any more perfect. It's just the right combination of sun and clouds, mixed with a slight chill. Best sleeping weather too, if you ask me. Nope," he said, after swallowing the last drop of his coffee. "There's nothing that can compare to fall in the Finger Lakes, least not for me."

"I never thought about it that way before, but I guess you're right."

"I'm always right. Remember?" He smiled at his own joke and stood up. "You need a refill?"

"No, I'm good. One cup is it for me."

"Suit yourself," he said, leaving her alone with her new thoughts of fall as he walked back inside of the cottage and poured himself a second cup.

Matthew had followed in their father's footsteps, choosing to work mostly blue-collar jobs. But, during his first five years of employment with SYSCO, driving trucks, he never missed a single day of work other than previously scheduled vacation days, which eventually caught the attention of upper management. Before long, due to nothing more than absolute grit, ambition, and God-given smarts, he settled into a desk job as an area sales manager and began earning upwards of six figures, years before older brother Jack had done the same. A luxury that funded Sandy—his high school sweetheart and wife—her weekly manicures, pedicures and monthly shopping trips to Manhattan with her many friends. They were comfortable.

After refilling his mug, Matthew rejoined Grace on the front porch and, as before, seated himself as far away from Bailey as he could manage. He lifted the hot mug to his lips and took a big gulp just as Grace 's cellphone began to chirp. "I bet it's Jack." He swallowed and rested his mug on the chair's ample armrest. "Bastard's always late."

Grace pulled her phone from her sweater pocket and checked the message. "You're right. It's a text from Jack." Realizing a second too late what she had blurted out, she added, "Please don't say it... I know, you're always right."

Matthew shrugged his shoulders and smirked. "He's going to be late again, right?"

She read Jack's text aloud: "Running late. Be there by noon. Tell Matty I said fuck you." Grace and Matthew shared a mutual smirk before she returned Jack's text with a simple "OK" and dropped her phone back into her pocket.

"So, that's that," she said, secretly relieved that Jack was going to be arriving late. It would give her some additional time to think.

While Matthew finished his coffee, they sat in silence enjoying the fall view together. The air was growing colder, but the trees were ablaze with color. Red and gold leaves licked at the bright blue sky. Grace stood up and stretched her arms above her head. "I'm going to head down to the lake for a little bit."

"You want some company?"

"Nah, I think I'll just take Bailey. I want to tire him out before Jack arrives. I'm going to walk him down to Taughannock Point and back."

"Damn Grace, that's like three and half miles each way. Are you trying to tire it or kill it?"

Ignoring her furry friend being referred to as an "it," she began walking towards her car. "Don't be silly, we take long walks together all the time at home. Six miles is nothing."

Matthew scowled. "First of all, I'm never silly, and second, I think it's a stupid idea. But, heck, have a nice walk."

Sarcasm noted, Grace ignored him, opened the back door of her car and grabbed the leash. "Come on Bailey, let's go."

Bailey jumped from his slumber, chased after her towards the lake, and they were gone.

CHAPTER 2

AUDREY
MONDAY, JUNE 23, 1969

Audrey McKenzie stretched her upper torso and leaned over the bench seat of her powder blue '65 Ford Cortina and glanced in the rear-view mirror. It was unusually warm for June, probably 90 degrees already, and very humid. Now that she had finally convinced Shea—her husband of seventeen years—to allow her to volunteer at a newly-created camp for blind children the entire summer, she wanted to be sure she looked the part: intelligent, prepared, and very professional.

The minimal makeup she wore appeared morning fresh, and her hair was still in place, but probably wouldn't be by the time she arrived. Especially after having no other choice than to open all four car windows; the only way she could possibly hope to gain any relief from the oppressive heat. Not exactly the weather she had hoped for her commute from Cincinnatus to Trumansburg, but at least it was a clear, sunny day. One which included the sharp, fresh scent of newly cut grass drifting on the summer's breeze. Besides, Audrey was happy with practically any weather conditions as long as nothing prevented her from finally being on her way. Which, naturally, a little heatwave could not.

Backing down the driveway of their rented home, Audrey was relieved that her two teen sons, Jack and Matthew, weren't home to watch her drive away. Pangs of guilt gnawed away at her gut as she turned the corner onto Telephone Road and headed west out of town. Even though she meant every word she had said to Shea only two weeks earlier, she still felt guilty leaving her family alone for the entire summer. Especially the boys. But her desire to get away for a little while wasn't because she didn't care about them—of course she did—but more to do with the fact that she didn't feel professionally fulfilled in her life. Never once had she accomplished anything that she felt particularly proud of, less her two sons.

She had explained to Shea that she intended to spend her days helping out around the camp in any way that she could: cooking, cleaning, doing dishes and the like, but her main objective (and the reason she was hired) was to read aloud, as often as would be tolerated, to the many blind children.

Shea didn't understand any of it, but then he never really did understand Audrey. In the end, he agreed to let her go, as long as she was back before the boys returned to school in the fall. Once she assured him that she'd be home in plenty of time before then, she immediately began packing for what would certainly be the adventure of a lifetime.

As she continued to drive, her guilt grew more intense. she hadn't been completely honest with Shea regarding her desire to get away. The real reason, she knew, was far more troubling, but also something she wasn't prepared to deal with. Not yet, anyway. Audrey shook her head as if to dislodge the unpleasant thought.

Her sudden need to get away for an entire summer was because she feared she was growing old entirely too soon; simply worn out from living with Shea. Deep down, she thought she still loved him. *But, shouldn't a wife know for sure whether or not she still loves her husband?*

A long time ago, she had known for sure that she loved Shea. Life had been simpler then, before the boys came along—nearly fifteen years ago now. In the early years of their marriage, they'd spent many loving hours beneath the sheets, enjoying quiet conversations all alone in the dark. But now, and sometime since year two of their marriage, Shea's true self crept into their union like a thief through an unlocked window. It was then that he began spending most evenings away from home, drinking. He'd drink with his friends or, if necessary, all by himself. He didn't care, as long as he could have a drink. *Or ten.*

It was true that most of Audrey's friends' husbands expected their wives to tend to their children's needs, as she has always done, but shouldn't her husband at least be home at night to occasionally help out? Audrey certainly thought so.

Shea had once truly been charming. In the early years, he used to tell her he couldn't stand being away from her for even an hour, and rarely ever was, with the exception of when he had to work. Now, though, all he seemed to want to do was drink and, of course, fish. It left very little time for her.

Audrey knew that if Shea could figure out a way to fish every day he would, but his day job got in the way of that. Thank God. It was true that he had always provided for she and the boys, well enough, anyway. They could have probably purchased a home of their own by now from what Shea earned as a supervisor, if he didn't spend so much of his money on whiskey and beer, leaving his family to eat dinner at home alone.

21

His drinking wasn't even the worst part of it. She winced, thinking about what was, and almost missed her next turn onto N.Y. Route 392: his drunken self, rubbing up against her naked flesh, his breath reeking of stale beer and whiskey.

"Damn it, Shea!" She took a hard left onto the county road leading her further west.

Shaking off the unpleasant memory of the night before, she decided she needed to stop thinking about Shea in order to pay attention to her written directions resting on the seat beside her. She would just have to figure out what to do about her troubled marriage later, when she had some quality time alone to think.

Resolved, and well on her way to the camp, Audrey began to smile again. Soon she would finally be sharing the marvelous words of Poe, Shakespeare, Whitman, and Austen with the children. Children she hoped would be unlike her own two, who didn't appreciate the finer things that life had to offer. Especially poetry. "Too much like their brash Irish father," she whispered.

She allowed her mind to wander some more, and soon she was thinking of nothing else but the many poets she adored. Their tender words meant so much to her; now and when she was a young child growing up. Words so special, no matter how many times she reread them, they always moved something deep within her. As if the magnificent pairing of such eloquent words, with perfect syllables so carefully selected by each poet, were gracing her ears for the very first time.

Classics such as *The Raven,* by Poe; or the graceful simplicity of *This Little Bag*, by Jane Austen; and, oh, the many sonnets of William Shakespeare! *How can one possibly select a favorite?* "Shall I compare thee to a summer's day?" The words slipped through her lips as a gentle whisper.

She'd have to remember to speak up when reading to the children. Her soft volume of speech was something she had grown accustomed to. A habit she acquired while Shea was at work and the boys at school, as this was when she pampered herself with her favorite pastime: reciting beautifully-written poetry.

Shea in particular didn't care for her poetry, or any other form of reading simply for pleasure. He felt that reading was "a nice to have, a skill, a necessity, if you will," he had explained. "In order to help one land gainful employment."

Audrey shook her head, thinking about Shea's position at the local dairy plant which required little to no reading at all. "What a joke," she whispered again. And just like that, her thoughts drifted back to reality; but this time, mainly, to the current whereabouts of her two sons.

Both boys had already headed out to their summer jobs earlier that morning. Jack, older and more practical, had successfully landed a position at nearby Doug's Dairy, the local ice cream joint operated by the Houck family. He was hired to arrive an hour before the small shop was scheduled to open, set up and scoop ice cream throughout the day. It was a simple enough job that paid fairly well and located only a few short blocks from their home; an easy bicycle ride to and from.

Matthew, her stubborn-born son, however, insisted that he would continue to work long, hard hours every day during the summer for Mr. Dalrymple, even though his dairy farm was located on the other side of Marathon, a good twenty miles away. No matter how much she pleaded with him to quit he wouldn't budge. *Matthew's heart was always in the right place but his head not so much.* It was true that Dalrymple needed him (and his dirt-cheap rate of seventy-five cents per hour) to survive and, she admitted, the free milk and eggs they received from time to time were always welcomed. However, she felt that it was time for Matty (as she called him) to move on from farm work. Matthew wouldn't even consider her logic, not while Mr. Dalrymple still needed his help. "Even if it does take me more than an hour to ride my bike each way, I'm not going to quit!"

Yes, Matthew was definitely the obstinate one; always trying to conceal his tender heart, too. But Audrey knew his true gentleness no matter how many times his bad temperament got in his way. A sentimental boy—a true Irishman—for sure, was her Matty. When she discovered him sneaking saucers of milk out each night for the stray cats in the neighborhood, he made her promise she'd never tell a soul, especially not Dad or Jack. She never did.

Unlike Shea, 100% Irish—third generation of those straight off the boat from Ireland, in fact—Audrey was a refined mix of English, Scottish and Welsh. As a result, she dubbed her children's unique ancestral blend as the 'The British Isles' very early on. A term Jack and Matthew felt equally proud of hearing her repeat time and time again over the years, especially while tucking them into bed each night. "Good-night, my darling little British Isle boys."

Audrey glanced down at her wristwatch and realized she must almost be to Trumansburg. Although it was hotter than ever now, making the drive entirely more arduous, she was surprised how quickly time had passed. Before pulling into Camp Vision (a very stupid name for a camp for blind children, she felt) at precisely 3:00 p.m., Audrey made a mental note to write a letter to the boys each and every week.

Once inside the camp grounds, she parked alongside a conspicuously fancy white motorcycle. She turned off the car's ignition, wondering who it belonged to, before turning her attention back to her rear-view mirror. Her once neatly-coiffed hair was now a wind-blown mess, just as she suspected it would be. Always prepared, she reached into her pocketbook and pulled out a few spare bobby pins, a hairbrush, and a tube of lipstick. After a few tucks of her hair here, a twist there and her favorite shade of lipstick, *Kiss Me Pink*, was evenly smoothed over her full lips, she regained her confidence and swung her legs out from the car and stood up.

In the peak of life, aged just thirty-seven years, Audrey McKenzie never looked more beautiful.

CHAPTER 3

GRACE
FRIDAY, AUGUST 31, 2018

Located a stone's throw north of Kingtown Beach—a seasonal resort offering a few rental cabins, cottages, and a couple of yurts— was where the McKenzie cottage had sat on the west shore of Cayuga Lake since 1971. Grace and Bailey began walking south past Kingtown, towards the direction of the point; another three miles further down the lake.

Taughannock Point was near the sight of a now defunct summer camp for blind children. Grace's mother had spoken of the camp often when she was very young; telling Grace of the time she'd worked there; the summer before Grace had been born.

As they walked, Grace realized it was useless trying to remember the brief conversations she had with her mother more than forty years ago about a summer camp that no longer existed. Impossible, in fact. Even so, she couldn't help trying to remember what it was her mother had done there. All she clearly remembered was how her mother's face would light up every time she spoke of the summer camp. The name of the establishment, Camp Vision, was a no-brainer. Grace had always felt it was a very stupid name for a camp for blind kids. Naturally, she never shared this observation with her mother. *Never make waves. Check.*

Growing up, Grace had been extremely focused, working very hard in order to secure a future for herself anywhere else than in Upstate New York. The mere thought of never leaving her small hometown had often made her feel physically ill. There was so much more elsewhere, she was certain—just waiting for her. She wanted to be somebody. So, according to her plan, after completing her bachelor's degree at SUNY Cortland and earning a master's from Upstate Medical in Syracuse, she quickly landed a job as a Physician's Assistant in Philadelphia where she still worked today. Jack and Matthew, on the other hand, never left New York state and chose to raise their nine children; Jack, four and Matthew, five, in Cincinnatus.

There were other ways that Grace felt she differed from her older siblings, besides her desire to move away. Little things, mainly, like the fact that they had blue eyes like their parents, and hers were very dark brown. But she also had a sort of feeling that something was amiss between them. It just wasn't anything she was willing to discuss with anyone, much less her family. Growing up in the McKenzie household, one didn't speak of things that would be considered "uncomfortable." A lesson Grace learned early in life, at the age of five, when her mother suddenly stopped attending weekly Mass with them.

"Why doesn't Mommy go to church anymore?" She had asked her father one Sunday morning as they walked the three short blocks from their home to Our Lady of Perpetual Hope. Her father's immediate silence signaled that he wasn't about to answer her insensitive question and, furthermore, she shouldn't have asked him in the first place. *Lesson learned.*

Once they were past Kingtown Beach, and people, Grace released Bailey from his lead and allowed him to roam freely in front of her. Soon, Grace 's memories returned to those of her dad, as they always did. It made perfect sense, she thought, considering she spent the majority of her days growing up with him and not her mother. Besides, the last years of her mother's life were too sad for her to think about right now. Especially the first two years leading up to her final diagnosis.

At the age of sixteen, when the diagnosis was finally made, it was too much for Grace to bear. Entirely too much. It still hurt, but she'd learned not to think of those days too often anymore. They only served as an unpleasant reminder that she never got to know her mother as a person, due to the early-onset of her illness at the appallingly young age of 54; one of the saddest realities of Grace 's life.

Grace had heard the many stories Jack and Matthew would tell ever year while gathered around the Thanksgiving table; about their mother, and the time they had spent with her growing up. But they were their memories, not hers, and always about the many wonderful things their mother had done years before Grace was even born.

Her brothers' memories included how their mother was always so kind to every child she ever met. Especially those less fortunate, they would emphasize. "She couldn't refuse a Girl Scout selling cookies door-to-door, that's for sure," Jack and Matthew joked on several occasions when the topic of their mother's fondness of children resurfaced. This particular memory of theirs had always disturbed Grace but, naturally, she never let on. Every time the statement was made about Girl Scouts selling cookies, and how their mother couldn't resist buying several boxes, Grace 's mind was forced to remember the mother she knew. The one that began surfacing a few years after her brothers had moved out of the house for good.

Clearly showing signs of extreme personality changes due to the Alzheimer's, her mother had once violently slammed the front door of their house in a little girl's face, screaming, "No, I don't want any of your fucking cookies!" Grace was fourteen.

Another memory she tried to keep buried was the time her mother served bloody and raw hamburger for dinner once. The meat hadn't even been warmed in the pan when her mother scooped it up with a spatula and placed the raw patties in buns on top of their plates.

The mother Grace knew was nothing like Jack and Matthew's version of the same woman. Her mother had been downright cruel at times, crazy even. Not the wonderful, three-course-meal-cooking woman with dinner ready and on the table every night by five o'clock, that her brothers so happily described. Her mother was weird.

Fortunately, there were some memories Jack and Matthew shared with Grace that she truly enjoyed hearing. Like about the many colorful costumes her mother had apparently sewn for the local theater group in town, refusing to ever accept payment in return. And how she used to volunteer her time at Cortland Hospital, where all three McKenzie children were born, to read to blind children…

"That's it!" Grace stopped dead in her tracks. "She read poetry to the blind kids at that camp."

Hearing her gasp, Bailey turned around and bolted back to her side, tail wagging in concern. "Sorry, boy," she said, realizing she had scared him. She bent over to massage the sides of his neck to calm him. "Everything is fine."

As the pair continued on their journey south, Grace abandoned what few fond memories she had of her mother and focused on her father again. Before long, she was smiling.

"I bet I can beat you in a race to the house, Dad," thirteen-year-old Grace had announced.

"You think so?" Shea asked, smiling down at his boisterous daughter.

"Yep. Are you ready, old man?"

"Ready as I'll ever be," he said with a wink.

"Okay then... ready, set, go!"

Grace took off in a flash, certain of her superior skill as a runner, and made the mistake of turning back around to check on her dad. To her surprise, he was right on her heels and gaining fast. Shocked, she faced forward and kicked it into high gear. But before she knew what was happening, he ran past her in a blur all the way to the house and won the race.

It remained her favorite memory of her father. The day he surprised her by teaching her one of life's lessons: never underestimate your opponent.

Looking ahead, she saw that she'd finally reached the point. In memory of her dad, she sprinted the rest of the way to the tip of the point as fast as she could.

Collapsing to the ground at the water's edge, soaked in perspiration, she began to laugh harder than she had in years.

It was about 11:45 when Jack finally pulled into the driveway of the cottage. And although he expected to find Grace waiting for him on the porch with a big smile, Matthew sitting beside her wearing his customary scowl in recognition of his tardiness, he was surprised when he found neither. Even after grabbing his gear and walking inside of the cottage, his siblings were nowhere in sight. *Whatever. They'll be back.*

Jack had enlisted in the Air Force after graduating from high school towards the end of the Vietnam War in '73. After serving two years of active duty, he returned home, moved back in with the family. He'd quickly settled into civilian life, working odd jobs while attending college on the GI bill. After completing his degree and passing the CPA exam, he'd opened a small tax firm in Cincinnatus catering mainly to farmers and other small business owners like himself.

Jack had always had a good head on his shoulders in regards to managing money, so serving as the town's chief tax and financial adviser matched his skill set nicely. Jack's wife, Chelsea, whom he met while attending Syracuse University, was also from western New York state (same as Shea and Audrey) and settled into small-town life in Cincinnatus effortlessly. Chelsea held a particular fondness for animals, especially those no one else wanted, and (quite unintentionally) had managed to fill her and Jack's first one-bedroom apartment in town with five feral cats, two dogs—one with only three legs— and a very plump potbelly pig.

"Either the pig goes, or you do!" Mr. Houck, their landlord, said after learning of the arrival of Chelsea's pig. Three weeks later, Jack purchased ten acres of farmland near the town of Pitcher, where the Mud Creek met the Otselic River and dropped two double-wides in the center of his land; one for humans and one for Chelsea's ever-growing collection of critters until which time a proper house and barn could be built for each. It took more than six years, but to this day the Jack & Chelsea McKenzie Farm was one of the nicest in Cortland County.

As Jack waited for his siblings to return, he decided the time was ripe to claim the largest bedroom for himself, if he could.

He walked into the only bedroom overlooking the lake and noticed no one's luggage lying about. Sure enough, their parents' old bedroom was apparently unclaimed. "What fools," he laughed, and began to unpack.

As was his habit, he neatly placed the clothing he had brought with him for the three-day weekend: three t-shirts, two pair of jeans, two pairs of shorts, underwear and socks, into the largest bureau. His two long-sleeve flannel shirts he hung on wooden hangers in the closet. After making up the queen-size bed, he placed his travel bag containing his shaving kit and other toiletries inside one of the two end tables, and sprayed the perimeter of the room for bugs—he hated spiders and the cottage bred them—he decided to see if anyone had thought to bring any food, which was where he found Matthew.

"Little brother," Jack said, nodding in Matthew's direction as he entered the kitchen.

Matthew opened the refrigerator door and looked inside. "Great. No food. The least she could've done is stocked the fridge," Matthew complained.

"Where is she anyway?" Jack asked.

"She took that hound of hers for a walk. Said she wanted to tire him out before you got here, but she was planning on walking all the way down to the point and back. Hopefully, the fuckin' mutt will collapse and die on the hike back."

Jack smiled, knowing full well when his brother was only trying to sound tough. "You don't mean that, little brother. That dog is all she has these days and you know it."

"For the love of God, stop calling me little brother… but, yeah, I know. She loves that fuckin' mutt."

"When did she leave?"

"Right after you sent her your text."

Jack checked his phone. "That was more than two hours ago. She should be back soon."

"Probably," Matthew said. "But I'm starved, how about you?"

"Yeah, I could eat. As soon as Grace gets here, we'll run into town and pick up some groceries. Maybe share a pie and some beers at that pizza place you like so much."

"Can't."

"Why not?"

"It's been closed for more than two years. Jesus, Jack, don't you ever read a newspaper?"

Jack knew that Matthew was pleased to know something about Trumansburg that he didn't, but let it pass. "Alright smart ass, where can we eat?"

"Don't worry, I know a place."

"Whatever," Jack said, as he walked away and took a seat in the living room next to the fireplace. "Fire's dying."

"Yep," Matthew said, joining him. "So, what's this all about?"

33

"What?"

"The weekend, Einstein. What are we doing up here?"

"I have no idea. All I know is that she called me up out of the blue about three days ago and said she needed to talk to me. Sounded important."

"I got the same call."

The two brothers sat quietly with their thoughts for a few moments until Jack finally broke the silence. "Do you think she knows?"

Matthew shot him a look as lethal as an automatic weapon in the wrong hands. "No, I don't."

"Well, it's possible. What is she now? Forty-five, Forty-six?"

"She's forty-eight," Matthew responded, being the only one of the two who remembered every family member's birthday. "She'll be forty-nine come next April."

"That's a long time not to know the truth," Jack said, folding his arms across his chest.

"Bullshit! I don't care how long it's been or how old she is. She's not going to hear it from me or you. Got it?" Matthew's blue eyes were now wide, appearing almost black with his pupils fully dilated. His chest pumped up, his large jaw tightly clenched.

Jack had seen this look on his brother's face many times, just before he threw a fast and devastating punch into something—or someone—with his mighty fist. "Alright, settle down, little brother. Don't go getting your Agent Orange up now. I'm trying to figure out, same as you, why the hell she'd invite us up here, is all. I won't say a word about it."

"You better not, or you'll answer to me," Matthew said, making his point perfectly clear. "And for the last goddamn time, stop calling me little brother or I'll knock that stupid smile off your face."

"Oh, you're scaring me. I'm shaking... see." Jack held his steady hand up for Matthew's inspection to demonstrate his point. But the hard and cold look still frozen across his younger brother's face suggested maybe Jack should be scared of Matthew, at least a little.

CHAPTER 4

AUDREY
MONDAY, JUNE 23, 1969

After grabbing her heavy suitcases from the trunk of her car, Audrey crossed the parking lot and headed towards what she assumed must be the main office: a one-story, log cabin which sat predominately between two larger, more expansive cabins of the same design. *They must be the dining hall and indoor recreation center I've heard about.*

Upon reaching the front door of the office, a painter finished nailing a handwritten 'Wet Paint' sign above the door.

"Be careful, miss," the painter said as he climbed down from his ladder and opened the door for her. "The paint on the trim is still wet."

She smiled politely before walking inside. "I'll be careful. I wouldn't want to ruin your handiwork."

Standing behind the counter inside was Jayden Scarsi, founder and owner of Camp Vision. Audrey had met him entirely by accident a month earlier while reading poetry at Cortland Hospital. It was something she enjoyed doing as often as her responsibilities at home would allow. Seeing her read to the blind patients, Jayden immediately introduced himself and offered her a position at his summer camp. And now here she was, standing in front of the wealthiest man in Homer, New York.

"Hello, Audrey. I'm so happy to see you made it," Jayden said, coming around the counter to greet her. "I hope you didn't have any trouble finding us."

"No trouble at all. Your directions were spot on," Audrey said, setting her two suitcases on the floor. "Thank you."

One of the people Jayden had met while traveling carefree from state to state only two short years ago, practicing his Bohemian lifestyle, was Ajei (Äh-hē) Yazzie, a shy Navajo girl who was partially blind and living in the woods of Colorado with her aging father, Ahiga. Currently ten years old, Ajei stood next to Jayden behind the counter, clearly excited to meet the pretty new lady who had just arrived.

"I'd like you to meet my daughter. Ajei, please come around and say hello to Miss Audrey."

Daughter? Audrey smiled, wondering about the little girl who ducked underneath the counter and walked up to her. He'd told her of Ajei at their first meeting, but she immediately realized how different to him the girl looked. Seemingly precocious, with brown eyes and naturally tanned skin, the little girl was uniquely delightful as she offered her outstretched hand. "Hello, Miss Audrey. My name is Ajei."

Audrey shook her tiny hand which, surprisingly, was quite firm. "Hello, Ajei. I'm very pleased to meet you."

"My dad says you'll be reading to us."

Audrey looked up at Jayden, who simply nodded. "Yes, that's right. I have some poetry I'd like to share with everyone."

"That's neat," Ajei said, taking a few careful steps backwards.

"Audrey, Ajei has been with us since we opened last year for business and knows her away around camp better than anyone. I've asked her to show you to your cabin, if you don't mind."

"No, not at all. I'd be delighted to have Ajei show me the way," Audrey said.

"Great. Ajei, here are the keys to Miss Audrey's cabin. You go on now and show her the way, but come right back. We have more guests arriving soon. I'll need your help with them, too."

"Sure," Ajei said, taking the keys and smiling widely. "Are you ready, Miss Audrey?"

"Ready," Audrey announced she lifted her suitcases and began following Ajei outside.

"Bye, Audrey," Jayden called from back around the counter. "I'll stop by your cabin a little later on tonight so we can talk."

"Sounds good," Audrey said, now hurrying to keep pace with her little guide who skipped a few paces ahead of her, clearly not hampered by her limited vision.

Ajei turned her head and looked back at Audrey, who was struggling to keep up with her. "The doctor in Syracuse says I have tunnel vision."

"Oh?" Audrey said.

"Yeah, it's pretty rare."

"What is tunnel vision?" Audrey knew what tunnel vision was, but sensed that Ajei would prefer to tell her.

"It's kinda hard to explain, but I'll try," Ajei began. "When I look directly at something, say that tree over there." Ajei pointed to a large sycamore. "I can see most of it, where I'm looking, anyway, but it's surrounded by this giant, black fuzzy circle. It's kinda like that."

"Oh, I'm so sorry," Audrey said. "That must be very difficult for you."

"Nah, not really. Better than most of the other kids here. Most of 'em can't even see a thing. At least I can see somethings." Ajei turned back to the lead position and continued with her skipping until coming to rest in front of a small, squarely-built cabin. "This one is yours, Miss Audrey."

Cabin No. 12, the plaque above the door read. "This is lovely," Audrey said, stepping inside. "All of this, just for me?"

"No," Ajei corrected. "You'll be sharing it with another lady, Miss Cori."

"Oh, of course, how pretentious of me," Audrey said, as she looked around the cabin. The aromatic scent of yellow pine seemed to be coming from everything: walls, floors, ceiling, and even the furnishings.

To the right, flanking a magnificent stone fireplace, were two small floral-print club chairs and a matching couch covered in the same, cheerful fabric. Two small rustic tables, made of pine, rested on each end of the couch. The furniture arrangement created a clever division between the living space and kitchen which was located on the left.

The kitchen was small, but equipped with a darling little blue stove, small icebox and an ample sink. Situated between the two front living spaces, further creating a sense of division, was a small, round dining table large enough to seat two comfortably, perhaps three if you were to squeeze in an additional chair. However, looking around, Audrey discovered there were no other available chairs to be had.

Walking to the back of the cabin, past the dining table, Audrey found an adequate-size bedroom on the right and a bathroom on the left. She paused in front of the bedroom door and looked inside: two twin beds covered with matching, sky-blue checkered bedspreads were placed on opposite sides of the room, two small pine dressers sat beside each bed, and ivory-colored lace curtains covering the one window of the room blew inwards due to the breeze coming off the lake. In the bathroom, she admired a pale blue shower curtain currently pulled to one side of a stand-up shower. Across from the shower was a tiny, blue sink and standard size commode, also blue.

"This is perfect," Audrey said, smiling brightly.

Ajei smiled too, obviously feeling very proud of her smart design. "Thank you, it was my idea to use blue to decorate it. Do you like blue, Miss Audrey?"

"Yes, very much."

Ajei clapped her hands "It's the color of the sky."

"Yes, exactly. It's perfect."

"Thanks."

"You're welcome," Audrey said, with a bright smile of her own as they walked back to the front of the cabin.

"Miss Cori is really nice, too," Ajei said. "She's our cook. On Tuesday nights she makes pizza."

"How wonderful. Is the pizza good, Ajei?"

"Yeah, but not the kind she makes sometimes with all the vegetables. I tried in once, last year. It's really bad." Ajei rolled her eyes. "You should tell Miss Cori not to make you that kind, with all the onions and stuff, and just make you a plain cheese one like she makes for us kids."

"Oh okay, thank you, Ajei. I'll remember that."

"Okay, bye!" Ajei announced, abruptly, signaling it was time for her to return to the office. Giggling, Audrey pulled the lace curtains away from the front window and watched the happy little girl with tunnel vision skip away.

Once Ajei was completely out of sight, Audrey stepped away from the window and sat down on the couch. *Would poetry be as distasteful to children as vegetables on pizza?* She began to feel foolish. *A dreamer who dreams of nothing more than spreading joy by sharing the things she loves.*

Suddenly, feeling much more than foolish, she stood up, began pacing the floor and seriously began to wonder if she should even bother to unpack. "I'm such a fool," she whispered, marching the pine floors of the small cabin. "Why did I think that any of this would matter to these children?" Her voice was growing louder. "Such an idiot!"

She lifted her favorite book, *The Complete Poetry of Edgar Allen Poe*, from her suitcase and threw it towards the front door, missing it. Instead, it crashed to the wall to the left of the door with a thunderous *thwack*, just as a woman entered the cabin.

"Whoa! What's going on here?" The woman ducked, holding both hands in front of her face. She peeked between her fingers warily. "Please don't throw anything else at me, doll."

"Oh... I'm so sorry! I wasn't aiming at you... really, I wasn't." Audrey quickly retrieved her book from the floor and tucked it back into her suitcase.

"Okaaay, who then?" The woman asked, looking around.

Something in the tone of her voice convinced Audrey she wasn't really angry. Maybe. "Can we please start over?" Audrey asked.

"Sure."

Audrey stretched her right hand to the woman and she accepted it. "My name is Audrey McKenzie. I was brought on this summer to read to the children."

"Oh, I see. My name's Cori Cohen. So, Audrey, when you're not throwing books around, what type of stuff will you be reading to the kids?"

Audrey dropped Cori's hand and turned away. She now felt completely horrified. It was a stupid idea, she knew it. "Poetry," she whispered.

Cori moseyed to the dining table and took a seat. "Sit down and tell me about it, Audrey. I love poetry."

Audrey swung around. "You do?"

"Yes, of course... you do too, right honey?" Cori tilted her head slightly to one side.

Audrey chuckled and took a seat at the table. "Yes, of course. I love poetry. But I'm beginning to worry the children may not."

"Oh, honey, don't be silly. They'll love it."

"Do you really think so?"

"Yes, of course I do," Cori said with authority. "If they don't, so what? Poetry isn't for everyone. But for the ones that it is, they'll be tickled to hear you read."

"Yeah, I suppose you're right. Thanks."

"You're welcome, kid." She pressed her palms to the table and stood up. "Now, let's figure out our sleeping arrangements. Shall we?"

Audrey smiled. She liked her. "Sure thing, right behind you."

CHAPTER 5

GRACE
FRIDAY, AUGUST 31, 2018

As the hiking duo, woman and dog, began walking back towards the cottage, Grace picked up a stone she spotted along the path perfect for skipping: flat, three inches in diameter, and no more than a quarter of an inch thick. She carried it in her hand as she continued walking back towards the cottage.

She had to have been sixteen at the time, she thought. *Yes, sixteen.* It was the summer her mother looked straight at her with a puzzled look on her face and broke her heart: "What's your name again, dear?"

Taking a few more steps in the direction of the cottage, Grace remembered the conversation she had with her father later in the day, when he took her down to the lake to skip stones.

"Why doesn't she even know who I am now?"

Seeing that she had abandoned any idea of skipping stones with him, Shea took a seat next to her. "Honey," he began. "Sometimes we don't understand God's plan. Remember Father Baker's sermon last Sunday? The one about why God lets bad things happen?"

"Yeah, I guess so," she said, unconvinced.

"He told us the story about a woman who had recently lost her son. The woman, he said, had cursed God and felt that it was impossible for her to continue a relationship with Him. Do you remember that part?"

"Yeah, Dad… but this is different."

"How is it different, Grace? What that woman must have been feeling after losing a child must have been as horrible as what you're feeling now. Maybe even worse."

Grace nodded.

"Do you remember the card she received later from a friend, and what it said?"

"Something about God concealing His purpose."

"That's right. When His purpose is concealed, we must continue to live based on His promises."

"I know… but I don't think I can do that."

"But you must. Remember what else Father Baker has taught us about the devil?"

Grace began to kick some pebbles at her feet. "No, not really."

"He told us that Satan is very real and very evil, and that he tries to hurt us every way he can. It's only by keeping your faith in the goodness that is God, that you'll be able to get through what's happening with Mom right now. Do you understand?"

Grace leaned her head on her father's shoulder and cried until there were no more tears left inside of her. "Do you think this happened to Mom because she stopped going to church all those years ago?"

Shea hugged his daughter a little tighter. "No, honey… I really don't think so. But, come on now, let's skip some stones together now."

Grace abandoned the trail near the edge of the property and finally freed the stone she had been carrying over the lake. She watched as it skipped in rapid succession, bouncing six times over the water, until finally disappearing to the bottom of the deep lake. "Come on, boy. Let's go."

"Here they come," Jack said, watching Grace and Bailey from where he stood at the kitchen window.

"Good. I'm ready to start eating my fuckin' hand," Matthew grumbled, grabbing the keys to his pick-up off the kitchen table. "I'll drive."

After Grace and Jack said their hello's, they jumped into Matthew's pick-up and headed towards the nearby town to grab some lunch.,

Within ten minutes, the siblings were seated around an outdoor table under a large umbrella, eager to sample some beer at a local brewhouse that had recently opened, according to Matthew.

Grace ordered the beer dubbed the *Atomic Blonde* while both men ordered a heavier, English stout called the *Stouty McStoutface.*

"I hate these stupid names they come up with for beer now-a-days," Matthew said. "Why not just call it a stout?"

Grace rolled her eyes and shook her head. "Why are you always so nasty, Matthew? Can't you say something nice once in a while?"

"And ruin my charming personality? I don't think so," he said, grinning. "It's tasty, though."

"There you go. I knew you had it in you," Grace teased. "So, what's everyone going to get to eat?"

"I'm thinking maybe the Mexican bowl," Jack said, as he continued to peruse the menu. "That sounds pretty good."

"Figures," Matthew said.

"Matthew... be nice," Grace pleaded. "For me, please?"

Now it was Matthew who rolled his eyes before waiving the waitress over to their table. "I'll try, just for you, Sis. But only for the weekend. After then, I'm back to good 'ol me."

"Good enough. Thank you." Grace said, before turning her attention to their waitress

After everyone had placed their order and the waitress was gone, Grace cleared her throat and looked up at her brothers. "So... I guess you're both wondering why I wanted to see you this weekend."

"Nah, not really," Matthew quipped. "I love driving fifty miles out of my way for overpriced beer and hipster food."

"You really can't help yourself, can you, Matthew?" Jack threw Matthew a stern look before returning his attention to his sister. "Go ahead, Grace."

Once again, she cleared her throat before finally speaking the words she had rehearsed several times before. "I've recently received some... information. And I'm hoping the two of you may be able to clear something up for me."

"That's it?" Matthew said, swallowing the last of his stout. "We could have done that over the phone."

Ignoring him, Jack asked, "What kind of information, Grace?"

Beginning to lose her nerve, she downed the last of her beer, too, and waved her hand above her head. "Waitress, could you bring us another round, please?"

"Sure thing, Hun. Be right back."

"Why do perfect strangers insist on calling people they don't know Hun?"

"Shut. Up. Matthew," Jack said. "You really are an asshole, you know that?"

"Yep," Matthew said, grinning again. "But enough about me, go on, Grace. Finish telling us your news."

Grace began to wonder why she thought her brothers would be able to shut up long enough for her to have a civil conversation with them. Never mind, it was nothing." She shook her head, dropping her gaze to her hands, clenched in her lap.

"Okay, great!" Matthew said, leaning back in his chair. "Glad that's settled... now where the hell is that girl with our next beers?"

"Screw that. What's on your mind, Grace?" Jack said. "It's obvious somethings bothering you. I've never known you to drink a beer with lunch, much less two."

The waitress returned to the table and began distributing the three glasses of beer from a brown serving tray. Meanwhile, Grace reached under her chair and pulled her purse onto her lap. From it she withdrew a plain, white legal envelope and placed it on top of the table in front of her. She then looked across at Jack's and Matthew's faces.

Both men were staring down at the envelope. Thinking what, she had no idea, but she had successfully gained their full attention. The mood around the table had clearly shifted. Grace was now in control. Something which felt completely incongruous and foreign to her, as it very rarely happened in the presence of her older brothers. They, she had always suspected, perpetually thought of her as nothing more than a little girl, not worthy of their respect. Even now, forty-eight years old, they still treated her like a child.

But they were silent now, staring down at the white envelope with the distinctive logo. Grace couldn't help herself, and shamelessly basked in their uneasiness for a little while longer before she broke the silence with words that shattered like glass: "I had my DNA tested."

Jack jerked his head upward, but Matthew remained perfectly still.

"Do you both remember Mom referring to the three of us as the British Isles?" She asked.

"Yeah, she said it all the time," Jack said.

Matthew remained stone-faced, saying nothing.

"Well, then…" She opened the envelope and withdrew two pieces of paper. Identical copies of her recent DNA test results. "Maybe one of you can explain this to me." She slid the papers across the table.

"What's this supposed to prove?" Matthew asked, clearly fully aware of what he now held in his hand.

"Just read it," Grace said, nervously lifting her second beer to her lips.

Once they finished reading the report, both men leaned back in their chairs and exchanged a quick glance.

True to form, Matthew was the first to offer up a possible alternative explanation. "Obviously it's wrong, Grace. They must have mixed your DNA up with someone else's."

"Oh?" She said, completely unconvinced.

"Why would you even want to have something like this done, anyway?" He said as he threw his copy of the report across the table to her. "You and your generation. Always having to have shit proven to you."

"We're from the same generation, Matthew," she said, calmly. For once she had the upper hand.

"You know what I'm talking about, Grace," he said. "Younger people... like you. Right, Jack?"

Jack studied the results from his sister's DNA report. According to it, Grace was 49.3% Italian, 26.9% English,

20.1% Scottish and 3.7% Welsh. No Irish. He lifted his head and smiled across the table at his sister. It was a well-known fact that their father, Shea, was 100% Irish; his parents having immigrated from Ireland to the United States in the late 18002. Suddenly, he began to laugh.

"Do you think this is funny, Jack?!" Grace snapped, grabbing his copy of her DNA report from his hand.

"No, it's not that, Grace. Honestly. I'm sorry I laughed. I wasn't laughing at you. I understand how you must be feeling right now."

She slumped back in her chair, covered her mouth with both of her hands and spoke between fingertips. "So, it's true then? Dad wasn't my biological father?"

"Does it matter?!" Matthew slammed his fist on top of the table. "Wasn't he good enough to you, his little princess?" His words stung, as he clearly intended.

"Leave her alone, Matthew, and keep your voice down. She knows how much Dad loved her... right, Grace? You do know that Dad loved you, very much."

"Yes, of course I do. And I loved him very much, too. I still do. Probably even a little more than Mom." She let that thought sink in a little before she continued. "These test results have done nothing to change the way I feel about Dad, and always will feel about him. But I'm more than just a little curious about my real father. I *need* to know who he is... and I think you both know, and always have. Honestly, I'm actually upset about the fact that even after Dad died you both chose not to tell me the truth." Now her voice was getting too loud, but she found herself launching into the speech she'd practiced on the drive up. "As far as I'm concerned, you both owe me an explanation. And furthermore, you need to tell me right now everything you know!" She sat back in her chair and crossed her arms across her chest.

"I'm not going to sit here and listen to this crap," Matthew said. He stood up, pulled his wallet from his back pocket and threw three ten-dollar-bills on the table. "I'm outta here."

"What'd ya mean? You drove," Jack said, following him out of the restaurant and down the street.

Matthew ignored him and continued to charge down the sidewalk, several yards in front of Jack. "I'm not going to have any part of this conversation, Jack!"

Jack stepped up his pace. "What the hell is wrong with you? You're acting like an idiot... she deserves to know the truth about her father." Both men now stood in front of Matthew's truck.

"No, that's just the thing... she doesn't, Jack. As far as I'm concerned, it died right along with Mom and Dad. Where it belongs!"

"You really are an asshole; do you know, that little brother? Always have been."

Jack turned to walk away, but Matthew rushed him before he could, and pinned him up against his truck, his right hand balled into an angry fist. "I swear, if you tell her any more than you already have, I'll..." His fist was inches away from Jack's face.

"You'll do what!" Jack yelled, pushing himself away from his brother's grip. "Kill me? Is that what this has come to, Matthew? You'd actually kill me over this!"

Matthew backed away from Jack and got into his truck. His blood now pounding intensely inside of his skull. "Just leave it alone, Jack. You'll be sorry if you don't. And I'm not talking about me now."

"Come on, it's always about you."

51

Matthew fairly pierced a hole in Jack's skull with his blue-black eyes. "There are so many reasons, and you know it, why she doesn't need to know anything more. Case closed." He turned away from Jack and lowered the window of his truck. "You know I'm right, Jack. It's for her own good."

Jack stood on the sidewalk, catching his breath as Matthew turned the key and the engine started. *Maybe the truth is too much.* He wasn't sure. "You're really going to leave us here?"

"Yes," Matthew said, and drove away.

CHAPTER 6

AUDREY
MONDAY, JUNE 23, 1969

After Audrey finished unpacking, she sat on her bed, examining her wedding band. Several of the prongs holding the tiny diamonds in place had become loose a few weeks ago. Unwilling to risk losing any of the precious stones, she pulled her ring from her finger and dropped it into a dish on top of her dresser before she changed into her bathing suit. She and Cori were planning to take a walk down to the lake for a quick swim and late lunch.

This summer, like the one before, Cori had arranged her own schedule for kitchen duty. She arrived every morning by six to prepare and cook breakfast, which was served between the hours of eight and ten. She then returned to the kitchen by three and cooked supper, served between five and seven. Therefore, her free time were the hours between breakfast and supper as her staff took care of preparing and serving lunch.

"Wow!" Cori exclaimed after Audrey emerged from the bedroom wearing her new two-piece swimming suit and twirled around the hallway floor. "Look at you. I'm as heterosexual as they come, sweetheart, but I'm thinking about banging you myself, looking like you do."

"Oh, stop it," Audrey said, blushing. "Are you sure it's not too much?"

Cori pretended to inspect the pink and white polka dot bikini seriously this time. "Ah, *too much* aren't exactly the words I'd use to describe it. Too little, maybe. Too much, definitely not."

Suddenly uncertain about her choice of swimwear, Audrey attempted to cover herself with both of her arms. "Should I change into my one-piece?"

"What for, honey? The kids are blind. Remember?"

"Oh, yeah, I suppose you're right. But are you sure I look okay? I don't want to…"

"Shut up," Cori said, cutting her off. "It's absolutely darling. I wouldn't change a thing." She grabbed the picnic basket she had packed, slipping her camera strap over her shoulder. "Besides, if I looked that good in a bikini, I sure-as-shit would wear it—and so should you. Let's go."

Smiling wide, certain she'd never met anyone quite as outspoken or as funny as Cori, Audrey grabbed her beach towel and a blanket and ran out the door behind her.

As they approached the lake, both women heard a loud boom from the sky. Frightened, Audrey turned to Cori. "What was *that*?"

"Nothing, just the Guns of the Seneca."

"What?" Audrey said, blankly.

"You know, The Guns of Seneca. Ohhh, I get it, you've never heard one before."

"I'm sure I haven't. Explain, please."

Before Cori explained anything further, having just arrived on the beach, she selected a choice spot next to the long dock belonging to the camp for them to rest. She set the picnic basket and her towel down in the sand while Audrey spread out the blanket. On such a sultry day, the lake was as flat as a mirror. It lay without ripple, blue-green and crystal-clear. "Isn't this beautiful?"

"Yes," Audrey said. "It's very beautiful and I can't wait to take a swim, but what's this about the Seneca guns?"

"Oh right, that," Cori said, taking a seat on the blanket and pulling two sandwiches from the basket and offering one to Audrey. "Tuna or chicken?"

"I'll have the chicken, please. Thanks."

"You got it," Cori said, handing Audrey one of the sandwiches as she began unwrapping hers. After she took a healthy bite and swallowed politely, she explained the mystery known as Guns of the Seneca.

"The boom that we just heard is actually known as a skyquake in other parts of the world, but here we call them the Guns of the Seneca. Don't ask me why, it's just what they've always been called. They're actually an unexplained phenomenon that sounds like a cannon or a sonic boom coming right out of the sky, like we heard. They happen all the time around here. I'm surprised you've never heard one before."

"Never," Audrey said, concerned. "Are they dangerous?"

"Nobody knows, but I doubt it. My father told me when I was young that it's not just in the Finger Lakes that they're heard."

"No?"

"No. They've been reported in several places all around the world; the river Ganges in India, the North Sea, Japan, Italy, Ireland, and even Idaho of all places, according to my father."

"Wow, that's the weirdest thing I've ever heard. And no one knows what they are?"

"Nope. Some say it's God, but I doubt that. I'm sure He has more important stuff to do than set off bombs in the sky above Trumansburg. My money is on the aliens."

Audrey started to laugh; certain Cori was joking with her again until she saw her face. "You're not kidding, are you?"

"No, of course not. I never joke about aliens. They're up there, believe me. They just haven't figured out how to communicate with us yet. Maybe the booms we hear is them trying to do just that."

"Interesting," Audrey said, wadding the foil from her sandwich into a ball and tossing it into the basket. "Maybe you're right."

"I'm always right," Cori said, smiling.

"Now you sound like my youngest son, Matthew. He's always right, too." Audrey sighed, thinking about both of her boys again while gazing out over the lake. "I'm already starting to miss the little hellion and his older brother, Jack. And I've only been here an hour. I think I'm in trouble." She giggled.

"You mean to tell me with a rockin' body like yours that you've already popped two babies out from your coochie?"

Audrey blushed, wondering if she would ever get used to Cori's choice of words. "Yeah, that's right. Two boys. But it was eons ago. Jack is already fourteen and Matthew, thirteen. Irish twins, my husband calls them."

"Okay, now you're just blowing my mind. What are you, twenty-three, twenty-four? You can't possibly have two kids that old. I'm not buying it."

Now very flattered, Audrey said, "I'm thirty-seven, but I'll be thirty-eight in December, thank you very much."

"Get the fuck outta here!"

"Cori, your language! The children... they can hear better than we can," Audrey warned, noticing a group of small girls playing down by the water with one of the camp counselors. "Please don't swear. At least not so loud."

"I'm sorry, that's the Jersey girl coming out in me. I apologize. But you must have some awesome genes, Jesus Christ! You don't look a day over twenty-four, I swear it."

Audrey corrected her again. "It's not good to say 'Jesus Christ' like that, either."

"Oh, yeah, sorry about that. I keep forgetting. That guy is pretty special to you gentiles."

They both laughed and fell back onto the blanket. "You're a good egg, kid," Cori said, sitting up and grabbing her camera. "Let me get a picture of you."

Audrey stood up, smiled and posed for a few shots and then reciprocated by snapping a few of Cori. After they had finished eating, their bellies full, Audrey brushed a few crumbs from her chest and stood up. "That was the best chicken salad sandwich I've ever tasted. What's your secret?"

"Finely diced red onion. I never make chicken salad without adding red onion. Surprised most people don't do the same."

Audrey shrugged her shoulders, realizing that she was one of those people that had never thought about adding onion to chicken salad. "I'll remember that. Thanks."

"Sure. Now, let's do this thing." Cori said, as she stood up, pulled her sundress off over her head and began running towards the lake, beating Audrey to the water.

"Wait for me," Audrey yelled, racing to join her. A young man nearby had arrived for a swim and stopped dead in his tracks, but Audrey just dodged past him without a thought.

"Cheese and rice, this water is freezing!" Cori screamed.

Audrey laughed and swam closer to her. "I think it feels grrreat!"

"Whatever, just keep an eye out for my nipples. I think they may have fallen off!"

Audrey overheard someone else laughing at Cori's remark from the shore. Turning around, she recognized him immediately. It was the painter she had seen yesterday, looking devilishly agreeable in a pair of navy-blue swimming trunks, trimmed in gold.

Without hesitation, the painter stripped his white muscle shirt off over his head and dropped it onto the sand. He then ran the full length of the dock and dove in, head first.

When he finally came up for air, Audrey released an unexpected gasp, loud enough for only herself to hear, *thank God*. When she realized he was watching her, too, she quickly turned around and swam back to Cori. "Who's that?" Audrey asked, being careful not to stare directly at him again.

"Who?"

"Him, over there… swimming in the water past the dock."

Cori swam a little closer to the dock for a closer look. "Beats me, I've never seen him before."

"I saw him yesterday when I arrived. He was hanging a wet paint sign above the door of the office."

"Oh, that must be Jayden's nephew then. I heard he'd be here this summer, helping out with some carpentry and stuff like that. Why, do you think he's fetching?" Cori teased, using her best English accent.

"Cori, stop! I'm a married woman."

"That doesn't mean you're dead, sweetheart," Cori said, before swimming towards the shore. "I'm outta here. This water is ridiculous!"

Audrey laughed at Cori, and herself, realizing she must be approaching middle age fast; gawking at a handsome young man, no matter how good looking. Turning her back to him once more, she swam to the shore to rejoin Cori on the blanket. Once settled in, Audrey turned her head to face her friend. "Cori, may I ask you a question?"

"Sure, kid. Fire away."

Audrey smiled. "How well do you know Jayden?"

"Not too well, why?"

"Oh, I don't know. I was just curious about his little girl, Ajei. I was surprised to learn he had a daughter."

"Oh, yeah, that." Cori sat up and leaned back on bent elbows. "I met Jayden about four years ago, after responding to an ad he placed in the paper for a cook. Not only did he hire me for the job, he also gave me a bonus to design the kitchen. A very nice bonus."

"He does strike me as a generous man."

"Absolutely. He's a good one, alright… anyway, after he hired me, I got busy working with his engineers on the kitchen. Then he abruptly announced that he was off again on another one of his many trips."

"Trips?"

"Yeah, the man is filthy rich. From what I learned from the guys building the cabins, Jayden hasn't worked a day in his life."

"No!"

"Yep, that's what they said. He went to college and all, but after that he spent his time galivanting from state to state. Trying to figure out what he wanted out of life, I guess."

"Interesting."

"Very." Cori stretched out on the blanket again.

"And Ajei? Do you know anything about her?"

"Oh, yeah. That." She sat up again. "When he returned home two years ago, he brought her with him… from Colorado."

"That's odd, don't you think?"

"Yeah, but that's Jayden. Apparently, he met her father, Ahiga, boxing in some joint known as Buckskin Joes about forty miles west of Pueblo, I think he said. Anyway, Jayden described the old man as quite the character. Apparently, his name is Navajo and actually means 'he fights'." Cori let out a small chuckle. "According to Jayden, the old man did fight, every Friday and Saturday night at Buckskin Joes. But, as Jayden soon learned after observing several of his bare-knuckle bouts, he was a very poor boxer. 'A very proud Navajo, but a terrible boxer,' were Jayden's exact words. An inconvenient truth for both himself and young Ajei, I suppose. Week after week, Jayden said he stood by watching as Ahiga gave it his all trying to win the nightly purse, upwards of $200 some nights, depending upon the size of the crowd. And almost every single time he lost. Even Ahiga's wife, Ajei's mother, had grown tired of her husband's foolishness and ran off with another man leaving Ahiga and poor little Ajei behind to fend for themselves."

"That's terrible. The poor girl."

"I know, right? But luckily for her, Jayden arrived around this same time."

"And he just decided to pick her up and bring her here?"

"Yes, sort of. I'm getting to that part."

"Sorry."

"Stop apologizing for everything, kid," Cori said with a wink. "Anyway, after Jayden realized the magnitude of the harsh reality of Ajei and Ahiga Yazzie's poverty, he knew he had to help them. He explained to Ahiga that he had the means to provide for both of them, if they would return to New York with him. But Ahiga apparently wouldn't even consider picking up and relocating to another land, no matter how much Jaydan pleaded with him. As Jayden explained it, Colorado was the home of the old man's people for generations, and where he intended to remain until the day he passed over and rested in the arms of the Great Spirit. He did, however, agree to allow eight-year-old Ajei make her own decision regarding her fate. I guess he knew he had failed to provide for her properly."

"That's one of the saddest stories I've ever heard."

"Yeah, I know. It's a killer. But, at least little Ajei has a chance for a normal life now."

"Has Jayden formally adopted her?"

"Yeah, I'm pretty sure he did."

"Wow, that's quite the story. Thanks."

"No problem, kid."

Cori lifted her sunglasses off of the bridge of her nose and looked towards the lake. "It looks like Pretty Boy has had enough swimming for one day."

"Huh?" Audrey lifted her head and looked towards the shore. Water dripped from the painter's naturally-tanned skin and glistened in the sun as he got out of the lake. "Ohhh, I see..."

Cori grinned. "Uh, huh. Ohhh, I *see* too."

"Oh, Cori, you're the worst!" Audrey laughed, side slapping her friend. "But he certainly is an attractive young man."

Both women smiled as they turned over onto their stomachs, their heads facing the lake. Gathered along the shoreline, several blind children dug in the sand together. Audrey and Cori watched as the young man took a seat next to them. Although the two women couldn't hear what was being said, they could hear the children erupt with laughter soon after the painter had joined them. They watched as he helped a little boy form a sandcastle with his hands. The man's hands cupped around the smaller boy's, helping him feel the shape of the tiny sculpture. Soon, several sandcastles dotted the shoreline. Each one built by a child, their tiny hands expertly guided by the painter's hands, while Audrey and Cori watched.

"Do you think he may be a counsellor, too?" Audrey asked.

"No. I'm pretty sure he's just here to help out with some finishing details."

The painter stood up and began walking towards them. "Is he coming towards *us*?" Audrey whispered.

"Kinda looks that way," Cori said, now staring directly at the young man as he crossed the beach. "Good boogity-moogity, he is a handsome devil." She turned over onto her back and sat up.

"Shhhh," Audrey whispered, sitting up as well. "He'll hear you."

"Too late," Cori teased, seeing he had already reached the edge of their blanket. "Well, hello handsome," Cori said, resting back on both of her elbows. "You Jayden's nephew?"

"Yeah, how'd you know?" He smiled.

Smiling back, Cori said, "Well, you're the spitting image of him, for one, but I heard you may be here helping out around the place this summer. Like to join us?"

Audrey threw Cori a look as if to say, *are you crazy?*

Unaware of Audrey's disapproval, the painter took a seat on the corner of the blanket closest to her. "Sure, thanks."

Up close, he was even more beautiful than Audrey had thought. Magnificently male, he had a classic jawline and high cheek bones. His chocolate brown eyes twinkled in the sunlight, matching his hair. His olive-colored skin contrasted with his white teeth and Audrey's heart skipped a beat as he smiled; two charming vertical dimples, framing his face.

"So, what's your name, honey?" Cori asked.

"It's Danny. Danny Pepitone."

"Cori Cohen," she said, shaking his hand. "Pleased to meet you, Danny."

Danny then turned his attention to Audrey, who had remained quiet "This is the second time we're meeting, miss... and I still don't know your name."

Audrey said nothing at first, until Cori jabbed her in her side with her elbow. "The man asked you your name, honey."

"I'm sorry," Audrey said, placing a hand in front of her face to shade the sun from her eyes, smiling politely up at Danny. "My name is Audrey McKenzie. Pleased to meet you."

"Are you both camp councilors here?"

Cori laughed. "Hah! Not a chance. I'm merely the humble chef." She faked a bow, bending slightly forward at the waist.

"Then it's you I need to thank for the awesome omelet I had this morning. Delicious." He was smiling again.

Cori nodded in appreciation. "You're very welcome. I'm glad you enjoyed it. We watched you playing in the sand with the kids and Audrey thought maybe you were a counsellor."

"No, afraid not. I'm just here to help out with some manual labor stuff, but I enjoy playing with the kids."

Growing more uncomfortable in her two-piece bathing suit, sitting so closely to him, and *that smile*, Audrey suddenly stood up and wrapped her beach towel around her waist. "Please excuse me. I think I'm going to head back to our cabin now, Core. I'm suddenly not feeling too well." It was the first time she called her friend this new nickname, and while she'd done it without thinking, Cori clearly liked the sound of it.

"Oh, okay, honey… I hope it's nothing serious. Should I come with you?"

"No, that's alright. I'll be fine. I think I just need to get out of the sun for a little bit."

Danny stood up. "I'm sorry you're not feeling well, Audrey."

"Thank you."

"I'm looking forward to seeing you again, sometime... when you're feeling better, I mean. Maybe, we'll run into each other here again tomorrow?"

"Maybe," she said, turning towards the direction of the cabin.

"So, what is it that you do here, Audrey?" Danny asked.

She turned around and smiled politely once more. "I'm here to read poetry to the children is all," she said, dropping her smile and walking away.

CHAPTER 7

SHEA
TUESDAY, JUNE 24, 1969

Shea McKenzie clocked out at the usual time, three o'clock, and returned his timecard to the metal rack hanging to the left of the clock. He had worked for the town's dairy company for fourteen long years before finally being promoted to first-shift supervisor, a position he enjoyed very much. He liked taking the lead and telling his men what, when, and how to perform a particular task. He knew the business very well and was considered a fair and honest man by the men he supervised. In return, they respected him more than just about any other man in the plant.

True to his beliefs, Shea was never one to come down too hard on any man having been found violating this or that company policy or procedure. Even when the man screwed up so badly and deserved to be firmly reprimanded, Shea was never too harsh. On the rare occasion that one of his men did need to be disciplined, Shea would do so in private out of earshot from the other workers. All men had their pride, the same as he, he figured. It was something Shea never forgot even after being promoted to the lead man and what his men appreciated the most about him. Some of the Italian guys began calling him 'Capo' shortly after he became their new boss. It stuck.

"Buona notte, Capo," Vic Campagna said, walking a few steps behind Shea as they exited the back door of the plant together.

"Good night, Vic. Have a good one."

"Okay, you too. See you in morning."

"You bet," Shea said as he turned south onto Lower Cincinnatus Road.

"Heading over to Charlie's, are you, Capo?" Vic called out before he rounded the corner.

"Yeah," Shea answered. "You wanna join me?"

"Not tonight, but thanks. The wife's cooking a family favorite: beef braciole, for our little girl, Sandra. She's turning fourteen already."

"Ouch," Shea said. "That's gotta be tough, Vic. Glad I've got only the two boys to worry about."

"Ah, but she's a good one, our Sandra. Thanks for the invitation. Another time?"

"Sounds good. Don't' forget to say happy birthday from Capo to your little girl for me now."

"Will do. Grazie, tanto, grazie," Vic said, with a wave, as he headed across the bridge in the direction of his home.

Charlie's Pub was where most of the other Irish in town would be about now, and even a few of the Italians, Shea thought. He continued to walk along Lower Cincinnatus Road which ran parallel to the Otselic River. The Otselic, as everyone knew, separated the two chief ethnicities living in town, with very few exceptions. Irish families lived on the east bank of the river, Italians on the west. It had been this way for generations. Very few times did either group cross over the river bridge unless it was to work, drink, or attend church.

Charlie's Pub, being the only bar in town, was on the east side of the river, same as the plant. The only Catholic church for miles around, Our Lady of Perpetual Hope, was located on the west side. Due to these inconvenient circumstances, the two groups eventually learned to coexist. Although privately, both sides continued to hold onto their outdated stereotypical ways of thinking just as the Otselic continued to flow from north to south through town. The Italians thought that the Irish were a bunch of lazy, stupid drunks and the Irish were certain all Italians were somehow connected to the Mafia—although they weren't exactly certain how—and that they regularly beat the women they claimed to love. But when it came to working, drinking, or worshiping the same God—at least while in Cincinnatus—the two groups put aside their differences and got along fairly well. Understanding clearly, after all, that they had no other choice.

Shea walked inside of Charlie's and grabbed his typical seat at the bar. "Hey, Quinn."

"Howdy, Shea. Boilermaker for you?" The young man asked. He always manned the bar when Shea stopped by.

"Yeah, thanks," Shea said as he placed his brown, leather wallet on top of the bar.

Quinn quickly returned with Shea's customary twelve-once Schlitz, shot of Jack Daniels and set the two drinks down on the bar before him. "Hey, was that Audrey I saw driving out of town yesterday afternoon?"

"Yeah," Shea said, throwing back his shot. "She's got this crazy idea to spend the entire summer up at some new camp for blind kids in Trumansburg near the lake."

"No shit?"

Shea chased the liquor with a large swallow of his draft. It felt great. "Afraid so. Reading poetry to the kids, no less."

"Ha! That's a good one. She's really into that stuff, poetry and all."

"Yep. The woman loves it."

"Well, I think that's pretty cool, you know? Giving something of yourself to blind kids. Good for her."

"Whatever," Shea said. "I'll be happier when she returns home, that's all I know. I hate to cook, but the boys and I have to eat, unfortunately."

Quinn wiped down the bar with a damn rag and rearranged a few coasters and straws. "When's she coming back?"

"Not until Labor Day."

"That long, huh?"

"Yeah," Shea said rubbing the back of his head. "Hell, if I didn't go and tell her it would be okay with me if she stayed the whole stinkin' summer. As long as she's back in time to get the boys off to school in the fall."

Quinn smiled. "That's a good man, Shea. Not many men in town would do the same for their wives."

"Probably not," Shea agreed. "Obviously much smarter than me."

"Nah, you're doing the right thing. Think about how happy she'll be to see you and the boys again in September."

Shea smiled, thinking about Audrey's return. How much he loved her was insane. It was something he'd known from the first day of December, 1952. He'd spotted her ice skating on Spring Lake in Perry, near where they both grew up. He had to talk to her, right then and there, so he did just that:

"Gosh, you might be the most beautiful girl I've ever seen in my life," he said, skating backwards a few feet in front of her, a grin on his face

Although clearly flattered, Audrey continued to skate straight ahead and ignored his cheeky remark. She did, however, manage to flash him a little smile and that's all it took. Shea's heart had been won. For the remainder of the day and into the evening, he continued to demonstrate his charming nature and quick wit; all wrapped up in his fetching good looks. Eventually he won her over, and by the time the sun set over the lake, they were dancing cheek to cheek.

A year later they were married. Ten months later, John Richard "Jack" arrived and ten months after him, they were blessed with the arrival of their second son, Matthew James.

Shea knew he would always love Audrey and be willing to do practically anything to ensure her happiness. He gave her everything she needed to be happy, he felt, less the one thing she wanted most of all—something he learned after only two years of marriage that hadn't changed. She wanted him to stop drinking, for good.

She explained her needs to him, several times. Pleaded, was more like it; if he were being honest with himself. But his drinking wasn't anything she should concern herself with, Shea felt. Despite enjoying a "wee nip from the fruit of the gods" from time-to-time, he went to work each morning, provided for his family both financially and spiritually, and never allowed his eyes to either wander or lust after another woman. *It was enough.*

Still, he knew that she prayed for his sobriety daily, but it did nothing more than put him on the defensive. As a result, he seldom drank in their home anymore and lied about how many times he actually did. No, he would never stop drinking, and Audrey would have to accept him exactly the way he was, He swallowed the last sip of his beer and wiped the corner of his mouth. "Another round for me, will ya' Quinn?"

"Sure thing, my man. Coming right up."

CHAPTER 8

GRACE
FRIDAY, AUGUST 31, 2018

Grace was staring into her third *Atomic Blonde,* twirling a section of her dark brown hair around her index finger when Jack returned to the restaurant.

"You look about sixteen years old again, doing that," Jack said, reclaiming his seat across the table from her.

"Ha, that's rich! I certainly don't feel sixteen," she said, releasing the ringlet of hair from around her finger and allowing it to fall and curl around her face. "So, did he really abandon us here?"

"Yep, afraid so."

"Nice."

"Well, you know Matthew..."

Grace drew a deep breath and exhaled it loudly through her nose. "I guess I really messed this whole thing up."

Jack smiled politely. "Well, in hindsight, it may have been better to wait until we were back at the cottage to break your news to us. At least then, when Matthew inevitably stormed off, as you must have known he would, we wouldn't be stuck here trying to figure out how we're going to get back."

"I checked with our waitress. We can call an Uber when we're ready to leave."

"That's good. Do you still feel like eating?"

"Sure, if you do. I haven't eaten anything but a protein bar today and that was around five o'clock this morning. I'm actually starving."

"Okay then, let's eat."

Instead of returning to the cottage, Matthew drove home, pulled into his driveway and turned off the pick-up's engine. Sandy wasn't home; another shopping trip into the city with some friends. He was grateful for the solitude. He knew he'd have to tell his wife everything about today. Not only that Shea wasn't Grace 's biological father and that he'd known for years, but the whole rotten story. He couldn't risk Sandy learning the truth in any other way, due to Grace's meddling. His wife would never forgive him if she did. He wouldn't blame her.

It was only two o'clock in the afternoon, but already he felt completely drained. There was a real chill in the air now, despite the warmth of the sun. He reclined the driver's seat of his truck and closed his eyes, trying to collect his thoughts. His head drooped, and then the visions flashed before him. The blood. His father's hands, covered in it… Heart pounding, Matthew opened his eyes and jerked upright.

Not wanting to relieve that day, he slowly began to regain his composure. *Forget about it.* Once settled comfortably into the driver's seat again, the sun radiated over his face, it felt good. Familiar. And helped to calm him. He easily closed his eyes once again. This time remembering how he and Sandy used to sneak down to the river's edge on fall afternoons, like today, when they were in high school.

They'd lay on their backs in tall, soft grasses and allow the warmth of the sun to lull them to sleep. Once they had remained that way for so long, sound asleep in each other's arms, that even after the sun betrayed them and set for the night, they remained sleeping. When they woke to total darkness, shivering, they were nothing but happy. It was after spending days together like that one that they both knew that they'd always be together.

Several warm minutes passed and, in his slumber, Matthew's unconscious mind returned to Palm Sunday 1975:

Jack had just returned from his tour of duty overseas. It was a Saturday, the day before Palm Sunday, and everyone was thrilled he was back in time to attend services with them. He moved back into the house their parents had finally purchased the year before he returned home, located on Deerpath Lane. It was the one and only house they had ever owned, besides the lake house. Matthew was nineteen by this time, but still living at home trying to save up enough money to propose to Sandy and get married in the fall. Grace had turned five the week before, on the first of April.

The day began like most other Sundays in the McKenzie home. Audrey was at the stove cooking a hot breakfast for everyone, while Shea sat outside underneath his favorite maple tree with Grace, pointing out different types of birds as he sipped Jack Daniels from a silver flask. Jack and Matthew brought one another up to speed regarding the intimate details of the past two years of their lives while getting dressed for church.

After enjoying their breakfast together, with everyone wearing their Sunday best, the McKenzie family walked the few short blocks together to Our Lady of Perpetual Hope, like they did every Sunday morning.

Seating inside of the church was at a minimum due to the holiday; the only time the less-devoted typically attended. Despite the overcrowding, Shea eventually found pew space near the back of the church large enough for the five of them to fit. There they sat, huddled together quietly, wide-eyed. Sandy and her family sat closer to the front of the church.

Grace and several other children waved their palm branches above their heads as the church organist, Mrs. McCleary, began playing a traditional hymn. As everyone sang along to *God the Father* the anticipation grew. By the time the fourth verse was finished, the door connecting the rectory to the church opened wide and everyone drew a collective breath.

With every eye in the church focused on the new priest, he took his place at the top of the altar and raised his outstretched arms to his congregation, asking them to rise. As everyone stood from their pew, even the smallest of children, Audrey remained frozen and suddenly gasped—entirely too loudly—and attempted to divert her eyes downward as she slowly rose to her feet. Matthew noticed his mother's face first; skin as pale a sheet of paper with her grayed lips slightly parted, her eyes as wide as they could stretch...

Matthew jerked awake abruptly and his eyes flew wide open again. For two or three seconds, he couldn't remember where he was and found himself searching his front yard for his mother. He'd had this dream before and it always affected him the same.

"God damn it!" He thumped the steering wheel, yanking the door open and slamming it shut behind him. As he marched up the driveway to his front door, he cursed freely. "Damnit, Grace! You had to come back here and stir everything up again!"

CHAPTER 9

AUDREY
FRIDAY, JUNE 27, 1969

By the end of the week, Audrey had memorized the names of all forty children currently enrolled at Camp Vision. They ranged from the ages of eight to eighteen and came from all over the country; one boy as far away as Seattle. Most were from the northeast, a handful from the south, and one little girl, Kati Cartwright, lived in Cortland County that Audrey knew from the many times she volunteered to read to the blind at the Cortland hospital.

Audrey was in the main rec room, rearranging the chairs in a circle for her first poetry reading which was about to start in ten minutes, when Jayden stopped by to check on her.

"Hi, Audrey… what are you doing?"

Audrey smiled. *Wasn't it obvious?* "I'm putting the chairs in a circle to create a warm, supportive space for the children while I read to them."

"I see. I'm not trying to tell you what to do here, you understand, but that may not the best idea for these particular children."

Audrey let go of a chair and put her hands on her hips. She didn't have time for this. "Why not?"

Jayden smiled. "Because it took us five days to teach them where the furniture in this room was located."

"Oh no! Quick! Help me shove them back where they were... I'm so sorry."

As Audrey was busy trying to put all the heavy wooden chairs, one by one, back where they were, Jayden lifted his walkie talkie to his mouth. "Danny, rec center. Stat. Over."

"On my way. Over."

Less than a minute later, Danny walked in wearing a pair of tan chinos and a white t-shirt. "What's up?"

"Put these chairs back in place. Audrey's poetry reading is about to start and somehow the chairs got rearranged." He smiled at her. "We don't want to confuse the kids."

"Got it," Danny said, as he lifted two chairs at a time and began putting them exactly as they were before. Audrey continued moving the chairs as well. "I can handle this, Audrey, if you need to prepare your readings or anything."

"Thank you. That's a good idea," she said, as she walked to the stage and grabbed her notebook. From the book *Sketches of Natural History*, by Mary Howitt, she had selected two poems: *The Garden* and *The Spider and The Fly*. They seemed like good choices to lead off with, and she hoped the children would enjoy the readings.

"Okay, you're all set. Every chair is back in place," Danny said, approaching the stage. "Would you mind if I hung out and listened to your poetry, too, Audrey?"

Audrey looked up from her notes, puzzled. All the men she knew hated poetry. "Sure, if you'd like. Thank you for putting the chairs back in place for me."

"My pleasure."

"I'm going to stick around, too," Jayden said, taking a seat in the back of the room.

Soon the children began to file in with their counselors, and suddenly the room was packed. Even Cori and a few of her staff took a break from the kitchen and found seats closest to the stage, next to Danny.

Audrey had never read to a packed room like the one she found herself standing before. She felt her heart beginning to accelerate, and wiped her suddenly sweaty palms on her powder blue skirt—*why did I wear a skirt?* She adjusted it, self-consciously, before taking a breath and moving forward to the front of the stage holding her papers in her hands, trying desperately not to shake as she addressed the crowd. "Hello. My name is…"

"We can't hear you," someone yelled from the back of the room.

"Speak up," another kid shouted.

Hearing this, Danny jumped from his seat, ran up onto the stage and disappeared off to the right. A second later, he returned carrying a microphone attached to a tall, metal pole.

"Sorry about that, everyone. I forgot to set up the microphone for Miss Audrey… it'll just take me a minute."

"Thank you, Danny," Audrey whispered as Danny got busy setting up the microphone. She was trembling.

After the microphone was in place, Danny tapped it a couple of times, releasing several loud booms. "I guess you all heard *that*," he quipped, and everyone laughed. He then smiled over his left shoulder to Audrey. "Your turn."

Audrey walked to the microphone, something she had never used before in her life, and leaned too far into it. "My name…" Her voice burst with distortion and high-pitched squeals. The children covered their ears and cried out in pain. Now terrified, she looked at Danny who was still standing beside her.

"It's okay," he whispered. "Don't lean forward so much and just speak naturally."

Audrey now felt as if every move she made was in slow motion, but she turned her head back to face the microphone, this time not leaning in, and started over. "My name is Audrey McKenzie. Today I'd like to begin by reading two poems written by Mary Howitt, an English poet and author of the famous poem, *The Spider and The Fly*. Maybe you've heard of it." The crowd remained silent.

"I have," Danny whispered.

Audrey looked down at the writing on the page and cleared her throat. "*The Spider and The Fly*, by Mary Howitt." Her hands where now trembling uncontrollably, causing the papers in her hands to shake so violently that she couldn't read them. People in the audience began to clear their throats in an effort to inspire her to begin speaking. But she remained silent, staring blankly into the crowd when the papers suddenly fell from her fingertips and landed on the floor below.

From where he stood, Danny began to speak. "Will you walk into my parlor, said the spider to the fly." His voice carried across the room with apparent ease. "Tis the prettiest little parlor that ever you did spy." He walked closer to Audrey and stood beside her. "The way into my parlor is up a winding stair, and I've many curious things to show when you are there."

He squeezed her hand, gently, and quickly released it as he continued. "Oh no, no, said the little fly, to ask me is in vain, for who goes up your winding stair can never come down again."

Softly, finding her courage, she began to recite it along with him. "I'm sure you must be weary, dear, with soaring up so high. Will you rest upon my little bed, said the spider to the fly. There are pretty curtains drawn around; the sheets are fine and thin, and if you like to rest awhile, I'll snugly tuck you in!"

Audrey could see Jayden smiling, and the look of awe on the children's faces. In response, her voice grew stronger and she smiled brightly at Danny, signaling she was okay to continue alone. Danny took a few steps backwards so that only Audrey spoke now. "Oh no, no, said the little fly, for I've often heard it said, they never, never wake again, who sleep upon your bed! Said the cunning spider to the fly, dear friend what can I do, to prove the warm affection I've always felt for you? I have within my pantry, good store of all that's nice; I'm sure you're very welcome—will you please to take a slice?"

The crowd held their breath. '*Would the fly accept the invitation?*' was the thought on every child's face, she thought.

"Oh no, no, said the little fly, kind sir, that cannot be, I've heard what's in your pantry, and I do not wish to see! Sweet creature! said the spider, you're witty and you're wise, how handsome are your gauzy wings, how brilliant are your eyes! I've a little looking-glass upon my parlor shelf, if you'll step in one moment, dear, you shall behold yourself."

"Don't do it!" one of the children screamed and everyone chuckled.

"I thank you, gentle sir, she said, for what you're pleased to say, and bidding you good morning now, I'll call another day. The spider turned him round about, and went   into   his   den, for well he knew the silly fly would soon come back again. So, he wove a subtle web, in a little corner sly, and set his table ready, to dine upon the fly."

The children leaned forward in their seats as Audrey continued, "Then he came out to his door again, and merrily did sing, come hither, hither, pretty fly, with the pearl and silver wing. Your robes are green and purple—there's a crest upon your head; your eyes are like the diamond bright, but mine are dull as lead! Alas, alas! how very soon this silly little fly. Hearing his wily, flattering words, came slowly flitting by; with buzzing wings she hung aloft, then near and nearer drew, thinking only of her brilliant eyes, and green and purple hue—thinking only of her crested head—poor foolish thing! At last, up jumped the cunning spider, and fiercely held her fast. He dragged her up his winding stair, into his dismal den, within his little parlor—but she ne'er came out again!"

Audrey smiled over the crowd as she recited the final stanza. "And now dear little children, who may this story read, to idle, silly flattering words, I pray you ne'er give heed:
Unto an evil counsellor, close heart and ear and eye, and take a lesson from this tale, of the spider and the fly."

The kids—and even the adults—exploded with cheers and claps and Audrey took a bow until the applause quieted down. "Thank you," she said, collecting her papers from the floor. "Now for my next poem, also by Mary Howitt, is *The Garden.*"

CHAPTER 10

GRACE
FRIDAY, AUGUST 31, 2018

Jack and Grace stood on the sidewalk in front of the brewhouse waiting for their Uber. They had carefully avoided any further conversation regarding Grace 's DNA results over dinner, but when their ride finally pulled up in front of them, she was ready to pick up where their conversation had left off.

She slid across the back seat and sat behind the driver. Jack sat beside her. The sun was beginning to set behind them as the driver headed east back to the cottage. "So, can we talk about this now?"

Jack wiped the corners of his mouth and stretched his neck backward. "I guess so."

Grace cleared her throat. "How long have you guys known?"

Jack turned his head away from her and stared out the window. The leaves on the trees in town had turned color several weeks ago and were beginning to fall to the ground. He watched as the wind picked up the many orphaned, colorful pieces of foliage and swirled them in the air while those still clinging tightly to branches turned upward. "It looks like it's going to rain."

Grace looked out her window. "Yeah, looks like it. Jack, please... tell me what you know."

Jack took a deep breath, released it through his nose and faced forward. "We've both known since the year I returned home from Vietnam."

Grace tried to remember when that was. "That would have been when I was about five or six, right?"

"Yeah, as a matter of fact, you had just celebrated your fifth birthday the week before I came home."

"Okay, right, I think I remember that now. Everyone was so happy you were home again."

"Yeah, I suppose they were."

"I remember how sad it was when Peter Campagna was killed over there. Mom started playing all of those sad songs on the piano after that. I'm sure she worried about you every day."

Jack shook his head in agreement. "It was a terrible time."

They sat a few moments in silence, both reflecting upon the war. Even though Grace had only been a child, she remembered hearing about Vietnam, at least what she could understand at such a young age. She particularly recalled the gruesome coverage that was plastered all over their TV screen each night. Until then, no one had ever seen such horrific images coming into their living rooms. It was awful, and did nothing more (at least in her household) than scare the crap out of them, especially her mother.

"How did you both find out I wasn't Dad's biological child?"

"Oh, Grace, does it really matter? It never changed the way any of us felt about you. Can't you just leave it at that?"

"No, Jack, I can't!" Grace snapped. "I'm sure this may not seem like a big deal to you, but it's a very big deal to me. I want to know who my biological father was."

Jack pulled at his collar for a second and cleared his throat. "I'm afraid I can't help you there, Grace. I don't know who he was."

"Does Matthew?"

"No."

"Are you sure?"

"Yes, I'm sure. Neither one of us has any idea."

Grace furrowed her brow. Nothing made sense to her. How could they not know who her real father was? Then a terrible thought entered her mind. "Mom wasn't raped, was she?"

Jack hesitated before answering. "I don't know. Maybe..."

"Oh my God!" Grace covered her face with both of her hands. "No wonder you guys didn't want to tell me!" She began to cry.

Jack sighed. "I really don't think it was a rape, Grace. If it were, I'm sure we would have known about it. Surely, there would have been an investigation or something like that, but there was nothing of the sort. I guess she somehow fell into the arms of another man, as terrible as that may sound."

"Are you sure it wasn't rape?" She wiped mascara from her face.

"Yes, I'm sure. We all would have known if it were. I'm sorry I gave you the wrong impression."

Grace regained her composure. "Well, that's a relief. But how could it be that Mom just decided one day to be unfaithful to Dad? That doesn't make sense to me either."

"I don't know, maybe she was already suffering from the Alzheimer's." He seemed to be grasping at straws now.

Grace consider the possibility. "But Mom was only thirty-eight when I was born. I've never heard of anyone being afflicted with Alzheimer's that young."

"I really don't know why Mom did what she did, Grace, but obviously it happened and you were born nine months later. That's all I know. I'm very sorry."

Grace knew he was lying, but thought about it some more and decided to take a step backwards. "Okay, I understand. Obviously, you couldn't possibly know why she did what she did. But you said you learned the truth about me when you came back from Vietnam. How did that come about? Did Mom and Dad just suddenly decide to come out with it? Wait a minute, did Dad *even* know!?"

Jack let out a little groan and rubbed his hand over his belly.

Further annoyed with her brother, Grace asked, "What's wrong with you?"

"I think I going to get sick."

"What?! Now?"

"Yes, driver, pull over... I'm going to throw up."

Hearing this, the driver immediately pulled onto the shoulder of the road and Jack jumped out of the car. Both he and Grace watched as Jack walked into some tall weeds and bent over at the waist. After a couple of minutes, he wiped his mouth a few times with the back of his hand before walking back to the car.

"Are you okay now?" Grace asked, hoping he wasn't faking a sudden illness.

"Yeah, I think so." He got back into the car. "Must have been that Mexican bowl. Wait until I get ahold of Matthew for recommending the stupid place. Let's just get back to the cottage, okay? Maybe we could continue our conversation tomorrow, when I'm feeling better."

"Yeah, of course," Grace said. "Driver, let's go."

CHAPTER 11

AUDREY
SUNDAY, JUNE 29, 1969

After the Mass held inside of the rec room in a make-shift church, Audrey walked to Jayden's cabin to use his telephone. She had promised Shea she would call him once a week on Sunday afternoons. At the time, however, she didn't know the office would be closed on Sundays and she'd be unable to use the phone. The only other cabin which had a telephone was Jayden's. She hoped he wouldn't mind the interruption.

Last week's heatwave had finally passed and the day was much more seasonable. She walked the well-worn trail below a cloudless sky. Rounding the corner at the end of the path where it came to a "T", she noticed Danny out front of his cabin polishing the white motorcycle she had spotted in the parking lot her first day at camp.

"Hi, Danny. What do you have there, a Bonneville?"

Danny looked up from his bike, holding a blue shammy in his hand. "Yeah, that's right. How'd you know?"

She walked across the grass to join him. "My dad owned a small engine repair shop in town when I was growing up. He loved working on old motorcycles. Especially the classics." She smiled as she examined his bike a little closer. The fuel tank was painted pearly white and the fenders were adorned with gold racing stripes lined with black pinstripes. "But none as nice as this one. He repaired old clunkers mainly, usually Harleys." She ran her hand gently over the tank, being careful not to smudge what Danny had so carefully polished. "She's a beauty. A '62?"

"Close, '63." He squinted one eye, seemingly trying to block the sun coming over her shoulders as he faced her. Danny cleared his throat and turned his attention back to his bike. "Thanks. The color is called Alaskan White. First year Triumph went with a solid color instead of their typical two-tone design."

"It sure is pretty. I really like it. You're a lucky guy, Danny, owning such a beautiful bike." She began walking back to the trail.

"Where are you headed?"

"To your uncle's cabin to use his phone."

"Oh."

"Why?"

"I was just thinking maybe you'd enjoy taking a spin on her with me a little later, is all." He looked down at his bike again. "I was getting ready to take a ride. There's a forest not too far from here. In Hector, I hear. Thought I may check it out. Wanna come?"

She hesitated, slightly, before answering him. "No, I don't think so, but thank you for asking. It's very kind of you. It's a perfect day for a ride."

"Yes, it is. I'm looking forward to it." He began polishing the handlebars once more.

"I bet." She began to walk away again and then suddenly stopped, remembering she hadn't properly thanked him yet for the night before. "Oh, I almost forgot. I wanted to thank you for coming to my rescue last night during the recital. I don't think I would have gotten through it had you not stepped in."

"Ah, it was nothing. But you're welcome. I was happy to help out."

"Well, thanks again. I really appreciate it. I honestly don't know what came over me. I've recited poetry to children dozens of times and not once did I become flustered."

"Well, it happens."

"Yes, I guess it does. I was very impressed that you knew the words to *The Spider and The Fly* well enough to recite it cold like you did. And very lucky for me, too." She chuckled.

"My mother and I used to read poetry together all the time when I was a kid. That one is a favorite. I know some others, too."

"Oh, yeah? Which ones?"

"A few of Shakespeare's sonnets, some of Walt Whitman and Emily Dickinson. But don't hold me to it." He laughed, revealing his charming smile.

She felt herself blushing and turned her head away. "That's incredible. Most of the men I know don't give a hoot about poetry."

"Well, their loss."

"Yeah," she said. "Well, thanks again, Danny. Enjoy your ride."

"Sure thing. Catch you later?"

She gave him a quick thumbs-up. "Sure."

When she reached Jayden's cabin, she knocked once and waited a few seconds until Ajei opened the door and greeted her.

"Hi, Miss Audrey. Come on in."

"Thank you, Ajei." She stepped inside.

The cabin was the same basic design as hers and Cori's, with the exception of one additional bedroom. But the furnishings, she noticed, where entirely finer. Jewel-toned rugs from the Orient, thick and plush, graced the floors in the living area and at the entrance where she currently stood. The dining table separating the kitchen and living area, same as she and Cori's, was made of solid oak, not pine, as well as the six matching chairs placed around it. In the center of the table rested a fine, Asian-style porcelain vase, currently boasting a large bouquet of yellow roses, baby's breath, and tall stalks of assorted greenery. Gold-framed original oil paintings, signed by each artist, hung on the walls. Drapes made of the finest silk flanked every window and fell elegantly to the floor. It was decadent.

"Hello, Audrey. What an unexpected surprise," Jayden said, joining Ajei at the front door. "Please come in and have a seat."

"Oh no, but thank you," she said. "I hate to bother you, but I told my husband that I would call him once a week on Sunday. I'm afraid I wasn't aware the office would be closed on Sundays. May I borrow your phone, please? I'll be brief."

"Well, of course. It's over here." Up against one wall of the living room sat a large, mahogany desk, was where the telephone rested. "Take your time, Audrey. Ajei, let's give Miss Audrey some privacy."

"Thank you," Audrey said.

"We'll be outside doing some weeding around back."

Jayden and Ajei walked outside and Audrey quickly dialed her home phone number.

Shea picked up on the third ring. "Hello."

91

"Hi, Shea. It's me."

"Hi, honey. How's it going?" He sounded happy to be hearing from her.

"Very good. I held my first poetry reading last night. The children really enjoyed it."

"That's great. How's the food?"

"Delicious. As a matter of fact, our chef, Cori, is my roommate. She's very nice, and very funny. You'd like her."

"I'm sure."

Audrey paused a moment, thinking of what to say next. "So, what are you and the boys have planned for the day?"

"A little fishing. How about you?"

She paused again, allowing herself some additional time to think. Truth was, she hadn't really decided what she would be doing today.

"Audrey?"

"Oh, I'm sorry. I'm standing in Jayden Scarsi's cabin admiring all of the fine furnishings… I got a little lost for a minute. I think I might hang out at the lake today with Cori and do some reading. It's such a beautiful day."

"Yeah, it's beautiful here, too. By the way, what did you do this morning? Are there services there?"

"Yes. Jayden converted one section of the rec room for church services. Area priests volunteer their time to conduct Mass for us each week. It's been very accommodating."

"That's nice, glad to hear it. Well, the boys are ready to go now. They're outside. Just finished loading the truck. Would you like to speak to them before we hang up?"

"Of course."

"Okay, hold on."

A few seconds later, Matthew picked up the phone. "Hi, Mom. How's it going?"

"Great. You and your brother would love it here, Matty. There's a sandy beach on the lake, canoes, kayaks, arts and crafts, pottery making, woodworking and, of course, my poetry readings."

"Sounds cool, except for the poetry. Sorry Mom, it's not my thing."

"Yes, I know. I hear you're about to go fishing with Dad. Can I get a quick word with Jack, please?"

"Sure, here he is. Bye, Mom. I love you."

"Love you, too, Matty." She waited until she heard Jack pick up the phone. "Hi, Jack. Holding down the fort there, are you?"

"You know it. Someone's got to." He chuckled.

"But, really, everything okay..." She sensed Jack knew what she was eluding to: Shea's propensity for drinking too much when she wasn't around.

"Yeah, Mom. Everything's fine, but Dad's cooking really sucks."

"Jack, your language," she scolded.

"Sorry. But it really is awful. We all think so, even Dad. We miss you... and you're cooking. But, other than that, everything is cool."

"Good. I'm glad to hear it. Well, I know you are all excited to get going to the river. Be careful, okay, Jack?" Again, another warning about Shea's drinking.

"We will, Mom. Please don't worry. Love you."

"I love you, too, Jack. I'm going to be writing a letter to each of you later on tonight. I'll mail them out tomorrow. That is if I can figure out how to get to a post office from here."

"Okay, cool. See ya later."

"See ya later," Audrey said, smiling, repeating her teenage son's exact words before hanging up the phone. Turning away from the desk, she suddenly remembered that she had forgotten to tell Shea that it would be better if she called him on Saturday. She considered about calling him right back, but figured it could wait. She'd just call him next Saturday and explain it then.

Stepping outside, she found Jayden and Ajei doing some weeding out back, as they'd said they would be. "Thank you again, Jayden. I'm finished with my call."

"You're welcome, anytime," he stood, brushing the dirt from his pants.

"Miss Audrey, will you be going to the lake today?" Ajei asked.

"Maybe, I haven't decided yet. Will you be there, sweetheart?"

"Yep, as soon as we finish here... we're both going!"

"That's wonderful. Maybe I'll see you then," Audrey said, happy to learn she may be able to spend a little time with the pair later on. "Thanks again, Jayden. For the use of your phone."

"You're welcome."

"Bye," Ajei said, waiving to Audrey as she walked away.

CHAPTER 12

GRACE
SATURDAY, SEPTEMBER 1, 2018

The next morning, Grace woke before sunrise in the smallest bedroom of the house. She had decided if Matthew did return, the least she could do is offer him the next-best bedroom with a queen size bed, seeing that Jack had already claimed the biggest one for himself. With a yawn, she sat up and stretched her arms above her head. Her muscles felt stiff and sore from being cramped up in the small twin bed she'd slept in. Bailey let out a little huff, but quickly abandoned any idea he may have had about getting up; it was still dark outside. He lay his head down once again and fell asleep.

Grace, however, was wide awake having suddenly remembered someone when she woke. Someone she hadn't thought about in years who may actually be able to help her. Excited, she leaped from the bed and dashed into the bathroom to take a warm shower

As the hot water cascaded over her sore body, she tried to remember where Cori Cohen, her mother's best friend, was living now. The last she knew it was somewhere in Albany, near Lincoln Park. After her mother died, Grace had kept in touch with Cori for a little while, like she promised she would, but eventually lost all contact with her. The last time she remembered seeing Cori was at Shea's funeral, six years ago. Grace wasn't even sure if she was still alive, she realized with a pang of guilt. *Although,* she realized, *I probably would have heard from Matthew if Cori had passed away.* He was always good about that sort of thing.

Stepping out from the shower, she tried to remember if she still had Cori's telephone number stored in her phone. Grace grabbed her phone off the dresser and began searching for Cori's name. *No luck,* there was nothing listed for Cori in her contacts. Still determined, she switched over to Facebook. Maybe Cori was active on social media; she was certainly the type that may, Grace figured. Sure enough, there was only one person listed with the name of Cori Cohen, currently living in Albany.

"Gotcha," Grace whispered, deciding to send her a private message later on, after getting dressed and eating some breakfast. For now, she sent her a friend request.

Still wrapped in a bathroom towel, Grace began scrolling through some of Cori's recent Facebook posts. The last thing the outspoken ninety-year-old woman had posted were some words from a World War II museum in Svolvaer, Norway, comparing Hitler's campaign style to the current administrations with her added caption which read, "Uneasily familiar?"

The post before it, she wrote, "Pay attention and read carefully!! Don't let Don the Con and Paul Ryan scam you!!" A picture of the Social Security logo, and a theory which claimed that the folks in Washington have pulled off a bigger Ponzi scheme than Bernie Madoff ever did was posted below it. Further still, was a post explaining how to defeat authoritarianism urging all of her friends to follow 'Occupy Democrats' now before it was too late.

Grace dropped her phone on the bed, relieved to discover that Cori's mind must still be as sharp as ever. *Same old feisty Cori; speaking her mind.*

By the time Grace had settled on the living room couch in front of a crackling fire, a toasted bagel and cup of joe beside her, the sun was beginning to rise over the trees. The sudden jingle of her cellphone startled her; it was a message from Cori!

Wow, that was fast.

"Grace! What a wonderful surprise it was to receive your friend request. It's been way too long. We MUST get together sometime soon to catch up. I miss you, beautiful girl!"

She smiled and began typing her response. "You must be an early bird, too. I'm sitting next to a warm fire at the cottage enjoying my breakfast. I would LOVE to get together with you, Cori. When can we meet?"

"You're in Trumansburg? If so, and you don't have other exciting plans for the weekend, how about today? I'm only a few hour's drive from you, but I can meet you half way if you'd like."

Grace thought about her response for a few seconds. She'd like nothing more than to spend the day, perhaps even the rest of the weekend in Albany with Cori, but she'd already pissed off one brother and wasn't sure how Jack would feel about her abandoning him here alone. Finally, she typed, "Let me see what I can do. I'd actually love to come to you... if that's ok. I have a chocolate lab now, Bailey, that I'll have to bring with me. Ok?"

"Are you serious? Of course! I love dogs, I just hope he doesn't mind a few cats. I have four. I'll be home the entire weekend."

"OK. I'll get back to you in a little bit. Waiting for Jack to wake up."

"You're with Jack? How nice! How about the ardent brother, him too?"

Grace smiled. "Sort of. I'll explain everything when I see you. Thanks."

"Sounds promising, can't wait. Hope to see you soon."

Grace set her phone down on the floor beside her and leaned back into the couch.

Within an hour, her coffee finished, Grace was half-dozing in the warmth of the fire when Jack lumbered out of his bedroom yawning and rubbing his fingers through his hair. "Good morning."

"Good morning, how'd you sleep?" Grace stretched.

"Pretty good. How about you?"

"Not that great, I tossed and turned a lot and woke up before dawn. How's the stomach?"

"Huh?"

"Your stomach… is it still bothering you?"

"Oh, that," Jack said, perhaps remembering his fake puking attack. "Much better, thanks."

"That's good. Would you like a bagel? I can toast one for you."

"Sure, but where'd you get the bagels? Last time we checked, there wasn't anything to eat here."

"I went shopping last night after you went to bed."

"You're kidding?"

"Nope." Grace walked into the kitchen and began preparing the bagel for her brother, and he joined her.

"Looks like it's going to be another beautiful day," Grace smiled as the sunlight began to pour through the kitchen window.

"Yeah, looks like it," Jack said, as he joined her, carrying his toasted bagel sandwiched together with a generous blob of cream cheese in one hand and a cup of coffee in his other. He took a seat on the love seat next to her and bit into his bagel. "Got anything special planned for today?"

"Well, I actually wanted to talk to you about that."

"Okay, shoot."

"I woke up this morning thinking about Cori Cohen."

"Huh, Cori? That's weird." He said, swallowing hard. "I haven't thought about her in years. How's she doing these days?"

"Good, I guess. I've actually lost contact with her too. I haven't spoken to her since Dad's funeral."

Jack nodded and continued chewing.

"Anyway, I got thinking about her and how well she and Mom got along... and, well, I thought that she may know something more about my biological father."

"Do you think?"

"Yeah. Don't you?"

"I don't know," he said, seemingly trying to downplay her brilliant idea. "She may not have told Cori about him, Grace," he offered.

Grace rolled the thought of this possibility around in her mind for a few seconds. "Sorry, brother, but what you don't know about women is a lot." She chuckled. "Sorry, couldn't help myself. That's one of my favorite movie quotes. Moonstruck."

He stared blankly at her. "What?"

"You know... Moonstruck. With Cher?"

Nothing.

"Never mind. But, anyway, I'm pretty sure Cori probably knows more about it than anyone else; women tend to share this type of thing with one another."

"I guess," he said, having nowhere else to go with the conversation. "So, what's your plan? Are you going to contact her?"

"Already did. Through Facebook."

"Cori's on Facebook?"

"Yep. Taking pot shots at the current administration, too." She smiled, remembering Cori's many anti-POTUS comments.

"I bet."

Grace smiled briefly, and then asked the one question that had been dogging her all night. "Jack, there's something I really don't understand. Maybe you can help me."

"Sure, I'll try," he said, half-heartedly.

"Can you please explain why you and Matthew both chose not to tell me about this? I mean, I get it. When Mom and Dad were both alive you must've felt like it wasn't your place to tell me. Maybe they even swore you to secrecy? But, hell, why didn't either one of you say something after Dad died? I truly don't understand. Obviously, you must have felt I deserved to know. It really bugs me that you didn't even try."

Jack hung his head and heart for a few moments. She was right, and he knew it. "Grace, I can't answer for Matthew, but I never said anything because I started to believe that you were better off not knowing. I mean, it's not like any of us ever treated you any differently because you weren't Dad's biological child. We all loved you with all our hearts. That's never changed."

"I know," she said. "But my God, the health issues alone should have been enough for you to want to tell me the truth. I mean last year, when I had that cancer scare, did it ever occur to either of you that perhaps knowing my complete family health history may have actually been important? My whole life, I've completed those stupid questionnaires in doctors' offices. Same as you, I've always stated there is no cancer in our family, but that there's heart disease on my father's side. You have NO idea what it feels like, Jack. To suddenly discover, at the age of forty-eight, that you know nothing about an entire other half of yourself. Nothing at all."

She stood up. "I feel you have both done me a great disservice by not telling me this sooner. Perhaps, oh, I don't know, say six years ago after Dad died! Maybe then I would've had a better chance finding my real father and been able to ask him some important questions. If for no other reason than to learn the other side of my family's health concerns. But now it's probably too late for that. He's probably dead!"

Grace was suddenly furious, surprising even herself, and no longer cared whether or not she had offended him with her words. *It's my goddamn life, who gives a shit how any of this makes Jack or Matthew feel?!* She was done embodying the sweet, perpetual little-girl persona that both of her brothers seemed to prefer. *Screw them!*

"And, by the way," she continued, towering over her older brother as he sat on the couch, looking up at her. He seemed somehow weaker now. "I've decided to spend the rest of the weekend in Albany with Cori. I'm leaving right after I take Bailey for a walk. You can do whatever you'd like, Jack, I really don't care." She marched from the living room into the kitchen where Bailey lay sleeping. "Come on, Bailey. We're outta here."

As she began walking towards the back door, Jack sat stunned on the love seat with his mouth fully agape, a bit of cream cheese stuck in the corner of his mouth. Before slamming the door behind her, Grace leaned into the room and yelled, "and another thing, did either of you geniuses happen to notice that the goddam cottage needs to be repainted again?!"

With that, she was gone.

CHAPTER 13

AUDREY
SUNDAY, JUNE 29, 1969

Audrey hurried back to her cabin hoping to find Cori still reading a book. Maybe she could convince her to head down to the lake with her again for the day. Knowing her distaste for the cold water, she wasn't sure Cori would agree, but it was worth a try.

As expected, Cori was sitting in one of the two club chairs reading a book when Audrey arrived. "Hey, kid. Did you get ahold of your hubby?"

"Yes. I caught them as they were heading out to go fishing. I was able to talk to all three of them."

"That's nice. Do they miss you?"

Audrey chuckled. "Yes, but I think it's actually my cooking they miss, not me. Apparently, Shea's meals haven't been too good."

"Ah, don't kid yourself. I'm sure they miss you."

"Maybe," she said, looking down. "But who knows."

Cori closed her book. "I'm beginning to think there's something troubling you. Do you want to talk about it? I'm a pretty good listener."

"Thanks, Cori, maybe later. Right now, I was hoping I could convince you spend the day down at the lake with me again. You can bring your book."

Cori sat in silence for a few seconds, perhaps considering her options. Finally, she agreed. "Yeah, okay, I'll join you. I've already made up some of that chicken salad you enjoy so much. Why don't I whip up us a couple of sandwiches and some other snacks while you get changed? I'm not planning on doing any swimming, though. I've had my fair share of the ridiculously cold water."

"Sounds great, thank you. It'll only take me a few seconds to change."

"Okay, but take your time." Cori stood up and walked into the kitchen where she began preparing their lunch while Audrey ducked into the bedroom to change.

As promised, Audrey reappeared wearing her swimsuit only a few seconds later—a one-piece this time, having felt very uncomfortable wearing her bikini the last time she and Cori went to the lake. Besides, Jayden may like the sophistication of her one-piece bathing suit of pale blue and white with the darling little silver belt. "All set?" She asked.

"Yep," Cori said as she dropped some drinks, a few snacks and their sandwiches into a cooler. "Let's go."

By the time they arrived at the beach, many of the campers and their counsellors had already arrived. Some were busy kayaking or canoeing, while others swam or played in the sand.

"Wow, pretty packed again today." Cori set the cooler down on the sand near the lifeguards' station. "Here good?"

"Yes, this will do," Audrey said, stretching out the blanket she had carried while looking around. There was no sight of Jayden.

"Do you want a sandwich now?" Cori asked.

"No, thanks. I'm going to take a little dip in the water first."

"Okay, suit yourself. I'll hang out here with my book."

"What are you reading?"

"Peyton Place."

"Oh, gosh, Cori. I heard that's a bit tawdry."

"No kidding. Why do you think I picked it?" She laughed and leaned back against the cooler. "You wanna read it when I'm finished?"

"Geez, I don't know…"

"Oh, come on, kid. Live a little."

"Whatever," Audrey laughed, pulling her sundress off over her head. "I'll be back."

"Okay, I'll be here."

As Audrey swam, Jayden and Ajei arrived. Seeing them, she couldn't help wondering about the strange arrangement. Jayden and his lifestyle intrigued her. She couldn't image not having to work for a living, or a man caring for a young girl all alone. Soon, moving past thoughts of his lofty lifestyle, she began wondering if Jayden drank.

Still very much lost in her thoughts about the mysterious Jayden, she didn't hear Ajei calling her name at first. "Miss Audrey, Miss Audrey!" Ajei repeated, calling from the shoreline.

Finally hearing her, Audrey swam in closer to the beach area. "Hi, Ajei. I see you made it."

"Yeah, just now. Can I come swimming with you, Miss Audrey? My dad says I can, if it's okay with you."

"Of course."

Ajei waded into the water and stood next to Audrey. "Miss Audrey, can you do a handstand?"

As Audrey dipped under the water and began demonstrating her hand stand, Ajei's laughter, louder than it had been since she arrived at camp, could be overheard by Jayden who sat on a blanket a few yards away. He stood up and walked to the lake.

"How was that?" Audrey asked, resurfacing from the water, startled to discover Jayden had joined them. He quickly averted his gaze from her legs, but Audrey saw a flash of admiration in his eyes.

"Wonderful," Jayden replied. "Do it again."

"Yes! Do it again, Miss Audrey! Do it again!"

More than happy to obliged them, Audrey dipped back underneath the water and performed another handstand. And another, and another... until, finally, she felt winded. "Now it's your turn."

"Who, me?" Jayden asked.

"Well, I'm looking straight at you," she said, splashing a little water in his face.

"Yes, Daddy! Do a handstand!" Ajei squealed.

As Jayden dove underneath the water to demonstrate his own skills, Danny arrived. Spotting the three of them together, he jumped into the water and swam towards them. Watching him approach, Audrey missed Jayden's handstand.

"Did you see it, Miss Audrey? My dad just did a handstand, too!"

"Yes," she fibbed. "I saw it. How wonderful!"

"Uh huh," Ajei said as she swam closer to her father. "Daddy, please take me out into the deeper water with you now... please."

"Sure, hold on," Jayden said, turning his back to Ajei as Audrey helped her wrap her arms around his neck. "Are you ready?"

"Sure," Ajei laughed. "Let's go!"

Audrey laughed as she watched them swim deeper into the lake.

"Cute kid, isn't she?" Danny asked. They stood beside one another, water skimming them just below their waists.

Audrey nodded.

"They're both so lucky to have one another. Best thing that ever happened to Uncle Jayden, if you ask me."

"Oh, yeah? How so?"

Danny shrugged his shoulders. "Well for one, his life seems to actually be serving a purpose now. Before Ajei, he simply drifted from state to state. Not a care in the world. Didn't seem normal to me."

"I see your point."

"And Ajei, forget about it." He laughed. "I mean, look at her... She's a much different little girl now than she was two years ago. It makes me choke up a little, you know?"

"Yes. I think I do." Audrey said thoughtfully.

Danny dove into the water and disappeared from sight for several, uncomfortable seconds. Audrey, beginning to worry, dove underneath the water and opened her eyes. Thankfully, the lake was clean and clear, not a bit murky, but Danny was nowhere to be found. It was as if he had suddenly disappeared. Unable to hold her breath a second longer, she swam to the surface and began calling his name. "Danny! Where are you? Danny!"

As she was about to call for a lifeguard, Danny swam between her legs and emerged from the water like a dolphin.

"Danny!" she scolded. "I thought you drowned!"

He chuckled. "I'm sorry. I didn't mean to scare you."

"Well, you did." She turned away and began swimming towards Jayden and Ajei.

"I'm sorry, Audrey. I would never intentionally scare you, or anyone." He swam closer to her.

She felt a little foolish. "It's okay, but you did have me worried." She shrugged with a smile, hoping to move past the topic. "How long can you hold your breath, anyway?"

"I'm not really sure, pretty long I guess."

"I guess!" She said, laughing now. "Golly…"

Another one of his irresistible smiles crept onto his charming face. "*Golly?* Only my mom uses that word." He began to laugh.

"Oh, you… you… child! How old are you anyway?"

"Twenty-five. How old are you?"

"Old enough not to answer that question, Mr. Rudy-mac-rudest."

"Ha! Now I'm a rude man?"

He swam underneath the water again. This time, however, she was prepared for his extended absence. Audrey stood in the water watching the surface, intently, wondering where and when he may suddenly pop up again. Then, much to her surprise, no more than five seconds later, she spotted him climbing the ladder of the floating dock, a good fifty feet away. Her mouth flew open. *How did he swim there so quickly?"*

CHAPTER 14

GRACE
SATURDAY, SEPTEMBER 1, 2018

Settled into her car, with Bailey and her overnight bags in the back, Grace sent a private message to Cori via Facebook again. "I've readjusted my schedule, can spend entire weekend in Albany. Leaving Trumansburg now. Please send your address for GPS, and your cell number. Mine is 215-555-0173. Thanks."

Before she was able to put the Land Rover into reverse, her phone jingled with a return message from Cori. "Terrific news! 518-555-0029. 62 Myrtle Ave, Albany. Please drive safely and see you soon!"

After entering Cori's address into her GPS, she backed down the driveway and drove away.

Jack secretly watched her from the living room window with a heavy heart. "Poor kid," he mumbled. Stepping away from the window, he walked back into his parents' bedroom and grabbed his cellphone. *Time to contact Matthew.*

Once on I-88 heading east, Grace began to wonder how much Cori may actually know about her biological father, if anything at all. She didn't think what Jack had suggested was true. Surely their mother would have shared with Cori, her best friend, who her biological father was. But still, she couldn't help wondering, with so many years having passed, how much a ninety-year-old woman could remember. Even one as razor sharp as Cori. Suddenly, she began to worry that this idea may end up as fruitless as her last attempt with her brothers.

Now frustrated with the possibility of Cori's memory failing her, she banged her hand on the steering wheel, startling Bailey. "Sorry, boy," she said. "Everything's okay. Lay down." Bailey followed her command and settled into the back seat again, but with both eyes watching her closely. "What would I do without you, boy?"

Grace returned her thoughts to Cori and her mother. They had met at Camp Vision in the summer of 1969, she remembered, where they became the best of friends after sharing a cabin together. *She must know about my biological father... She has to!*

She stepped on the gas petal harder and increased her speed. Hopefully Cori would remember him, someone Italian. *Mediterranean people are so very attractive.*

Totally lost in her head with thoughts of Cori knowing something, Grace didn't notice the state police car following her, even with its lights flashing and siren blaring. She continued driving as she had been, at a very high rate of speed, until Bailey began barking. Back to reality and horrified at what she had unintentionally done, she pulled over onto the side of the road and prepared herself to take her lumps. *So reckless.*

Her heart rate speed up as she waited for the trooper to emerge from his car. After a few minutes longer, which felt like years to Grace, the trooper stepped out of his cruiser and began walking the shoulder of the road. Once he was standing beside her car, she lowered the driver's side window and began smiling, uncontrollably, with nerves.

"Hello, officer." Bailey leaned over the top of her seat and sniffed in the man's direction a few times.

The trooper leaned one arm on top of the Land Rover. "Do you have any idea how fast you were going, miss?"

"No, not really, but I'm very embarrassed about this. I never speed."

"So, what's the rush today?" He asked. "Where are you headed?"

"To Albany to visit an old friend." Grace shrugged, "This may sound nuts, but I just found out that my father wasn't really my father. Both of my parents passed away several years ago and my friend in Albany... actually, she was my mother's best friend, Cori Cohen, is the only person still alive who may know who my biological father is, or was. I'm not sure about that either. Whether he's still alive or not, but I..."

"That's okay, I don't need to hear any more," he said, interrupting her. "I'm very sorry to hear about your father. DNA results?" She nodded. He cleared his throat. "This is what I'm going to do. Even though I clocked you at 92, a violation that could easily add 8 points to your driver's license, I'm going to ticket you at 72, which is only 3 points."

"Thank you, officer. I really appreciate it."

"I'll need your license and registration to go write this up."

Grace leaned over and opened the glove compartment. "Here you go," she said, handing him her papers.

"Thank you, I'll be right back." He walked back to his car.

While she waited, she blocked the handsome trooper's smile and green eyes from her mind and grabbed her cellphone, wondering whether or not she should send Cori a text letting her know she'd be arriving a little later. Deciding against it, she threw her phone back inside of her purse resting beside her on the passenger seat.

With her window still open, she looked around and suddenly realized where she was and recalled the day when she and Shea travelled together to the New York State Museum in Albany. On this very same stretch of highway the traffic was moving at a snail's pace that day, open only to one lane of traffic while fresh asphalt was being laid.

She remembered the thick, suffocating fog of exhaust fumes from the heavy equipment as they creeped by. She'd watched them closely from the car window, covering her nose. New asphalt fell to the road in huge gooey lumps as thick as syrup, eager to stick together. Two giant steel wheel rollers operating in tandem began rolling over the ebony goo, transforming it. It lay as smooth as a typing ribbon and as flat as icing, yet still bitter to her eyes and mouth. Now, as she glanced out her window, after so many seasons, what was once dead black and glossy had become gray and cracked, aging just like her.

She let out a shaky sigh as the trooper returned to her car and handed her the speeding ticket.

"Here you are, miss. Please slow down while you continue driving to Albany to visit your friend. And good luck finding your father." He tipped his hat and returned to his car.

Was he smiling? Grace wasn't sure, but she rolled up her window, tucked the speeding ticket into her purse and resumed driving towards Albany.

In another speed-limit-driven two hours, Grace pulled into the city of Albany and parked in front of Cori's New Orleans-style shotgun home. The house was a stunner with its bright turquoise walls, creamy white trim, black window panes, and a welcoming red front door.

Bailey, now eager to get out of the car, stood up on all fours and began whining. "I'm coming, boy," Grace said, stepping outside and opening the back door. After securing his leash to his collar, she looked around and spotted the park she remembered only a few blocks away and began walking in that direction.

"Grace! Is that really you?" Cori was an old woman now, but not the kind you pitied. She was very slender with medium-length gray hair, neat and thick, skimming the tops of her shoulders. Her face was not made up, with the exception of her lips which were painted a soft shade of burgundy. If she had been paler, her choice of lip color would look tasteless, but against her naturally tanned skin it looked just right. Greeting Grace on the sidewalk, she extended both arms and gave her a long hug.

"Cori!" The two women embraced a little longer as Bailey tugged on his leash. Noticing some dirt beneath her finger nails, Grace asked, "Are you a gardener now, too?"

Cori hid her hands behind her back. "Oh, yes, that. I'm constantly getting soil underneath my nails. Don't look."

"Oh, don't be silly. I bet you work very hard to gain that dirt and have the very best rose garden on this street."

"Well naturally, of course I do."

Grace laughed. *Same old Cori.* "I can't wait to see it, but I need to take this guy for a well-deserved walk. I was just about to head down to Lincoln Park. Do you want to join us?"

"Absolutely," Cori said, bending over to pet Bailey. "Nice pup you've got here," she said, rubbing the top of Bailey's head. "Let me grab my inhaler first. The cut grass tends to flare my allergies."

"Okay, sure, we'll wait."

When Cori returned a few seconds later, the pair smiled brightly at one another and began walking—now with a very anxious Bailey in tow—to Lincoln Park where he could play and they could talk.

After returning from the park, Cori, Grace, and Bailey walked into Cori's house and were greeted by the first of Cori's four cats; a short-haired white one. He rubbed up against Grace 's leg, keeping a steady eye on Bailey, who was nothing more than curious. "This is Rev," Cori said. "He's my oldest rescue."

"Grace smiled, petting the top of Rev's willing head.

Cori beckoned for Grace to follow her further into her narrow but surprisingly spacious city home. The front door opened directly into the living room, which boasted a long, button-tufted gray sofa along one exterior wall, and two matching chairs directly across from it—all very modern in design. The walls were painted a bright, creamy white, with a black trim. Instead of heavy drapes, the tall windows—floor to ceiling, almost—were covered modestly by retractable honey-comb, gray shades.

The pair walked past the living room, and Cori stopped at cat tree next to one of the tall windows, where two more cats sat. "These are Kitta and Burt," Cori said, petting one with each hand.

Grace and Bailey stopped in front of the cat tree. Kitta, as gray as Rev was white, threw back her head, revealing sharp, white teeth. Startled, Grace lowered her hand and took a step backwards. "Does she bite?"

"She can," Cori warned. "She's always been a feisty one, but I don't think she really intends to do any real harm." Cori continued to pet Kitta, moving on to her cheeks which she massaged with both thumbs until the little cat settled down. "She has the most beautiful green eyes, did you notice?"

"Yes, I see," Grace said, still leery of the toothy cat. "They're beautiful. And she's so fluffy."

"Tell me about it. Cat hair is everywhere in the house. I hope this won't bother you too much."

Looking around, Grace didn't notice any cat hair or smell a litter box. "Well, I certainly don't notice any. Your home is immaculate."

"I try," Cori said.

The countertops in the kitchen—a long, narrow island and L-shaped working space—were covered in milky gray soapstone. There were no upper cabinets; only one long steel rack attached to the wall left of the gas stove top. There, three black cast iron frying pans hung, neatly organized according to size. Above the center island hung an industrial style, aged-pewter caged pendant light. Its retro-looking rivets and wire cage gave the room a very rugged and hip vintage appeal. "Your home is beautiful," Grace said. "I'm envious. Did you hire a decorator?"

"Nope. I did everything on my own, including painting every wall and refinishing the hardwood floors."

Looking down, Grace admired the natural, unstained color of the wood floors and smiled. "Just lovely."

"Thank you," Cori said. "Are you hungry?"

"Yes, I actually am, but I don't want to put you to any trouble. Maybe we can order in?"

"Oh, never. There's no one that delivers around here that I can't make something tastier than anyway."

Remembering that Cori was a chef, Grace nodded. "Of course, I forgot what an excellent cook you are."

"Why don't you take your things upstairs to the guest bedroom while I whip something up. Second door on the right. It'll only take me a few minutes."

"Okay, thanks."

Grace grabbed her bags from the living room and headed up the open staircase. There were two bedrooms on the second floor; one clearly the master bedroom, so Grace entered the second. The room was beautiful; wispy grey curtains framed two large windows and puddled to the floor on the far wall, a crystal chandelier hung from the ceiling above a white poster bed. Grace sat down on the plush grey comforter and leaned back with a sigh.

"Isn't this beautiful, boy?"

Bailey, disinterested, began sniffing under the bed, and let out a low growl.

"What is it boy? Another cat?"

Sure enough, upon inspection, Grace found Cori's fourth and final cat snuggled safely underneath the bed, curled up inside a cushion. Grace tried to coax the tiger-striped cat to come to her, with no luck. "Poor thing looks scared, Bailey. Most likely of you. Come on, let's go," she said, standing up and walking away.

However, Bailey was clearly still very interested in the shy cat and remained where he lay, fishing underneath the bed with an outstretched paw.

"Bailey, come," Grace ordered. Reluctantly, Bailey came away from the bed and followed her back downstairs where Cori stood chopping cilantro, tomatoes, and onion on a chopping board at the island in the kitchen.

"We found another cat upstairs under the bed. Beautiful room, by the way, I love it."

"Oh thanks, I hope you'll be comfortable. And that's our Fink. He wandered up to a local dog groomer last December." She smiled and transferred the chopped vegetables into a bowl and squeezed a lime over it. "Do you like Mexican?"

"Love it, it's one of my favorites." Grace took a seat at the island.

"Good. Soft shell, bean and cheese burritos, fresh salsa and chips, and sweet tea coming right up. Sound good?"

"It sounds delicious, thank you." Grace considered bringing up the topic of her biological father, but decided the time wasn't right. *Later.* "It smells delicious," Grace sniffed appreciatively.

"Thanks," Cori said, taking her seat at the island. "Your mom used to tell me the same thing whenever I prepared this meal for her. I miss her so much."

"Me too," Grace said, taking a sip of sweet tea. "In so many ways. Something I was actually hoping to talk to you about a little later on."

"Sure, nothing more I'd rather do," Cori said honestly. "After we eat, I'll show you my gardens and then we can talk about your wonderful mother."

"Deal," Grace said. "I can hardly wait."

CHAPTER 15

AUDREY
SUNDAY, JUNE 29, 1969

Audrey finished up with her daily reading for the day, a memorial of Saint Gregory the Great, Pope of the Catholic Church. She tucked the day's reading back into her bible, kneeled beside her bed, and began to pray. As always, she prayed for Shea's sobriety and the health and happiness of her children. She also prayed for the many blind children she had met and have learned to love, especially little Ajei, her secret favorite. Just yesterday, she had learned that Ajei's name means 'my heart' in her native Navajo tongue.

"Oh, that's lovely, Ajei. Your parents must have loved you very much, giving you such a name."

"Yes, I guess they did," Ajei had said. "Especially my dad. He never left me like my mom did." The little girl's face turned so sad that Audrey felt her own heart breaking. It was for reasons such as this, one little girl having to endure so much pain in her life, that challenged Audrey's faith. This type of suffering by an innocent child—Ajei was only ten—was almost too much for Audrey to bear. How could God, who claimed to love his people, cripple a child with not only blindness, but the profound heartbreak she must feel every day by being abandoned by her own mother? Audrey was certain that she would never understand how any mother could do such a thing, much less how God allowed it to happen in the first place.

She made a mental note to speak to Father Finnegan back home, as soon as she returned to Cincinnatus, about the topic. Maybe he could explain it in a way that made sense to her. "We'll see," she whispered, as she rose from her knees and stood up.

"See what?" Cori asked, entering the bedroom. Her shift in the kitchen had just ended.

"Oh, nothing. Just talking to myself again."

"Ah, I see. You know they have medication for that."

"Very funny," Audrey said. "I'm going to take a walk down to the point. Wanna come?"

"No, not now. I've actually got a little bit of a headache. I'm going to lie down for a little while."

"Did you take some aspirin?"

"Yes, two. I'll be fine. It's just that time of the month."

"Oh, yuck, I'm sorry. But you're right, you'll probably feel better if you rest. Is there anything I can get for you before you leave?"

"Nope, I'm good. Please shut the bedroom door on your way out, honey. Thanks."

Audrey grabbed her sunglasses off her dresser and headed out, closing the bedroom door behind her. She was excited to take a long walk along the shoreline of the lake.

She checked her look in the full-view mirror hanging on the back of the bathroom door before leaving. She looked very cute today, she concluded, in her white shorts dotted with red cherries and a red tank top. Audrey decided against wearing shoes, preferring to walk barefoot along the lake. She grabbed her favorite book of poetry, the same one she had thrown against the door when she met Cori, and headed outside.

Although she had initially intended to head south, towards Taughannock Point, she turned north in the direction of Jayden's cabin first. If he was outside when she passed by his cabin, she'd thank him again for the use of his telephone. *No harm in that.*

As Audrey continued to walk, she found herself hoping he would be outside, and thought about praying for it, but that somehow seemed like a bad thing to do, so she decided against it. However, it turned out to be a moot point. Jayden was outside of his cabin, sitting with Ajei on the front porch. She waved to them both, "Another beautiful day."

"Yes, we were just saying the same thing," Jayden said. "Would you care to join us? I have mimosas."

Audrey wasn't interested in drinking a mimosa, or anything alcoholic at all—ever. *Why is he drinking alone on a Sunday?* "No, thanks. I'm headed down to the lake for a little walk along the shore."

"Okay, then. Have a nice walk," Jayden said.

"Thanks."

With as much nonchalance as she could muster, she turned around and began walking back in the direction she had come, towards Taughannock Point.

Danny sat on the front porch of his cabin whittling a chunk of oak he found in the woods while hiking. Carefully, he followed the direction of the grain as he sliced away at it with his pocket knife. He had learned how to whittle from his grandfather, Anthony Pepitone. His grandfather was an expert whittler, having carved both large and small pieces in his ninety-three years.

121

Danny remembered being fascinated by his many collections He carved about every living creature there was: dogs, cats, foxes, turtles, bears, fish, mice, squirrels... the list went on and on, as did the miniature pieces lining the shelves of his study when Danny was a child. When Danny took an interest in whittling, Grandfather Pepitone was thrilled to teach him how. He'd said he hoped Danny would carry on the tradition as he had done from his father before him. Danny was nine years old when he received his first lesson.

The first animal Danny successfully carved was a bear. Grandfather Pepitone had suggested it because it was basically one big ball with a tinier one on top for the head. "The legs and feet you'll learn later," Grandfather explained. "For now, Daniel, just focus on making the shape of the body. The rest will come in time."

Danny chuckled, remembering how crazy looking that first bear had been. But as always, his grandfather was correct. Eventually, by taking his time with each carving, each cut, his skills improved. Before long, he was making sculptures that rivaled his grandfather's.

Today he planned to sculpt a pelican. According to the Christian legend he had heard as a child, when a mother pelican cannot find food for her young, she thrusts her beak into her breast and nourishes her little ones with her own blood. The early church, he was taught, saw in this story a beautiful picture of what Christ did for us and what we, in turn, should do for one another. Many Catholics, like Danny, have taken this a step further and believe that because of our sinful nature, we were characterized more by greed than by self-sacrifice. But that could change, because there was nothing that God loved more than self-sacrifice.

As Audrey approached the "T" near Danny's cabin, she found him outside sweeping off his front porch with a broom. "Cleaning day?"

Danny rested the broom against the side of the cabin and jumped off the porch. "No, not really. Just cleaning up some wood shavings. I just finished doing a little whittling."

"You whittle?"

"Sure do, ever since I was a kid. Learned from the best, my grandfather."

"What kind of stuff do you whittle?"

"Animals, mostly," he said, running back up onto the porch to retrieve his latest project. When he returned, he held the newly-carved pelican in the palm of his hand.

Audrey stared down at the little creature. "Oh, Danny, it's precious." Taking it from him, she examined the delicate carving carefully. Danny had captured every detail, right down to the tiny eyes that weren't much larger than grains of sand. On the bottom of the pelican's adorable little feet, he had carved 1969, marking the date. "This is truly amazing, Danny. You're very talented." She handed the pelican back to him.

"Thanks." He shoved the carving into the front pocket of his jeans. "I wanted to apologize, Audrey."

"For what?"

"For spooking you in the lake yesterday and rudely asking your age. It was pretty stupid. I'm sorry."

"Oh, don't be silly. I wasn't really angry."

"Glad to hear it." They both smiled. "So, what are you up to today?"

"I was about to head down to Taughannock Point."

"Care if I join you?"

She hesitated, but then said, "Sure, if you'd like."

Seeing her bare feet, Danny kicked off his shoes. "Let's go. It's a great time for a walk."

"Yes," Audrey said, forgetting what she was thinking about before and began walking towards the lake. A little breeze was blowing from east to west, cooling them as they walked. There were a few clouds in the sky, but mainly it was a bright, sunny day.

Several other people were enjoying the nice weather by boat; there were several different types on the water: canoes, kayaks and even one sailboat. Further down the lake, past the campgrounds, they saw many people swimming from their own private docks and one young woman flying a kite shaped like an angelfish.

"Wow, that's really up there," Audrey said, watching the kite glide through the air

"Sure is. It's gotta be at least fifty or sixty feet up. I hope she doesn't lose it."

"She seems to know what she's doing."

Danny looked back over his shoulder. "Yeah, I suppose you're right."

As they continued walking, Audrey began growing a little curious about him and why he, too, had decided to spend an entire summer at the camp helping Jayden. "Tell me about yourself, Danny. What is it you do when you're not helping your uncle around camp? Are you a student?"

Danny picked up a clump of sand and let it sail over the lake. "I was a student," he began. "I graduated last year from a small school in Yonkers. I haven't exactly figured out what it is I want to do with my life. That must sound pretty lame to you."

"No, not at all. You're very fortunate to be able to take your time while you decide." She pressed further.

"What are your interests? Regarding your future, I mean. I hope you don't mind me asking."

"No, I don't mind. But I don't know, maybe something to help mankind, as cheesy as that may sound."

"Not at all. The world needs more people like you."

"Thanks. But like I said, the problem is I haven't discovered what I'd like to do or what I feel most passionate about. After the assassination of Martin Luther King last April, I'm leaning towards becoming active in the civil rights movement somehow. Maybe..." He turned his head to face her.

Audrey could hardly believe her ears. The civil rights movement was something she, too, felt passionate about. Something else that Shea didn't understand besides her love of poetry. Despite her husband's views, she made sure she educated her children about the horrors inflicted upon those in their country, and elsewhere, simply due to the color of their skin. She began to quote her favorite line from Dr. King's famous speech:

"I have a dream, that my four little children will one day live in a nation where they will not be judged by the color of their skin, but by the content of their character."

"Exactly," Danny said. "I intend to raise my kids, should I be so blessed with any, with those exact words. I think everyone should be judged strictly by their character, don't you? What a brilliant man the world lost when he was assassinated. Terrible."

"Yes. People should be judged by who they are. Not how much money they have, or their profession, but by their character."

They both smiled, and their eyes locked for a moment. Audrey's heart thudded in her chest for a second, and she abruptly announced, "Race you to the point!"

"You're serious?" Danny laughed, but Audrey was already tearing past him.

She spoke so quickly, and unexpectedly, Danny was a good fifteen feet behind her by the time his brain kicked in and he started to run. He seemed surprised to learn how fast she was and struggled to catch up with her. "You cheated!" He laughed, as he began to gain on her.

"Oh, excuses, excuses," she screamed as she continued to sprint as fast as she could. A clap of thunder overhead was their only warning as the sun disappeared behind a rapidly approaching storm cloud, and by the time they reached the point, the rain had started. "I win!" Audrey gasped, already drenched from the sudden storm.

The phone rang from the desk in the Scarsis' cabin. Excited, Ajei ran to the desk and lifted the receiver to her ear. Even though it had been two years since living in the woods of Colorado, speaking on the telephone to another person still enchanted her; the further away the person was calling from, the better. "Hello, Camp Vision. Ajei speaking," she said politely.

"Please put an adult on the phone." The man's voice sounded frustrated.

"Yes, right away sir, but may I ask where you are calling from first?"

"What the…" the man went quiet for a second, then sighed. "Cincinnatus, New York. Now put an adult on the phone."

Disappointed that the caller wasn't from somewhere further away, Ajei rested the receiver on top of the desk and ran out onto the front porch where she found Jayden reading the newspaper. "Some man is on the phone and would like to talk to you. He sounds kinda mean."

Jayden gave her a puzzled glance. He walked into the living room and picked up the receiver from off the top of the desk. "Hello?"

"Who's this?"

Jayden suspected Ajei was correct; the man on the other end of the line did sound a bit rude. "This is Jayden Scarsi, owner of Camp Vision. Who's calling?"

"This is Shea McKenzie, Audrey's husband. Is she there?"

"Well yes, she's here somewhere, but I'm not exactly sure where she is at the moment. But I did see her earlier. I believe she said she was planning to take a walk along the lake. May I get a message to her for you?"

"Yeah, I guess that'd be okay. I really wanted to talk to her now... have her call me back as soon as she can."

"I will," Jayden said, to the sound of a dial tone. Shea had already hung up.

CHAPTER 16

GRACE
SATURDAY, SEPTEMBER 1, 2018

Grace moved into the living room as Cori continued to prepare their afternoon meal. She took a seat in the living room, next to one of the large windows overlooking the backyard, as Cori shooed her out of the kitchen. Bailey followed and lay at her feet. More of a courtyard, the area out back was city-home small but as equally as inviting as the interior of Cori's home. Although the windows in the living room were all closed, Grace felt she could actually smell the roses; the blossoms were so large and plentiful.

Closing her eyes, she remembered the last pleasant day she had spent alone with her ex-husband, Paul. They had been at Longwood Gardens, outside of Philadelphia, touring the rose garden. The intoxicating fragrance of hundreds of roses filling the garden had been intoxicating. filled their senses, too. The resulting, cheerful effect was demonstrated by their many smiles and endless laughter. They explored the collection of roses, some dating as far back as the 1930s, feeling very much in love. At least Grace did. She couldn't even imagine, then, that they would be divorced six short months later.

Paul had made his fortune building custom, million-dollar homes as the nearby suburbs of southeastern Pennsylvania, near where they lived, continued to expand. Private wine cellars? Expansive great rooms? Carrara Marble, soapstone, or Vermont granite throughout? Pools indoors as well as out? Designer kitchens? Bathrooms including with gold-plated toilet seats, if you'd like? No problem, was Paul's motto. He did it all, whatever it took to make a sale.

As he continued in this fashion, making millions on his real estate investments, he ignored Jack's many warnings to dump his overpriced luxury homes, fast, as the market was about to crash. Paul, thinking Grace 's brother was foolish and nothing more than a country bumpkin, did nothing of the sort and continued to build his lavish homes, one after the other in rapid succession. Grace, not really understanding money matters as well as either her husband or brother, remained neutral; uncertain which man had the correct answer. When the real estate market finally did crash in 2008, as Jack had predicted it would, Paul and Grace lost everything, and their marriage found rockier ground. It became even rockier two days after their tour of the rose garden at Longwood Gardens.

It was a warm day in June, 2016, when Grace returned home from work in the middle of the day to pick up some important patient paperwork she had left on her desk in the den. Pulling into their driveway, she was surprised to see Paul's truck still there. Walking into the house, through the garage, she hung her keys on a nearby hook. "Paul? Are you home?"

He didn't answer, and she noticed a white sweater hung over the back of a kitchen chair that she didn't recognize. "Paul, is there someone here with you?" Hearing a sound coming from their bedroom, she entered the room and received the shock of her life.

There they lay, completely naked, currently engaged in intercourse on top of *her* bed. Paul, completely unaware that his wife was now watching him, continued to pound away at his lover with his ridiculously eager hips. She, the other woman, looked up and saw Grace standing in the doorway and let out a loud gasp.

"Oh my God... I'm going to kill you, Paul!" Grace lunged at him and began slapping away at his stunned face. "I hate you!" She screamed, while the other woman cowered beneath 1800 thread count Egyptian the sheets—the very ones Grace had purchased the year before in honor of the fifteenth wedding anniversary. "Get out!" Grace screamed. "Both of you!"

"Grace, please listen," Paul stuttered, as the shameless woman clung tightly to her Grace's husband and expensive sheets. Grace ran from the bedroom and out of the house, forgetting all about her patient's paperwork again. Once outside, she jumped into the Land Rover and drove directly to her lawyer's office. Six months later, in December of that same year, they were officially divorced.

Even now, as she stared out the window at Cori's roses, she could only see the image of the other woman clutching tightly to Paul. Cheryl Bain, she later learned, was her name: her husband's lover for more than seven years. How Grace hated her, and Paul. She jerked her head away from the window.

and stared down at Bailey, still curled up at her feet. "But I love you, Bailey Boy. Very, very much."

"What?" Cori called from the kitchen. "Everything okay?"

"Yep, just petting Bailey and telling him how much I love him."

"Ah, well, that's nice, but come on in. Our lunch is ready." Cori's voice, a welcome distraction.

CHAPTER 17

AUDREY
SUNDAY, JUNE 29, 1969

Once Danny and Audrey both reached the point, they collapsed to the ground and collectively tried to catch their breath but a pair of Canadian geese appeared from the underbrush, squawking loudly. The angry birds, apparently, seemingly very unhappy with the two humans they had just found, began chasing them.

Danny and Audrey jumped back as far from the squawking birds they could, while simultaneously trying to shoo them away from their feet. But the geese kept coming, trying to attack. "Quick!" Danny laughed. "Run as fast as you can and jump into..."

Audrey took off in a mad dash before Danny could finish his sentence and jumped into the chilly water. She began to swim, making her way deeper into the lake, with Danny right behind her. They swam as fast as they could until they were about fifty feet out. Danny was the first to turn around. "Okay, I think we're safe now. You can stop swimming."

"What the heck just happened?!"

"We must have been in their nesting spot. They weren't about to give in," he said, shaking his head. "Did you see the look on the biggest one's face?"

"Yes! I thought we were both goners for a minute."

"No kidding! That was crazy," Danny laughed. "I've never seen such angry geese."

"Me either. What now?"

While they continued to tread water, Danny checked the shoreline. "It looks like they both returned to their nest, but to be sure, let's swim back in the direction of the camp a little further. Are you up for it?"

"Sure," Audrey said. "No problem." She began swimming, parallel to the shoreline

"Did you know that Canadian geese are one of the few species that actually mate for life?" Danny asked, swimming beside her.

Audrey shook her head "No."

"Yep. Fascinating, right?"

"Sure, I suppose so," she said, hoping the topic of the loyal geese would soon end. For some reason, she suddenly felt a little guilty about spending so much time alone with Danny. "Good for them." *I'm married, is it seemly to spend so much time with him?*

"Are you ever going to tell me how old you are, Audrey?"

"Why so curious?"

Danny swam ahead of her a few laps, turned around, and began treading water again. "I don't know. I guess it only seems fair, now that you know how old I am."

"That's on you, my friend. You didn't have to tell me your age." She swam past him.

He sped up passing her again. "Well, that wouldn't hardly seem very gentlemanly, considering you asked. Is that even a word, gentlemanly?"

She laughed. "Yeah, I think it is."

"So?"

"So, what?" She turned and looked back towards the point. "I think we've gone far enough. Let's swim towards the shore now."

"Oh, I get it. You're changing the subject so you don't have to tell me how old you are."

"Seriously? That what you're thinking?"

"Yep. Sure is." He smiled.

"Well, you're wrong. I'm ready to get out of the water now because I'm freezing." She turned away from him again.

As they swam, the sun that once was shining so brightly earlier was now nothing but a blur. The water was deep and very cold. Audrey's arms began to ache. "I need to get out of the water, Danny." Her voice was barely a whisper.

"Put your arms around my shoulders. I can carry you on my back."

Her thoughts were beginning to feel incoherent, her lungs trying to remember to find air. Danny was pulling her now, her arms fastened around his shoulders. "Hold on, Audrey. We're almost there."

Her limbs began to shake. "I'm so cold."

Once they finally reached the shore, Danny pulled her from the cold water and carried her to a dry spot in the sand. Audrey opened her eyes and looked up. Danny was kneeling above her head, his face parallel to hers. "Hi." She murmured, shivering uncontrollably.

He smiled down at her. "Hi. Great walk, huh?"

"The best," she said. "Except for those terrible geese."

Danny laughed. "Yeah, except for them. Golly."

She laughed. "Golly?"

"You heard me. I'm bringing it back, just for you." The dimples on his cheeks grew longer as his smile grew larger.

"You're a nice person, Danny. I'm so glad we've met." She felt her body beginning to regain some feeling.

By now, a small crowd had gathered around them, worried about what had happened to the young woman. Audrey turned to face Danny and rolled her eyes. "Let's get going."

"Right behind you," Danny said, helping her to her feet. "Are you okay?"

"Yes." She said determinedly, trying to keep from stumbling in front of so many.

Danny turned his head to look at her as they left the beach. "Hey, have you ever heard about the legend of the door at Taughannock?"

"No, what's that?"

"Well, let me tell you." He smiled again. "There's an overlook where you can view the 215-feet-high Taughannock water fall. Have you been there?'

Remembering her trip with Shea and the boys last summer, she answered right away. "Yes, last year. It's quite beautiful."

"Did you happen to notice the outline of a door high on the wall of the ravine to the right of the falls?"

"No," she said, honestly. "I don't remember seeing anything like that."

"Okay, this is how the legend goes. A chief by the name of Ganungueguch once existed many, many years before the white man entered this region. He and his tribe lived along Taughannock Creek in the area of the waterfall. They, being Iroquois, were continually at war with the Delawares from Pennsylvania. Once, when Chief Taughannock and his Delawares raided the Cayugas and Senecas, they were defeated by Chief Ganungueguch and his braves. Most of the Delaware braves were killed in the battle, but some of them survived and were adopted by their captors, the Iroquois."

"Interesting, I never knew this."

"But wait, I haven't told you' the whole story yet. One of the adopted Delaware braves fell in love with White Lily, a Cayuga maiden. The Cayuga braves were jealous of this union and watched the pair closely to prevent them from running away together, because it was tribal law that a Delaware may never marry a Cayuga maiden. Knowing this, one dark night, the two lovers ran toward the Delaware's canoe on the shore of Cayuga Lake. They planned to escape southward to Delaware country, but an early alarm frustrated their attempt to escape."

"How terrible," she said, enjoying the story.

"There's more. They didn't know whether a jealous brave sounded the alarm, or the barking of one of the tribe's dogs alerted the village. But soon the entire village was chasing them through the pine forest. From the shouts of the braves in pursuit, the couple knew that they would be overtaken before crossing the creek above the falls. They ran from the protection of the pine forest and could be seen together in the moonlight. They stood on the edge of the falls, embraced, and leapt to what they thought was certain death on the jagged rocks below."

She gasped. "How terrible. They committed suicide?"

"Yes, but they preferred death to capture and the torture that would be inflicted on the Delaware brave especially, according to the code of the Iroquois. The villagers gathered near the pinnacle from which the two had jumped, and the squaws of the tribe wailed at the death of their beloved maiden. When the lamentations subsided, the people returned to their village. They planned to return to the base of the falls to bury the young couple in the morning.

When they came back after dawn the following day, however, they found no mangled bodies or any trace of the brave or the Cayuga maiden. The tribe's storytellers said that the Great Spirit was aware of the young couple's love and of their attempt to elope. The Great Spirit sympathized with them. He opened the door high on the side of the ravine, and when they jumped, he ushered them through the secret passageway and closed the door tightly. The passageway led to a domain where White Lily and her Delaware lover could live in peace and happiness forever. Next time you go there, look for the imagined door."

Audrey's heart hurt, and she nodded. It was a beautiful tale, but really quite terrible.

Looking ahead, she saw the outline of the cabins in the distance. "We're here."

"So, we are. Thanks for inviting me along for a walk, Audrey. Getting attacked by a couple of angry water fowl has been the highlight of my day so far."

She laughed. "So happy to have obliged."

"Well you'd better get right back to your cabin now. Get into something dry."

"Yeah, thanks for the walk. It was fun... but don't forget who won the foot race."

"Only because you cheated," he said, walking in the direction of his own cabin. "I'll get you next time, you just wait!"

"Oh, what a big man!" Audrey retorted. "We'll see about that, Danny Pepitone!"

Danny returned her smile, waved, and walked back to his cabin.

Audrey sat beside Cori on the front porch. They rocked in their chairs, knee deep in silence. A pleasant, easterly breeze blew summertime across their faces. From where they sat, they could just make out the edges of the crystal-clear lake and long dock. Audrey let out a slow controlled breath, gave her shoulders and neck a little wiggle and rolled her head in circles a few times. It was a decent effort, but she was still feeling very tense.

"You're one of the few people I don't despise, Audrey," Cori said, breaking their silence. "I find your quirks very cute."

"Thank you, I think... I feel the same way about you."

Cori nodded. "Is there anything you'd like to talk about, kid?"

Audrey continued to rock, trying to collect her thoughts on some key points and where she could begin. Finally, yet sheepishly, she began. "The last time Shea and I... were intimate, he was so drunk, he repulsed me. The mere touch of his clumsy hands, his horrible breath, his overall demeanor..." She stopped and drew a deep breath. "He's an alcoholic, Cori. I hate it."

"Oh, honey. I'm so sorry. Does he hit you when he's drunk?"

"No, never. He's never been mean to me."

"Does he hold down a job?"

"Yes. As a matter of fact, he's very well-liked and respected at the plant where he works. He was promoted to lead supervisor last year. But..." She paused again.

"But, what?"

"I'm not sure I still love him, Cori." Her harsh admission startling even herself. "And he hates my poetry. I think I may hate him for that."

Cori leaned over and put a reassuring hand on her friend's shoulder. "It's okay, let it out."

"I'm sorry, it's just that I've never said that out loud before. Oh, what am I going to do, Cori? We've been married for fourteen years... and the children, oh, this is just terrible." She began to cry.

"Audrey, naturally I don't know Shea, but if this is how you truly feel I think you owe it to yourself, and your children, to do what's right for you."

"But what's right? We're Catholic, Cori. Catholics don't believe in divorce."

Cori folded her hands in her lap and considered a different tack. "Have you tried discussing how his drinking affects you? Maybe he can stop. As to the poetry..."

"Yes, plenty of times. For years, in fact. His answer is always the same. He thinks that because he gets up and goes to work every day and maintains a roof over our heads that he's doing his part. He truly doesn't understand that he's actually an alcoholic. It's a very difficult situation... for both of us. He doesn't know how his drinking adversely affects me, even though I've tried to explain it many times." She sighed. "He'll never stop drinking. He's told me as much. To him, it's an Irish thing."

"Oh, I see. That is a very difficult situation. I guess you need to decide which is the worse of two evils."

"What do you mean?"

Cori cleared her throat. "Ask yourself, Audrey, is it worse to remain in a marriage that makes you feel so horrible you can no longer stand to lay with your husband, or is it worse to ask for a divorce despite both of your religious beliefs? I think it really boils down to that."

Audrey nodded her head. "You're so right. That's what I need to do. Starting right now, I'm going to think very hard on this and try to come up with the correct answer. Thank you." She stood up. "But, first, I'm going to go lay down for a little while. Do you mind?"

"Of course not, honey. Do what you need to. Meanwhile, my lips are sealed."

"Thank you, Cori, for everything." She turned to walk into the cabin.

"Oh, before you go—I almost forgot to tell you— Shea called while you were gone. He wants you to call him back. Jayden stopped by here earlier with the message."

"Great. Perfect timing," Audrey said, looking out over the lake. "I really don't want to call him back right now. Oh, Cori, what should I do?"

"I don't know honey, but as hard as it will be to talk to him, feeling the way you do right now, you have to start somewhere… right?"

"Yes of course, you're right again. I need to call him back now. But what should I say?"

Cori lifted her head up and shrugged her shoulders. "I have no idea, Audrey. I'm afraid that's something you'll have to figure out on your own."

"Right again. I'm sorry to have become so needy." She then went inside to wash her face before walking down to Jayden's cabin to make the all-important phone call.

The phone rang in their home in Cincinnatus only once before Shea reached it and lifted it to his ear. "Hello?"

"Hi. It's me."

"Where have you been? You worried me when you didn't call me right back. I've been waiting to hear from you for hours."

"Yes, I'm sorry. It's been such a nice day, I decided to take a walk down to Taughannock Point. You remember it, right?"

"Yeah, of course. We took the boys there last year, they loved it. It's close enough for you to walk to?"

"Uh, huh. Only about a couple of miles south of camp. I ended up sitting next to the lake reading from one of my poetry books," she lied. Instinctively, she thought it best not to tell him about sharing a walk with Danny. He wouldn't understand that it had been totally innocent. "I was enjoying myself so much I lost track of time. I just got back and heard you had called."

"That's okay. I understand. You and your poetry..." She could hear the smile on his face. "How are the poetry readings going? The blind kids seem to enjoy it, do they?"

Once again, she decided it best not to tell him about Danny and how he practically rescued her the night of her first reading. "Yes, I think so. They applaud every time I finish a poem, anyway."

"Great. I'm happy to hear it. I'm very proud of you."

Her heart couldn't bear hearing more sweet words coming from Shea. Somehow, it would be so much simpler for her if he were a terrible, horrible man. But he wasn't, and she knew it. "Well, I'm sorry, Shea, but I really should be going now. As a matter of fact, I'm

141

feeling a little tired. I think I may head back to my cabin and hit the sack."

"Okay, but there was a reason for my call. I wanted to ask you if you'd like me to come visit you one weekend. Maybe the boys, too?"

She was a little startled by his request, and stumbled over her own thoughts before answering him. "Well, yes. I think that would be very nice. But do you think your mom may be able to stay with the boys?" She cleared her throat. "There's something I need to talk to you about."

"Is there something wrong?" He sounded concerned. "Do you need me to come sooner? If so, I'll…"

"No," she said, interrupting him mid-sentence. "It's nothing like that. What weekend would you like to come?"

"Well, they've scheduled mandatory overtime the next two Saturdays at the plant, so how does July ninetieth sound?"

"That long?"

"Mandatory means mandatory, Audrey. That's the soonest I can come."

"Okay." She paused. "What time should I expect you, early?"

"Probably closer to noon, if that's okay."

Audrey, remembering that he'd probably still be in bed by 10:00 a.m. on a Saturday morning nursing a hangover, agreed to noon. "Okay, that'll be fine. I'll be waiting. Goodbye, Shea."

"Goodbye, Audrey. See you in a couple of weeks."

"See you then." Slowly, she returned the receiver to the phone and hung up, more convinced than ever that she needed to make a dramatic change in her life.

CHAPTER 18

GRACE
SATURDAY, SEPTEMBER 1, 2018

Grace helped clear the kitchen island of their dishes and silverware as Cori leaned over the sink, clinking together heavy frying pans as she washed them.

"That was delicious, Cori. I don't think I've ever tasted a better burrito."

Cori smiled. "Would you care for a glass of wine now?"

"Yes, please. What kind do you have?"

"Pinot Grigio, dry Riesling, and Merlot."

"I'll have the Merlot, please." She began drying the dishes with a towel. "I love the dry reds."

"Me too. After we're done here, let's take the bottle out back to the garden with us."

"Sounds perfect."

The courtyard was no more than twenty by fifteen feet. On the right, close to the house, was a tall, weeping silver tree. Its branches were cut high and neat, exposing a variety of plants beneath it. Hosta in blues and greens, a few bleeding hearts, purple and white impatiens, and several other types of night shades Grace couldn't identify. A brick pathway swirled around the silver tree on the left and hugged the fence where English roses draped precociously. "This is beautiful," Grace said. "And it smells delicious."

"It's the English roses," Cori said. "They're dormant now, being so late in the season, but you can still smell their seduction."

More blowsy, pink and white rose blossoms sprung up in the distance from high balustrades surrounding the boundary of Cori's property. In the back-right corner, sat four comfortable lawn chairs covered in bright turquoise and red cushions matching the house. "Let's sit here," Cori said, taking a seat.

Grace took a seat next to her, in a chair facing the house. Bailey rested by her feet. "Just beautiful."

"Thank you. I enjoy it." Cori said, smiling as she took a sip of wine.

Grace ran her fingers through her hair and checked her watch. 1:20. She stood up, walked to the back fence and sunk her nose into the center of an English rose, inhaling deeply. "Delicious. Are these difficult to grow?"

"Not really. All they need is a sunny location, plenty of water, well-drained soil, some plant food and, of course, your time and attention."

Grace caressed a soft pink bloom in her hand and gently massaged the petals. "I think I'd like to try growing some when I get home."

Cori nodded, "I remember how much Audrey enjoyed coming here and sitting with me in the rose garden. I planted those roses in the fall after the summer I met your mother at Camp Vision."

"Oh?" She turned around to face her. "That long ago?"

Cori nodded again. "We started a rose garden at the camp that year, too, towards the end of the season."

Grace returned to her seat. "Really? I don't remember Mom mentioning anything about a rose garden."

Cori leaned back in her chair and lifted her face to the sky. "It was mid-August. Cool, but still very sunny when a few of us, your mother included, went into Ithaca to buy the rose bushes."

Grace took a sip of her wine and settled in.

"None of us knew that much about roses, except Danny, whose mother had grown them in their yard his entire life."

"Who's Danny?"

"He was Jayden Scarsi's nephew. Jayden was the owner of the camp. He brought Danny on that summer to do some projects around the camp. Painting, hanging shelves, carpentry. Things like that."

"Mom never mentioned him."

"No, probably not."

"The only people I remember Mom talking about were you, Jayden Scarsi and, of course, Ajei... my namesake."

Cori smiled. "Grace Ajei, what a beautiful name your mother gave you."

"My heart," Grace said, as she rubbed her finger around the rim of her wine glass. "Cori, I need to ask you something. There's a reason why I'm here, besides wanting to see you again."

"I thought there might be," Cori said. "You can ask me anything, Grace."

Grace shook her head. "Thank you." She took a deep breath. "The reason I was at the cottage with my brothers is because I arranged for them to join me there. I needed to ask them about something... important. But we ended up getting into an argument, and it went downhill from there. Then I thought about you."

"I don't understand."

"I'm sorry, I'm not making myself clear." She sat her wine glass down on the table next to her and patted the top of Bailey's head. "I had my DNA tested a few weeks ago. When no Irish showed up in my heritage, but Italian did, I began wondering about Dad. He was one hundred percent Irish, you know."

Cori nodded.

"Eventually, I realized that it wasn't possible for him to be my real father." She frowned. "I loved him very much, Cori."

"I know you did. And he loved you, too."

Grace dropped her chin. "Yes, he did. If he knew he wasn't my real father, doesn't that speak volumes about his fine character?"

"Yes, it does."

"For sure." Grace lifted her wine glass and took another sip. The full-body, savory red wine began warming her. She held her glass in both hands as she continued. "I invited Jack and Matthew to the cottage to confront them with my DNA results. Somehow, I suspected they may have always known that Dad wasn't my biological father. Something just told me they knew."

"What did they tell you?"

"Not much. We ended up in Trumansburg yesterday, having lunch together. When I presented them with my DNA results, Matthew tried to convince me it was wrong and Jack started laughing."

"Laughing?"

"Yeah. Man, did that piss me off. But I think he was just nervous. Anyway, Matthew ended up storming off and leaving Jack and I stranded in Trumansburg. He was so angry."

Cori shook her head. "He does have a bad temper, that one."

"Yes," Grace said, shaking her head. "But later, after Jack and I finished eating, we took an Uber back to the cottage and he eventually told me they both knew Dad wasn't my biological father. Since I was five, in fact. The same year Jack returned home from Vietnam. I have no idea what prompted them to learn the truth then. He wouldn't tell me anything more. It's all so weird."

Cori sat silently, lost in her own thoughts.

"I still have trouble believing it's true, but I know it is. What's more, I got a notification on my phone this morning from AncestryDNA®." She pulled her phone from her sweater pocket and stared at the screen. "Apparently I have a first cousin living in Homer by the name of Danielle DeLorenzo. Do you know her?"

"No," Cori said, honestly.

After rereading the details of her first cousin, which weren't many, Grace dropped her phone back into her sweater pocket and sat up straight. "Cori, I have to ask you this. Do you know who my real father is? Or was?"

Cori refilled their wine glasses. The sun disappeared behind a dark storm cloud and the wind began to swirl around them. "Yes, Grace, I do."

CHAPTER 19

AUDREY
WEDNESDAY, JULY 16, 1969

Two weeks had passed since Shea had made plans to visit Audrey. He'd be arriving this coming Saturday, as Audrey was well aware. But today, the Mets were scheduled to play the Cubs at Wrigley Field in Chicago. The third game of a three-game series would be broadcasted live on TV beginning at 2:00 p.m. Luckily for her, the rec room was available for those who cared to watch it and Audrey, for one, intended to be there. She could think about her troubled marriage later, after the game.

As she settled into her selected seat closest to the television set, Cori arrived carrying a large bowl of fresh, buttered popcorn and a few small serving bowls. "Has the game started?"

"Not yet. About five more minutes to go."

"Good. I hate missing the players take the field at the start of the game. Especially the Tugger," she said, referring to the Met's pitcher, Tug McGraw. "Man, do I like to watch that man strut." She took a seat next to Audrey.

Audrey smiled and dipped one of the small plastic bowls into the popcorn, serving herself. So far, they were the only two people in the room. "Good as always," she said, tasting a few savory pieces of her favorite snack.

"Seaver is pitching today, you may not see Tug McGraw."

"So he is," Cori said, as they watched their team take the field. "Damnit, Tug must be seated inside the dugout. Too bad."

Audrey knew a lot more about baseball than her friend, especially details regarding the New York Mets. "Probably. But then, he never starts. He's a relief pitcher."

"Oh," Cori said. "Too bad. He's got a nice ass.".

Audrey rolled her eyes and giggled just as Danny walked in covered in grass clippings. He wore a pair of ratty pair of jeans and brown duck boots, and nothing else. His bare chest glistened with perspiration. "What's so funny?" He asked, moving to stand beside the couch.

"We were commenting on Tug McGraw's fine-looking ass." Cori smiled coyly as she dropped her hand into the large popcorn bowl. She grabbed a generous handful and shoved it into her mouth. "You gonna just stand there, handsome, or are you planning to join us?"

Audrey smiled, shook her head and diverted her eyes away from Danny's half-nude body.

"There you go again. Noticeable body language," Cori warned.

Danny put his hands on his hips. "What body language?"

Cori laughed. "Nothing. I'm just messing with Audrey... I think she fancies you."

"Cori!" Audrey warned. "Stop that. Danny and I are just friends. Right, Danny?"

Danny remained silent.

"Uh huh," Cori said. "Well, are you planning on joining us or what, Danny?"

149

"Yeah, but I need to shower first." He turned and faced the television. "Did the game just start?"

"Yeah, it's the top of the first," Audrey said, munching on her popcorn.

Danny looked around the rec room again. Seeing that it was still only the three of them, he bent over and placed both hands on the side of Audrey's stunned face. He smiled at her and then kissed her squarely on the lips. "How's that for body language, Cori?" He said, licking his lips as he walked away. "Be right back, ladies."

Cori leaned forward in her chair and laughed while Audrey sat speechless beside her. "Ha-ha, I told you he liked you!"

"He was just joking... he's like that. Way too young for me and besides, I'm married. Remember?" Audrey turned her attention back to the game, trying to forget the salty taste of Danny's warm lips.

"Well, it looked pretty real to me. Steamy, in fact."

"Don't be silly," Audrey insisted. "Let's just watch the game."

Both women were engrossed in the baseball game when they were interrupted by Ajei, who walked in carrying an orange kitten in her arms. "Look, Miss Cori, Miss Audrey! My dad got me a kitten!" She ran to them, cuddling the tiny cat carefully in her arms. "Would you like to pet him?"

"I sure would," Audrey said, petting the top of his tiny head. "He's beautiful, Ajei. What's his name?"

"Morris."

"What a lovely name. May I hold him?" Cori asked.

"Sure. But be careful, he only likes me," Ajei said proudly.

"I'll be careful."

Audrey asked Ajei, "I love your new kitty's name, but why not give him a Navajo one?"

"Oh, I did. His middle name is Mósí. That means cat."

Carefully, Audrey practiced pronouncing the Navajo word. "Mósí. Did I say it right?"

"Yep."

"What's his last name?" Cori asked, still petting and loving on the kitten.

Ajei giggled. "Scarsi, like me, Miss Cori."

"Oh, of course. How silly of me." She handed Morris back to Ajei who took a seat next to her. "Where's my cousin, Danny? He loves baseball."

"He'll be joining us soon," Audrey said. "He went back to his cabin to get cleaned up. He just finished mowing the grass.

"That's good. He probably stinks."

The women smiled.

"And he bites his fingernails, too. Gross."

"Well, I suppose none of us are perfect," Audrey said, suddenly feeling compelled to speak on Danny's behalf. "I smell funny sometimes, too."

"No, you don't, Miss Audrey. You always smell pretty."

"Well, not always," Audrey said, smiling. "After I've been working hard in my yard back home, I don't smell so good."

Ajei thought about that for a minute. "I bet you don't ever smell as bad as Danny does. Sometimes, he--"

Ajei's story was interrupted by the loud crack of a bat. It was the bottom of the first and the batter for the Mets, Bobby Pfeil, hit a double into center field advancing the runner on third base. Audrey jumped to her feet and watched number twenty, Tommie Agee, tag home plate, scoring the first run of the game. "Mets one, Cubs zero!" she cheered. "We're off to a good start."

More children, mostly boys, and a few of their counsellors, began entering the rec room and finding their seats. Although they couldn't watch the game, they were excited to be together listening to it. As Cori began doling out individual bowls of popcorn, Danny re-entered the room. His dark brown hair, slightly shaggy and still wet from his shower, was currently slicked straight back across the top of his head. With his hair combed this way, Audrey thought he resembled old Hollywood movie stars, like Clark Gable. He wore a pair of navy-blue gym shorts and a gray T-shirt, making him look far more modern than Clark Gable, not to mention extremely rugged. While talking to one of the counselors standing close by, he flashed Audrey his usual wide smile.

She began feeling extremely anxious in his presence and tried to refocus on the game, but after he finished his conversation with the counselor, she continued watching him as he made his way from child to child, making each one laugh with his endless and ridiculously silly knock-knock jokes. The outlandish things he was doing secretly made her chuckle.

Entertaining the children obviously came extremely easy for Danny. The crazy noises he made deliriously funny for the boys especially; they were laughing uproariously. Audrey began thinking about her own boys and how much they would probably be laughing right now, too, if they were here. But the girls, she noticed, were turning up their smug little noses at Danny with each crude-sounding noise he made. In response, he gently pinched the tip of each opinionated nose, one by one, making each girl laugh as hard as a boy.

It wasn't just Audrey that liked him, everyone did. Danny was special. His smile and handsome face could light up any room but, in the end, it was his fine character that people responded to. Including Audrey.

"Character," she muttered.

"What?" Cori asked.

"Oh, nothing. Just talking out loud again."

It was the bottom of the second inning by the time Danny made his way back up front and took a seat next to Audrey. He smelled of Irish Spring. Sitting so close to him, she found it even harder to concentrate on the game.

With runners on first and second, Tom Seaver stepped up to the plate. He hit a single to right field and the runner on second scored. Audrey jumped to her feet again and began clapping and laughing.

"Go Mets!" Jayden yelled, as he entered the room. "What's the score?"

"Mets, two. Cubs, zip," Danny reported.

When the Met's player, Agee, stepped to the plate for the second time, he hit a double to right field and Al Weis scored another run. "Three to nothing!" Audrey yelled, hugging Danny around his neck. "Oh, I'm so sorry, Danny. I get really excited watching the Mets. Please excuse me." She dropped her arms to her side.

Danny laughed. "It's okay."

She smiled as they continued watching the game together, inning by inning, while the warm, summer night lingered on. They sat closely to one another until the game was over. The Mets won, four to nothing.

"Wow, great game," Danny said, taking to his feet and stretching his arms above his head.

Many of the children, too tired to remain the entire time, had already gone back to their cabins with their counsellors.

"Sure was," Audrey agreed. "Ready to head back to our cabin, Cori?"

"No, not quite yet. I need to collect all of the popcorn bowls and take them back to the kitchen first."

"Oh, let me help you." Audrey stood up and began gathering some of the discarded bowls.

"No, honey. You go on ahead. I'll get this."

"Are you sure?"

Cori put her hands on her hips. "I never lie," she quipped.

"Right, okay, thanks. I think I will head back now. I'm getting a little tired myself."

"Me too," Danny said. "I'll walk with you."

"Goodnight, kids," Cori said, turning her attention back to the scattered and empty popcorn bowls.

Outside, the moonlight twinkled and the stars hung like a string of diamonds in the sky. They followed the path leading back to the cabins in peaceful silence, and once they reached the T where he would turn left, and she right, Danny turned to face her.

His hair looked jet black; his eyes wider than ever before in the light of the full moon. Audrey wished she didn't have to leave just yet. It was then that she realized she really wanted him in ways she knew were completely wrong. Suddenly, Danny took her in his arms and gently began kissing her. Her surprised but eager lips welcomed him and she returned his passion. "Danny, we shouldn't..."

"Shhhh," he whispered. "It's too late. I think I'm falling for you, Audrey. Please tell me you feel the same."

Inside her head, opposing thoughts were waging a brutal war. On one hand, she knew this was terribly wrong. But on the other hand, she knew that she, too, was beginning to fall for him, too. And the taste of his breath, so fresh and new, intoxicated her in a way she had never known. She leaned into him and returned his kiss again. "I should go," she whispered.

He slowly backed away, dropping his arms from around her body. "Alright, if you must..."

She looked down at her feet, feeling ashamed, and began walking in the direction of her cabin. Daring one glance back, she saw Danny still standing there, alone in the dark, watching her leave. Tomorrow she would tell him that she was married. But tonight... tonight belonged to her.

CHAPTER 20

MATTHEW AND JACK
SATURDAY, SEPTEMBER 1, 2018

Matthew sat next to Jack on the front porch of the cottage enjoying a few beers with him. After calming down over the shock of Grace 's news the day before, Matthew had decided to drive back out to Trumansburg and enjoy the rest of the weekend with his brother. Matthew cracked his beer and took a satisfying sip as he watched.

The late afternoon sun begins its descent over the western hills, streaming through the empty patches of the tall trees where leaves had already fallen. Long, black shadows washed over their faces. Jack had already told Matthew everything that transpired after he stormed away from the restaurant, including Grace 's decision to travel to Albany to visit Cori Cohen.

"I didn't tell Grace this when she brought up Cori's name, but I actually ran into her a couple of months ago at Saratoga Springs. Apparently, the old woman still loves a good horserace, and is there practically every weekend," Jack said.

"Yeah, I remember her and Mom's fascination with the horses," Matthew said, leaning back in his chair. "Well then, I suppose that's that. Cori's as sharp as ever. I follow her on Facebook, the old coot. It won't be long before Grace knows everything."

"Right," Jack said, taking another sip of his beer. "You're okay with this now?"

"I wouldn't exactly say that, it's going to suck if everything gets stirred up again, but seeing there's nothing much we can do about it then, yeah, I guess I'm okay with it." Matthew sighed and massaged his forehead with his fingertips; trying to chase away a burgeoning headache. "Sorry about the other day. I still had the crazy idea that we could actually continue to keep it a secret from her."

Jack nodded. "Forget about it. I already have."

Matthew pulled his ballcap away from his head and scratched behind his ear. "We've done everything we could for a long time, Jack, keeping our promise to Dad. if she finds out on her own, so be it. We tried to protect her from the truth."

156

"Don't I know it. Have you said anything to Sandy?"

Matthew grabbed another cold beer from the cooler resting beside him and popped it open. "Yep. Told her last night."

"How'd it go?"

"Not too bad. I thought her reaction would be far worse. But I guess that's because she doesn't think Dad had anything to do with it."

"That's cool. I guess I'll have to tell Chelsea about it now, too. Honestly, I don't think she'll give a shit."

"Why?"

"Because she probably would've done the same as Dad, if he did it, that is. She'll probably end up being a little prouder of him, I bet."

Matthew chuckled. "Yeah, I can see that about Chelsea." He took another gulp of his beer, wiped his mouth with the back of his hand and leaned forward. "You really don't think he killed him, Jack?"

Jack stared straight ahead, watching the red and orange leaves swirl around the oaks and maples from which they fell. He had forty-three years to think about this question; they both did, but still, he had no idea. "I'm not sure, but I don't think so. Dad wasn't that kind of guy, you know?"

"Honestly, I don't know either I hope he did do it. Christ. Can you imagine if that guy was still around here? Snooping into our lives, trying to get involved in Grace's?"

"No, I can't, but I don't think ol' Shea had anything to do with his disappearance." Jack threw his empty beer can into a nearby trash can and grabbed another from the cooler.

"Yeah I hear you. I'll never forget the look in his eyes that night, though. Pure evil." A chill ran down Matthew's spine. "I've never seen him so angry, Jack."

Jack nodded. "I know. I remember you telling me about it. Either way, he was a hell of a man."

"Yes," Matthew said. "None better."

The two brothers sat in peaceful silence for a while longer as the sun sank deeper into the distant hills. On the other side of the cottage and across the glass-like lake, a loon wailed. marking the arrival of dusk. The silhouettes of trees on the mountain tops and the last fading ray's sunlight spiraling through the sky was all that they could see now. Darkness was upon them.

"Sometimes I wonder why we didn't tell Grace sooner, you know? It sucks, but now that Mom and Dad are both gone, what did it matter?" Jack asked.

"Yeah. But like I said, she'll know everything soon enough, and it'll finally be over for us." Matthew lifted his can of beer into the air. "To Dad."

"To Dad," Jack said, somberly, as he clinked his can against Matthew's. "And to Cori."

"Yes, to Cori," Matthew said, as they drank a toast to their long-lost father and their mother's best friend.

CHAPTER 21

AUDREY
THURSDAY, JULY 17, 1969

The next afternoon, after eating lunch together in the cafeteria, Danny and Audrey walked the familiar path leading to their cabins again. It was another hot day. "After I get finished painting the trim outside of the rec room, I'm going to take my bike out for a spin. Would you like to join me?"

She knew she shouldn't, but it *was* such a hot day. "I don't know…"

"Oh, come on. It'll be fun. I'll take you down to that forest I was telling you about. I think you'll enjoy seeing it, and besides, with all the high trees it'll be very cool inside. Much better than here." He wiped a bead of sweat from around his neck. "What do you say?"

She paused at the T-intersection of the path, and looked in the direction of her cabin. *Shea won't be here for a couple of more days, and it really is hot outside.* "Okay, I'll go."

"Great," Danny said, looking at his watch. "It's half-past noon. Meet me at my cabin at two."

"Alright."

"And don't forget to wear long pants and boots, if you have them."

"What about a jacket and a helmet?"

"I have extras of both. Don't worry, you'll be all set." He smiled and tried to kiss her again but she leaned backwards, away from him.

"Just a ride, okay, Danny?"

"As you wish, my lady," he said, bowing at his waist.

She turned around, quickly, so he couldn't see her smile.

[scene break]

Danny was waiting for her on the porch, two leather jackets and helmets at his feet when she arrived. It was a few minutes past 2:00. "There you are. All set?"

"I sure am," she said, smiling large. "I'm actually very excited. I haven't been on the back of a bike in a long time."

"Well then, let's get going." He handed her one of the two jackets. "This one is slightly smaller, but I'm sure it'll still float on you."

She took the jacket and put it on. He was right, it hung off her shoulders and rested at mid-thigh. "How do I look?"

[keep it in Audrey's point of view] *Stunning.* "Better, now that the Mets T-shirt is covered up, that's for sure," he said.

She frowned.

"Sorry, but I'm a Yankees fan, through and through. I just watched the Met's game on Wednesday night because you were there."

"Oh, I see... but the Amazin' Mets are really something this year. You'd have to at least agree with that." Audrey smiled.

"Yeah, I suppose you're right. They really are. Did you bring a pair of sunglasses?"

"No, I didn't think of that. I can run back and get a pair."

160

"Not necessary," he said, handing her the helmet he typically wore. "Take this one, it has a face shield. I'll just wear my sunglasses."

"Are you sure?"

"Positive."

She put the helmet on over her head, adjusting her pony tail and the chin strap until she felt it fit snugly. Danny put on a pair of gold-rimmed aviator sunglasses, his jacket and other helmet, and smiled at her. "All set?"

"Yep."

He let out a little laugh and mounted his bike, his eyes twinkling. After checking both mirrors, Danny kick-started the engine and the bike responded with its trademark, rowdy purr. "Now you get on by just swinging…"

Before he could finish his sentence, she swung her long leg over the back of the seat and seated herself correctly behind him. "Like this?"

"Looks like you've done this before."

"Uh huh."

"Then you also understand how to lean into the curves with me?"

"Sure do, it's the best part."

[keep in Audrey's point of view; what does *she* feel?] As he pulled away from the cabin, she put her arms around his mid-section and held on tightly "Here we go." He dropped the clutch a few more times and the Triumph roared out of sight from Camp Vision and down the dirt road leading them to open highway.

"This is great!" Audrey yelled, wind rushing through her hair and in her face. When they rounded the first curve, she leaned into it perfectly and she wondered if he could feel her smiling. Once the long road straightened out again, he opened up the throttle, giving the Triumph all it had. They roared west together, across the state road leading them to the forest.

The route offered many twists and turns, as well as a picture-perfect view of the wide-open land they both loved: The Finger Lakes region of New York State. Long and low rolling hills surrounded them, dotted with dairy farms and unexpected waterfalls which Danny pointed out as they zoomed past. They glided past breathtaking and unusual combinations of scenery; quaint small towns, horse-drawn buggies, and spectacular lake views from higher roads seemingly designed by a touring motorcyclist, winding with elevation gains and drops without being too steep on pool-table smooth pavement. A rider's paradise, and a wonderful escape for anyone on a hot and sunny day.

Danny turned his head around, shouting over the roar of the engine. "The forest entrance is just ahead. We'll stop there for a little while."

She stretched her neck and looked at the road in front of them. "I see it."

He embarked on the trail leading into the forest, slowing down a bit. The trail was narrow, about a single car width, but relatively smooth and straight. He descended the trail to a clearing in a pine grove, alongside a large pond and slowed down, stopping the bike. "Let's take a break here."

Audrey dismounted and removed her helmet. The forest looked ancient. Thick and old trees, verdant with leaves, surrounded her. The scents of musky earth and pine drifted around her, and Audrey could hear the soft burble of running water nearby—the pond, fed by a small stream. Canopies of green, so dense that only the occasional streak of sunlight touched the forest floor, cooling the air. "How beautiful."

"Yeah it is," Danny said, retrieving a thermos from a leather saddlebag strapped to the side of his motorcycle. He unscrewed the top. "Take a sip."

"What is it?"

He smiled. "Just water."

"Oh, okay. Thanks." She took a sip. The water was glacier cold. She drank a little more before handing it back to him. "That was an unexpected surprise. Nice and cold."

"Never leave home without it." He took a healthy swig. "Let's take a look around."

They removed their jackets and rested them on the seat of the bike. Danny hung a helmet on each handle bar and then led the way along a well-maintained path leading into the pine grove. Under a canopy of tall trees, the air felt about five degrees cooler. Audrey crossed her arms around her chest.

"You're not cold, are you?" Danny noticed; his eyebrow raised in concern.

"No, I'm fine. Let's keep walking."

They walked a little further, until Danny stopped short. Audrey stopped a few feet in front of him after she noticed his footsteps halt, and turned around. "What are you doing?"

"Thinking," Danny said, smiling large enough that she could see his long dimples again from where she stood.

"So, let me get this straight, you can recite poetry on a moment's notice, swim underwater at the speed of light, rescue me from a freezing cold lake, but have to stop walking in order to think?"

"Yep, that's right. How about this one?" He began walking again. "Shall I compare thee to a summer's day?"

She was certain she felt her heart skip a beat, but she continued to walk straight ahead as Shakespeare's beautiful words flowed flawlessly from Danny's lips behind her:

"Thou art more lovely and more temperate. Rough winds do shake the darling buds of May, and summer's lease hath all too short a date; sometime too hot the eye of heaven shines, and often is his gold complexion dimm'd; and every fair from fair sometime declines, by chance or nature's changing course untrimm'd; but thy eternal summer shall not fade, nor lose possession of that fair thou ow'st; nor shall death brag thou wander'st in his shade, when in eternal lines to time thou grow'st: so long as men can breathe or eyes can see, so long lives this, and this gives life to thee." Danny jogged a few feet to catch up with her. "How's that?"

She turned her head to face him. "It's my favorite. Sonnet eighteen. How'd you know?"

"I didn't, but it's my favorite, too. We have a lot in common, Audrey."

"We certainly do." Looking down, she noticed the fringe edges of her jeans were dragging along the path behind them, creating a small trail. "I feel a little like Gretel," she chuckled.

"I guess that makes me your brother, Hansel," he shrugged.

"I guess so."

They continued walking, until he suddenly stopped again and turned to face her. "I don't feel like your brother, Audrey."

"I know," she said. "But we can't... not now."

Then, just as suddenly as he had kissed her once before, Danny held her closely and leaned in again for another. Audrey didn't try to stop him this time. Not even when he scooped her up in his arms and carried her to a small knoll. There, where the grass was cool and soft, he sat her down and continue to kiss her.

Instinctively, without any words, she lay back on of the bed of grass and allowed him to gently crawl on top of her. His tongue was so hungry for the sweetness of her tender mouth; he kissed her deeply and lovingly for a very long time. She returned his kisses with an equal desperation, blocking all other thoughts from her mind.

He pulled his shirt off over his head, and then hers, exposing her breasts. Even more cold now, her nipples stood erect, Danny took his time and prolonged loving each one with his mouth, slowly, while stroking her body passionately with both hands. Her back arched with desire, begging him. Finally, Danny acquiesced; sliding her jeans and dainty panties off in one quick movement, and entered her.

She had never felt lovemaking like this before; the rhythm of his slender hips matched her own without flaw, and their passion grew. Faster and faster they moved in frantic cadence, until their breath became labored and thick. "I love you, Audrey," Danny whispered.

She felt her heart breaking all at once and began to cry. "I know, I love you too," she breathed, as they climaxed together and collapsed in each other's arms. Audrey knew that she would have to tell him very soon that she was married with two children of her own; but not today. Today, she was simply a woman falling in love with a wonderful man.

Once they arrived back at the camp, it was already dark, so Danny pulled the Triumph up to his cabin as quietly as possible, the engine fairly idling. "Let me walk you to the T," he offered.

"Okay." She handed him his jacket and helmet and they began. "Danny, I think we should keep our relationship quiet. It may not be viewed very favorably by the others in camp. Especially your uncle."

"Why would my uncle be displeased? I don't understand your concern. I'm sure he'll be very happy to learn…"

"I'm thirty-seven years old, Danny," she blurted out, cutting him off.

Danny looked ready to excuse that, despite his clear shock at her revelation, but Audrey blurted, "Danny, you know how the world is. I really don't feel like being judged here. I hope you can understand."

"I don't understand. Why do you care about what other people may think?" Having reached the T, he stopped walking and put his arms around her.

The mere scent of him, slightly musky and erotically male, overtook her senses again and she melted into him. "It's just that it's all so new, for both of us. I'd really like to keep it our little secret. At least for now, while we're both still employed by your uncle."

"I'll quit tomorrow, if that's what you're worried about."

"It's more than that, Danny. I know it's difficult for you to understand, being a man, but I can't bear to be judged by people I barely know and possibly viewed as a cradle robber. Please try to understand how I feel, won't you?"

"For you, I'll do anything. You have my word. For the remainder of the summer, we'll interact as nothing more than co-workers and friends. Agreed?"

"Yes," she said, smiling. "Thank you."

"You're very welcome, my fine friend," he said, mockingly, as he dropped his arms and began walking again. "Stay away from me, old lady."

She laughed.

"I can't tell you how much I want to carry you back to my cabin and have my way with you."

"Danny, we can't..."

"Oh, don't worry. I'm not going to. Besides, your way may be fun. Sneaking around the camp like White Lily and her Delaware brave." He smiled a naughty smile.

Audrey blushed, slightly embarrassed by his suggestion but aroused all the same. "We shall see," she said.

He returned to her side and kissed her one last time before allowing her to walk away. "See you tomorrow?"

"You know it," she whispered, now standing a few feet away from him, walking backwards along the path. "I'll see you then." She blew him a kiss which Danny pretended to catch before waving goodbye.

She walked in silence the rest of the way to her cabin. Once there, she carefully opened the door, being careful not to wake Cori. Audrey decided to sleep in the living room for the night. Stripping down to her bra and panties, she curled up with a light blanket and throw pillow on the couch and settled in. The Righteous Brothers—*Unchained Melody*, a song from her youth—begin playing inside of her head. She hugged both arms around herself and remembered Danny's loving embrace, his lips, his mouth, his gentle tongue. Her belly responded with a flurry of butterflies, fluttering wildly inside of her. Audrey convinced herself that everything would work out fine. It was time for her to sleep.

CHAPTER 22

GRACE
SATURDAY, SEPTEMBER 1, 2018

Cori leaned back in her chair and pulled a knitted shawl over her shoulders. "It's getting chilly. Would you like to go back inside now?"

"Only if you do. I'm fine either way," Grace said.

Cori smiled. "My old bones will be a little more comfortable inside." She grabbed the bottle of wine and both women began walking towards the house, Bailey trailing closely behind, as always. Grace looked up at the sky; there were dark clouds beginning to form overhead. "It looks like a storm's coming."

"It's good we're moving inside now," Cori said as she locked the French doors behind them and took a seat on the sofa in the living room.

They sat quietly for a few minutes until Grace couldn't stand the silence any longer. "So, you were saying... you know who my real father was?"

"Yes," Cori began. "But first, I'd like to tell you a little about your mother... if you don't mind."

"No, please do. I know very little about her, due to..."

"The Alzheimer's. I know. So terribly tragic, for everyone. You all lost her way too young."

"Yes, we did."

Cori turned her head away from Grace and stared into the empty air. "The first day I met your mother, she threw a book at me."

"What?" Grace giggled. "Why?"

"Well, she wasn't really throwing the book *at* me. It just appeared that way when I walked into our cabin the first day we met. Apparently, your mom was having doubts about her poetry... and herself, most likely. She was worried that the children at camp may not enjoy listening to her poetry. That's when, in her frustration, she picked up one of her books and threw it at the front door. Unfortunately, it was at the exact same time I was walking inside the cabin." Cori laughed and looked down at her lap. "Oh, the look on her face when she realized she almost hit me... it was very comical."

"I bet. What did you say to her?"

"Oh, I don't know. Something funny I suppose. I remember us sharing a good laugh together only minutes later. I liked your mother immediately, Grace. She was very special."

"So I've heard. Unfortunately, many of my memories of her aren't so nice."

"Well, let me tell you all about the way she used to be. We'll try to replace those bad memories of yours with the good ones of mine."

"Okay. That would be nice." Grace leaned back against a generous-sized pillow and began to relax. The wine was very good. "Please, go on."

Cori continued. "Not too long after I met your mother, she began opening up to me about your father."

"Which one?"

"Shea, naturally."

"Oh, really? What did she have to open up about? Dad was great." Grace asked warily.

"You really can't guess?"

Grace looked up at the ceiling fan and watched the blades spinning around and around. "I suppose his drinking may have been a problem."

"Well of course it was, Grace. You do remember he drank every night, right?"

"Yes, but..."

"But, nothing. Although it's true that Shea was a good man, his constant drinking certainly was not. It had a very negative affect on your mother."

"I guess."

"You guess? I'm here to tell you, Grace, it did. Your mother told me everything. As a matter of the fact, one of the main reasons she accepted Jayden's offer to read poetry at camp that summer was because she desperately needed to get away from Shea for a little while."

"Why? He was never mean to her."

"Grace, she needed time to think... alone. When I met her, she was seriously considering asking your father for a divorce."

"What? I never knew that." Grace sat up straight, her eyes bulging.

"Well, of course not. By the time you were born, they settled into sort of a routine. An agreement to coexist."

Grace let out a loud sigh. "I guess that explains why they were never very loving towards one another."

"Yes, I'm sure it would."

"Cori, did my Dad know he wasn't my biological father? From the beginning, since the time Mom was pregnant, I mean?"

Cori took another sip of her wine. "No. Neither of them knew for sure."

"But I figured she must have been pregnant with me when she left camp that summer. How could she not have known who was the father? My God, did she sleep with more than one man?! Please tell me she didn't..."

"I wish I could, Grace. But I'm afraid everything became a little more complicated for your mother."

Grace stood up and walked to the window, giving herself a little time and distance. Suddenly, she was no longer certain she wanted Cori to tell her everything. She considered asking her to just reveal her biological father's name and she'd be on her way.

"Grace, do you want me to go on?"

She wasn't sure. All she could think about was that her mother had cheated on her Dad, just like Paul. She wanted to run upstairs and bury her head in one of those gorgeous pillows, but she turned away from the window and retook her seat on the sofa next to Cori. "Complicated, how?"

CHAPTER 23

AUDREY
SATURDAY, JULY 19, 1969

It was 5:15 in the morning when Audrey woke from her bed with a start. The fact that Shea was due to arrive by noon made it impossible for her to sleep. She still hadn't summoned enough courage to tell Danny the truth, and it had been two full days since they had made love. They had come close to a repeat performance last night, too, but she faked a headache in order to return to her cabin to think. It hadn't helped. She still didn't know what she was going to do.

Now her head really was pounding relentlessly, and she felt she may become physically ill. Quickly she jumped from her bed, ran into the bathroom, and hung her head over the toilet bowl; dry-heaving. *This can't be happening!* But it was. She was falling in love with Danny and Shea would be arriving in less than seven hours.

As she continued to vomit, Cori woke and rose from her bed. Following the sounds coming from Audrey, she stumbled, blurry-eyed, into the bathroom. "What's up, kid? You sick or something?"

"Something like that," she mumbled. Audrey flushed the toilet and grabbed the top of the sink to pull herself up. After splashing a little cool water over her face and mouth, she felt much better. She turned around to face her friend.

"What's going on, honey?"

"Oh, Cori. I've really made a mess of things," she began. "I don't know what I'm going to do..." tears began to flow down her cheeks.

"About what? I'm not following you." Cori's eyes were fully opened now. "What have you made a mess of?"

Audrey walked past Cori into the living room and plopped down onto the couch. With one hand draped over her face, she confessed her sin. "I... have been unfaithful to Shea."

"Oh, I see," Cori said, taking a seat next to her. "With Danny?"

Audrey dropped her head to her chest. "Yes. Two days ago. We took a ride on his motorcycle together, and it just happened."

Cori began rubbing Audrey's back, allowing her to weep. "How did it make you feel?"

"What, making love to Danny?"

"Yes. Did it make you feel good or lousy afterwards?"

Audrey wiped the tears from her face, considering Cori's question. "Good, I guess. It was beautiful. I've never experienced anything like it, as a matter of fact, but..."

"But, what?"

Audrey reached for the tissue box on the end table and blew her nose. "But I did feel terribly guilty afterwards. I mean, I'm still very much married."

"Yeah, you are. Let me ask this... do you love him?"

"Danny?"

"Yes, Danny. Do you love him? Because you already shared with me that you aren't happy with Shea."

Audrey put her head down. "Yes, I love Danny. And he said he loves me, too."

"Does he know you're married?"

"No," she whispered. "I never told him."

"I see." She paused. "Well, although we both know it wasn't wise to begin a new relationship while you're still married, what's happened has happened. It's in the past now. As I see it, all you can do now is move forward. I'm guessing that's where you're stuck... right?"

"Right," Audrey sobbed. "And now, with Shea due to arrive in less than seven hours, I have to decide right away. I wish I had more time." She began to cry even harder and, once again, Cori gently rubbed her back.

Audrey cracked a little smile. "I'm so happy we met, Cori. I love you, you know."

"Yeah, I know. I love you, too, kid. Would you like my advice?"

Audrey nodded. "Of course."

"You need to take your lumps, Audrey... beginning with Danny. I think you should get something in your tummy, get cleaned up, and walk over to his cabin and tell him the truth. And, if I were you, I would tell him how unhappy you've been with Shea and that you need some additional time to decide what you're going to do about your marriage. If Danny loves you as he says he does, he'll wait."

"He loves me. I'm certain."

"Okay, good. Then he should understand. Although, I'm certain he will be very hurt that you didn't tell him sooner that you were married, I'm sure he'll realize that you made a horrible mistake. If he's the man we both think he is, he should agree to give you all the time you need to do what's right for you. Should you decide to end

175

your marriage to Shea, then you and Danny can pick up where you left off. If that's what you both still want to do."

Audrey sat up a little taller and wiped her tears away from her face. "You're right, Cori. That's exactly what I need to do."

"Great. And, who knows, maybe one day you and Danny will look back at this time and have a good laugh... should you go in that direction, I mean. Now, let's get up and have our coffee. I'll make us each something quick to eat before I leave for work. You're going to need your strength today, that's for sure."

Audrey let out a little sigh. "That's for sure. It's going to be one of the hardest things I've ever had to do in my life, but I'll do it. I'll tell Danny the truth."

"It's the right thing to do, honey."

While Cori started a pot a coffee, Audrey took a seat at the table, realizing she was still a little shaky. It felt as if a wolf were eating away at her chest, tearing away pieces of her heart, bit by bit.

"You look pale," Cori said, taking a seat beside her.

Audrey dropped her head to her chest. "It's so cruel, you know, when a heart keeps on beating even after it has been broken in two. Mine aches for both Danny and Shea. It feels like my heart has literally been split apart, but still it continues to beat. Thump. Thump. Thump."

"You've really fallen hard for Danny, haven't you?" Cori asked.

"Yes, I have. I've never felt this way before. Not even with Shea. Danny just seems to get me, you know? It's as if he sees right into my soul, and I into his. It's such an incredible injustice. Why are we only meeting each other now?" Tears began to roll down her face again.

"Oh, honey, I don't know. I don't think anyone can claim to, but you need to think about your decision very carefully. After all, it's not just you, Danny, and Shea here. You need to consider what's best for your children, too."

"I know. I've been thinking about them the most, and how a divorce may negatively affect them. Even saying that terrible word: divorce. It makes me want to throw up again." She rubbed the goosebumps from her arms. "Oh Cori, I love Danny, desperately."

Cori cupped her hands around Audrey's, the same way they had witnessed Danny do a few weeks earlier while building sandcastles with the children at the lake. She seemed to choose her next words carefully. "All I can tell you is that life is like a roller coaster. Wild and wonderful, fast and furious, but filled with extreme fear from time to time. When I'm faced with such a challenge, I do my best to hold on tight, come what may, and enjoy the thrill of the ride. I think you need to take some time alone to reflect upon your life and decide, as only you can, what's right for you and your family. Let your heart be your guide."

"You're right, Cori. I think I know what I need to do."

"Is it also what you want to do, honey?"

"Yes, I think it is."

After they had finished their coffee and had a small bite to eat—rye toast with several slices of sharp, New York state cheddar cheese spread across the top—Cori changed into her uniform and set out for work. She needed to get breakfast started for the children. "Good luck today, Audrey," Cori said as she began walking towards the front door. "I'll be thinking about you."

"Thanks, Core. I think I'm going to need all the luck I can get."

"You'll do fine. Just remember to follow your heart." With that, Cori winked and walked out the door.

Audrey waved goodbye and carried their dirty dishes into the kitchen. According to the clock hanging on the wall, it was 6:30 already, and she still needed to get a shower before heading over to Danny's cabin. After rinsing their dishes out in the sink and setting them aside to dry, she went into the bathroom to shower.

After Audrey's hair was dried and the little make-up she typically wore was applied, she selected her favorite pair of bell bottom jeans from her dresser drawer and a pretty, yet conservative, white blouse which—after much consideration—she decided to button all the way up to the top. Pausing only briefly to check her look in the mirror, she slipped into a pair of canvas shoes and drew a deep breath. *You can do this.* With that, she walked outside and headed in the direction of Danny's cabin with a heavy heart.

The morning felt untouched and unspoiled, like a newly-printed dollar bill; crisp and clean, which helped lift her mood. With each additional step she took along the winding path leading her to Danny, Audrey became more resolute to make the change in her life she so desperately wanted. The physical distance between she and Shea now paralleling the emotional void she felt for him in her heart.

Thinking of Shea mostly, and how badly this would affect him, she began to tear up again. She cared for him deeply. And the boys naturally loved their father very much. He was a good father and, if she were being honest, a decent husband too. It was his drinking that she hated, not him. But now, feeling the way she did about Danny, Shea didn't stand a chance. Her heart, she knew, already belonged to another man.

As the sun burst through a heavy cloud above, it seemed to wrap around her like a warm blanket. Audrey knew she needed to hardened herself to the task at hand. She'd have to think only of what was right for herself and her boys. She had to tell Danny the truth the moment she saw him. She felt more and more in command of her own destiny, giving her the strength to do not only what she felt in her heart but in her head now, too. When she turned at the T, leading to Danny's cabin, Audrey was a woman walking confidently into her future.

Danny opened his front door. "Wow, what a surprise. Come on in." He opened the door a little wider, smiling large.

"Thank you. I hope you don't mind me popping in like this," Audrey said, stepping inside.

Danny closed the door. "Are you kidding?" He put his hands on her hips and drew her closer. "I wish we could spend every day like this, all alone together."

"That's actually why I'm here. We need to talk."

"Okay, but first..." He kissed her again. Slowly, lovingly, and before she knew what was happening, his love and entire being seemed to flow through her faster than the speed of light; besieging her with thoughts that she'd rather die than let go of him, wilt away to nothing but dust before losing his love and affection. Somewhere between kisses, Audrey succumbed to him, and lost her nerve to tell him what she had planned. She couldn't possibly tell him the truth right now. She wanted him again, one last time.

Slowly, Danny worked his way up and down her neck, kissing it softly. She opened her mouth, released a soft whimper and lifted her head to his ear. "I need you," she whispered. Then, working her way back to his lips, she kissed him with everything she had.

They stood in the front room of the cabin kissing for several more minutes until they began taking quick, shallow breaths together, hearts racing. Unable to contain his desire for her any longer, Danny put her hand in his and led her to his bed.

There, her hands quickly found their way to his body, exploring it, feeling every cleft and crevasse of him. She rolled over onto her back as he undressed them both. His hands soon rediscovering her every curve, venturing slowly as he moved on top of her "You're so beautiful," he whispered.

They stared into each other's eyes, full of love, wonder, and lust, and slipped once again into their perfect rhythm, communicating more than mere words ever could, until they were both deliciously satisfied.

Moments later, Danny wrapped her tightly in the cocoon of his warm arms and kissed her forehead. "Was there ever a time when we didn't know each other?"

Audrey draped one arm over his naked body. "What do you mean?"

"I've been laying here, looking at you and thinking about the day I first saw you. You were carrying a heavy suitcase in each hand. I knew there was something special about you, even then. As if there was a light in your eyes meant only for me, something to carry me throughout my entire life."

She looked up at him. "I know, I felt the same way when I saw you. I thought you were so handsome." She drew lazy figure-eights on his stomach with her finger.

He hugged her tighter. "I would give up anything for you. I would do anything to keep you safe…"

Audrey's mind was screaming, demanding she tell him the truth. *Now!* But her heart wouldn't allow her to take such a risk. Not yet. It would have to wait. She blocked the nagging thought from her mind as best she could and spoke directly from her heart. "I don't ever want to leave you or your bed, Danny. And I'd like nothing more than to always be with you, but I think I'd better head back to my cabin now before we fall to sleep or something."

"Please, not yet. Stay with me a little longer, Audrey. Just for a little while?"

Easily persuaded, and with some time to spare, she crawled on top of him and straddled his torso with her slender legs. Her pendent, full breasts dangled above his chest, clearly arousing him. He kissed each one, toyed with them, intoxicating her. She moaned for more. The erotic way he then lifted her hips and lowered her onto his full erection, devouring her, was more than she thought she could bear.

Audrey leaned into him and thrust her pelvis downward to match his passion with her own. There was no stopping her now. The ecstasy she felt, unlike anything she had ever experienced before, was leading the way. Her hips responded rapidly, instinctively, heightening her own pleasure. Unable to stifle herself once she reached full orgasm, coming in waves over and over again, Audrey cried out in ecstasy. She had never experienced such a thrill during intercourse before. After she collapsed on top of his chest, fully satisfied, Danny skillfully, not exiting her once, lifted her and gently turned her onto her back, extending their lovemaking until he, too, was once again satisfied.

It was a little past twelve when Shea pulled into Camp Vision. Without any trouble, he found a place to park near the office, next to their family car, the Caprice. As Audrey had driven it here, he had no other choice than to rely on his old pick-up to get around, but he didn't mind. He liked the familiar feel of his old Chevy, rust and all. Besides, normally he had nowhere else to go than to work, the bar, and to church. To those places, he typically walked.

As Shea stepped out of the truck and slammed the door shut—the only way it would actually close—the old, rusty hinges creaked loudly, as always, drawing the attention of the many blind children standing outside of the office. "Sorry, kids. She's a noisy old clunker," Shea laughed as he approached them. "Is the man in charge inside?"

"Yes," Ajei said. "He's my father."

"Oh well, aren't you a lucky little girl." Shea smiled. "Will you let him know I'm here, please? I'm looking for my wife."

"You're Miss Audrey's husband, right? I talked to you on the phone last week, remember?"

"Yes, I do remember. I'm sorry if I was a little rude. I was just feeling a little anxious that day."

"How come?"

Shea looked at the faces of the other children. They too, like the little girl who asked too many questions, seemed to be waiting for his answer. "Can you please just get your father for me?"

"Sure," Ajei said. "I'll be right back."

A few moments later, Jayden stepped outside. "Hi, you must be Shea."

The two men shook hands. "That's right. Are you Jayden?"

"Yes. You're here to visit Audrey?"

"Yes. Can you tell me where I can find her?"

"Sure, no problem." Jayden walked out into the grass. Shea followed. "If you take this road," he pointed to the left of the office. "Walk as far as the T in the road and then take a right. Audrey's cabin will be on your left after that. Number twelve. You can't miss it."

"Okay, sounds simple enough. Thanks."

"You're welcome." The two men shook hands again and then Shea was on his way Following Jayden's directions, he was soon standing on the front porch of cabin number twelve.

Regret washed over Audrey, sending shivers up and down her spine. How she desperately wished Shea wasn't standing outside—but he was. It was all happening too fast. *What if Danny should see him? Figure out who he is?* She was in a full-blown panic, longing to go back to the forest and change what had happened between she and Danny. *Impossible. It has happened.* Now the fact remained that she'd never felt more alive or more loved than she did in Danny's arms. What's more, she knew that she loved him entirely. Much more than she had ever really loved Shea.

Rising from her seat at the table, Audrey exchanged a long glance with Cori and walked to the front door. She knew what she needed to do.

"I'll be in the bedroom, kid. Good luck."

"Thanks." Slowly, Audrey turned the doorknob and opened the door. There, standing before her, was a smiling Shea. A bouquet of her favorite flowers—white roses—were in his outstretched hands. A small detail she hadn't even shared with Danny yet. "Shea, you shouldn't have…"

"Don't be silly," he said, handing her the flowers and walking inside. "Nice place." He turned to kiss her on the cheek, but she quickly ducked and walked into the kitchen and began looking for something to put the flowers in.

"I don't think we have an actual vase." She opened several of the cabinets until she settled on an empty coffee can. "This will have to do." Audrey walked back into the main room and set the tin can boutique of flowers in the center of the dining table. "What do you think?"

"Beautiful." Shea said. "Like you. I've missed you, Audrey." He walked closer to her and took her in his arms. His embrace was warmer, gentler than the last time.

"Thank you. But you really shouldn't have spent so much money… roses are very expensive."

"Ah, come on. If a man can't surprise his wife with some pretty flowers now and then, what good is he?"

"Right," she said, tugging at each of the flower stems until she felt they looked just right. "There. Are you hungry?"

"I could eat. What do you have?"

Audrey opened the refrigerator and looked inside. "We have some leftover chicken salad. It's really good, I think you'll like it. It has red onion. My roommate, Cori, made it. You remember, she's our chef here."

"Sounds great. Will you join me?"

"No, I'm sorry. I already ate," she lied. Her stomach was far too upset to eat anything. "But I'll sit with you while you do."

"Would you mind if I ate out front on the porch? It's such a beautiful day."

Audrey dropped the knife she was using to spread the chicken salad across a slice of bread, and it clattered to the floor at her feet. "Ah, outside, really? I think the bugs may eat your sandwich before you get a chance to if you did that."

"Oh, I didn't think of that. Inside is fine."

Audrey picked up the knife from the floor and dropped it into the sink. Grabbing a clean one from a top drawer, she quickly finished making Shea's sandwich and poured him a glass of lemonade. "Here you go," she rested his plate and drink on top of the table where he was seated. "I hope you like it."

"I'm sure I will."

While he was eating, Audrey tried to think of the best way to break the news to him. Without realizing it, lost in a maze of her own thoughts, she had been staring at him the entire time he was chewing his sandwich.

"What are you looking at? Do I have chicken stuck in my teeth?"

"No, I'm sorry... I didn't realize I was staring at you. I was just thinking."

"About what?"

"Us, Shea. I was thinking about us."

"What about us?"

Cori opened the bedroom door and walked into the dining area. "Hi, you must be the husband. I'm Cori, Audrey's roommate." She held out her right hand.

Shea stood up and shook her hand. "Nice to meet you, Cori. My name is Shea. I didn't realize you were here."

"Oh, sorry about that. I was just cleaning up a little in our room. Audrey, I think I'm going to head over to my friend's cabin now. You know the one, with the motorcycle?"

Audrey knew she looked a little flushed, but quickly jumped on board with Cori's ruse. "Yes, I think I do."

"Well, it's such a nice day I thought he may like to take a ride on his bike with me. A long ride."

"Oh. That's nice," Audrey was unsure what else to say.

"That way you and Shea can have some time all alone to yourselves. Sound good?"

"Yes," Shea said. "That's very nice of you, Cori."

"Yes, very nice." Audrey added, smiling.

"Alright then, see you two later on? I'll probably be gone for about three or four hours."

"I'll probably be gone by then," Shea said. "I promised our boys I'd be home before seven."

"Oh, okay. Well then, I guess this is hello and goodbye. Nice meeting you, Shea."

"Same to you, Cori. Enjoy your motorcycle ride."

"I'm sure I will," she said, before walking out the door.

Finishing the last bite of his sandwich, Shea wiped away a few crumbs from the corner of his mouth and stood up. "I guess this means we're all alone?"

"Yes."

Shea began to smile. "I've really missed you, sweetheart." He walked closer to her. "What do you say we head back into your bedroom for a little while?"

"You must be joking. It's the middle of the day."

"That never stopped us before, remember?"

"Yes, but I need to talk to you..."

He lifted her from her seat. "We can do that, too. But first, I want to show you how much I've missed you."

Audrey sat on the front porch of the cabin envying the tiny pebbles scattered about her feet. Hard and lifeless, unable to feel any pain. She stretched her bare feet as far as she could and began spreading a few around, not certain how she should be feeling right now. Not only had she not told Shea anything she had planned to, she had actually managed to have sex with him as well. Reflecting on it, she knew it felt nothing like it did when she was with Danny and she found herself back at square one: neither man knew the truth. *How have I become so spineless?!*

Looking in the direction of the T, Audrey saw Cori walking towards the cabin. She never felt so happy to see a friend approaching in her entire life. She stood up from the rocking chair and waved.

"All clear?" Cori asked.

"Yeah. Shea left about an hour ago."

Cori stepped up onto the porch. "And?" She took a seat in one of the rocking chairs. "How did he take it?"

Audrey sat down in the other chair and looked down at the pebbles again. "I didn't tell him."

"What? You've got to be kidding me! My ass is raw from that fuckin' bike of Danny's. And all that time I was covering for you, you never told Shea anything?" She leaned back in her chair and began rocking faster.

"Oh, Cori, please. Don't be angry with me. I'm feeling so desperately alone right now and even more guilty than before."

"You should be feeling guilty!" Cori snapped. "You *are* guilty."

"Do you think I don't know that, Cori? Even though I'm certain it's Danny that I want to be with for the rest of my life, it's not that easy to do." She stopped rocking. She couldn't admit to Cori that she even went as far as having sex with Shea today. "This is a very complicated situation."

Cori stopped rocking too. "Yes, and it's only going to get more complicated the longer you put off telling these men the truth."

"I know, I know, I know!" Audrey felt herself beginning to come unhinged. "Why have I been such a coward, Cori? Why?"

Cori resumed rocking. "I guess it's because admitting you've made a terrible mistake is hard. Especially to those you love. But you need to tell them, Audrey. Soon."

Audrey stood up and leaned against the porch railing. "I'm going over to talk to Danny now."

"Are you sure you can do it this time?"

Audrey stepped off the porch and into the grass. It was cool against her bare feet. Looking up at the full moon, she turned around to face Cori again. "I'll try."

By the time Audrey and Danny woke after making love again, somewhere in the distance, a hoot owl called out, and its shrill cry awakened Danny. After a few minutes, he stood up and walked to the bedroom window.

The full moon had slowly descended into the night sky. He watched its reflection shimmer across the dark water of the lake. Looking back over his shoulder, Danny knew he would one day marry the beautiful woman asleep in his bed.

He smiled, staring back up at the moon as he pictured their future together.

Hearing her stir, Danny turned away from the window and grabbed his clothing from the bed. "I'll walk you back to your cabin."

"No, I don't think that's a good idea." Audrey smiled, watching him dress. "I'll be fine."

He pouted, bent over the bed and kissed her. "Just to the T?"

Audrey lost herself in his sparkling eyes and delicious pout. "I guess that would be okay. But just to the T." She got up and got dressed and then walked into the bathroom. Danny walked into the kitchen for a drink of water.

Standing in front of the mirror in the bathroom, Audrey stared at herself, shocked to see her hair haphazardly pushed in every direction into a state of chaos. The realization that Danny had never said a word about her ridiculous hair, made her smile. She tried to run a comb through it. "Danny," she called out. "Do you have a hairbrush?"

"No, I'm afraid not. Just the comb."

"How about a hat or a scarf?"

He walked back into the bedroom, grabbed his Yankees ballcap off of the dresser and walked to the bathroom door. "Will this do?"

Seeing the Yankees logo, she asked, "Is this the only one you have?"

"Afraid so." He laughed, knowing how much it pained her to wear anything Yankee.

She took the cap and put it on, shoving her hair into it the best she could. "How do I look?"

"Beautiful," he said, kissing her cheek. "Like always."

She rolled her eyes at him and shrugged her shoulders. "Well, I'm just happy it's dark outside. I'd hate anyone to see me wearing this hat. We'd better getting going."

"Right," he said, leading the way.

She had to figure out a way to break the news to him, she thought, as they walked. Audrey hated herself for continuing to keep her marriage a secret, but mainly, she was still scared of losing Danny once he discovered the truth. There had to be a way to make him understand. Besides, once she explained her plan to divorce Shea, all would be forgiven; she should just tell him. Instead, she looked deeper into his dark brown eyes, noticing small flecks of copper for the first time. "I love you, Danny," she breathed.

He stared back into her brilliant blues. "I love you, too, Audrey."

No more words were spoken between them. He dropped his hand from hers and she simple walked away. Tomorrow, she would tell him for sure.

CHAPTER 24

GRACE
SATURDAY, SEPTEMBER 1, 2018

"Our first full day at camp, your mother and I went to the beach together for a picnic lunch," Cori said. "I remember it being very hot that summer. Hotter than normal, and your mother convinced me to join her for a swim in that wretched, cold lake. How I hated it. I wasn't in very long, so I returned to our blanket almost straight away after getting wet. That was the first day we met Danny, Jayden's nephew." She took another sip of her wine. "I'll never forget the look on your mother's face the first time he shared a blanket with us." Cori smiled and looked far away at her memories.

"Why's that?"

"I'm not exactly sure why she looked so frightened, but I think she may have been feeling a little overexposed... due to the bikini."

"What bikini?"

"The one she was wearing, naturally. Oh, what a beauty she was..."

"Wait. *Mom* was wearing a bikini?"

"Yes, of course. Why do you ask?"

Grace shrugged her shoulders. "I don't know... I guess it's just difficult for me to picture Mom in a bikini."

"Well, she wore that tiny pink and white number like nobody's business, I can tell you that. But like I said, once Danny joined us on our blanket that day, I think she may have felt uncomfortable."

Grace thought a little while before speaking. "He just decided to join you? Not even knowing you?"

"Well, yes, he was like that. Very friendly. It was later on in the day, after your mom rejoined me on the blanket after her swim. We sat and talked a little while, but soon found ourselves fascinated with Danny. He was building sand castles with several of the children at the water's edge. I remember us commenting about what a natural he seemed to be... around the kids, I mean. It was quite beautiful to watch."

Grace smiled.

"When he finished playing with the kids, he surprised us both by walking directly towards us. We didn't even know his name at this point, but I had already assumed he must be Jayden's nephew. He looked a lot like a younger Jayden."

"Oh?"

"Yes, the family resemblance was remarkable. Wait, hold on a minute... I have an old photo album." She walked upstairs and into her bedroom. A few seconds later she returned, carrying the album. She snuggled closer to Grace and began leafing through the pages. "Here we go," she said, pointing to one of the black and white photographs. "This is Jayden Scarsi."

Grace leaned over Cori's lap and into the album. There were two people pictured in the photograph; a man and a woman, standing next to a sign which read 'Office' on the side of a cabin wall. The man was smiling, revealing perfectly-straight teeth. He appeared much tanner than the woman and had very dark hair. She couldn't tell the color of his eyes. She wondered if he was her father. "Who's the woman?"

Cori leaned in for a closer look. "Oh, that's Sophia. He was dating her that summer, but it didn't last. I heard they broke up soon after this picture was taken."

"Because of my mother?" Grace asked.

"No, not at all. But it was no secret that Jayden thought very highly of your mother. Especially her willingness to play with Ajei whenever she asked. Something I don't remember Sophia ever doing. Jayden loved his little girl."

Grace stared at the photograph a little longer. "Did my mother sleep with him?"

"No, Grace, she didn't. He's not your biological father."

Audrey stared into Cori's eyes, knowing full well who must have been. "Was it his nephew, Danny?"

"Yes."

"But you said he was only twenty-three. How could..."

"You must remember how young your mother always looked. As a matter of fact, I remember being quite surprised to learn how old she was when I first met her, and that she had already bore two children. She didn't look a day over twenty-five then."

Grace thought a few seconds. "But in '69, Mom must have been thirty-seven, right?"

"That's right, but she truly didn't look it." Cori turned another page in the album. "Here, look at her."

Grace bent over again and stared at the photograph of her mother wearing that darling little bikini and posing for the camera. "You're right. She doesn't look a day over twenty-five here. I remember my brothers talking about how she used to get carded buying alcohol almost into her forties."

"Yes, I remember that as well." They both sat in silence for a little while, remembering Audrey's youthful looks as Cori continued turning the pages of her book. "Here's a picture of Danny, Grace."

This time, Grace lifted the photograph from the book and examined the picture closely. He was wearing a swimming suit, standing on the beach with the lake in the background. His hair was slicked back, probably wet, and specks of water glistened on his bare skin. He was squinting against the sun, but she could tell he was very handsome. Dark hair and eyes. Dark skin. Strong. Young. He looked strangely familiar. "Wow, I don't know how I should be feeling right now. He's gorgeous."

"Yes, he really was."

"I've never experience this before," she said, still staring at the photograph. "I mean, all those old family pictures Mom stored in an old cardboard box in our house growing up. I remember looking at them with my brothers, thinking none of the people resembled me in any way. Not even a little. Most of them were blonde and had blue eyes, like Jack and Matthew. But this..." She examined his picture closer. "This is remarkable. I have his cheeks, his nose, even his broad forehead. And his eyes are brown, right? Like mine?" She turned her head to face Cori, who was smiling.

"Yes, Danny had very dark brown hair and eyes, just like you."

"Wow." Audrey leaned into the back of the sofa. "May I keep this?"

"Certainly. You can keep any of these photographs."

"Thanks. I'll take the one of Mom in her bikini, too, if you don't mind."

Cori turned back to that photograph and handed it to Grace. "It's all yours, honey."

"Please tell me more about him. About Danny, my father."

"Certainly... Now, where was I? Oh, I remember, the first day we met Danny at the beach."

Grace nodded and took another sip of her wine.

Audrey was torn in two, Grace." Cori sighed as she finished her tale. "She loved both men, but differently. Shea, after all, was the father of her two children and deep down, I suppose, she still loved him. But Danny, that was a completely different story. She loved him with everything she had..." Cori paused, noticing that Grace was tearing up. "I want you to know this, Grace. Because I think it's very important that you do. Your mother loved your biological father with all her heart and wanted nothing more than to be with him for the rest of her life."

"Then why didn't she?"

Cori let out a loud sigh. "Because once Danny discovered your mother was already married..."

"He didn't know this by the time they..."

Cori shook her head. "No, he didn't. She tried so many times to tell him, but her heart wouldn't allow the words to leave her mouth."

"She eventually did tell him, right?"

"No, not exactly."

CHAPTER 25

DANNY AND AUDREY
FRIDAY, AUGUST 1, 1969

Danny lay in his bed at Camp Vision, convinced more than ever that Audrey was a gift from God, He couldn't imagine life without feeling the warmth of her embrace every single day. Tasting her, drinking her in as he made love to her as often as she would allow. The time spent at Camp Vision had served him extremely well, directing him with a clear, unobstructed vision of what his future could hold.

Excited, Danny sprung from his bed ready to begin a new day infused with the passion and the love he felt for Audrey, and jumped into the shower. He had planned something very special for Audrey that he wanted to execute before the camp closed for the season. Something he hoped would be very memorable that they would one day tell their grandchildren. If only he could figure out how to get her away from camp a little while without raising suspicion.

And then came the miracle.

"Danny, I was thinking," Uncle Jayden began when Danny reported for work. "With the success of Audrey's nightly poetry readings, I think we need to design and build some sort of outdoor structure. Like a pergola or something, so that the kids can enjoy the great outdoors while she reads."

Danny thought about telling Jayden about his love for Audrey now, but decided it could wait. He was too excited to learn more about his uncle's plans. "That sounds terrific. I'm sure everyone would enjoy it."

"Yeah, too bad it won't be up and ready this summer. But while I decide where on the property, I'd like you to build it. Take Audrey into Ithaca today and take a good look around. I know some of the homes have a few nice outdoor structures, especially in Cayuga Heights. Maybe Audrey will see something she especially likes."

Danny couldn't believe his ears. "Yeah, okay. I'll do that."

"Here's my camera. Be sure to snap a few pictures of whatever you find and like."

"Sure, no problem." Danny tried not to smile too widely and hung the camera strap over his shoulder. "Where's Audrey now? Do you know?" Naturally, he knew precisely where she was—he always did—but faked ignorance.

"Yeah, I think she's with Cori and Ajei in the rec room. I saw them there earlier," Jayden said.

"Okay, I'll go tell her the good news now and we'll be on our way."

"Here." Jayden threw him the keys to his truck. "Take Cori and Ajei, too. Cori would like to plant a rose garden. Pick out some nice English roses for her."

Danny tried to hide his disappointment. He had hoped to take Audrey into town alone, on the back of his motorcycle again. "Okay."

When he entered the rec room, his smile returned; the sight of her made him happy. He'd have to figure out another way to get her alone later on.

"Hi, Danny," Audrey said, spotting him.

He approached her, trying to subdue his smile. He wanted to pull her closer to him, but Cori was nearby reading a book to Ajei. Little Ajei didn't know about he and Audrey's relationship, nor should she. "Hi, everybody. Jayden would like us to take his truck into Ithaca to look at pergolas for me to build here."

"Why?" Audrey looked confused.

"He thinks we should have an outdoor structure for you to read poetry in next summer. He thought we might be able to get some ideas by visiting Ithaca."

"Oh, that's great!" Audrey clearly couldn't help herself, and threw her arms around Danny's neck and hugged him. "Cori, did you hear that?" She turned to her friend, disengaging her arms, much to Danny's regret.

"No, what?" Cori looked up from her reading, and Audrey repeated what he'd said.

"He wants us to pick up some rose bushes, too, Cori. He said you're thinking about planting a garden," Danny added.

Cori closed the book that she and Ajei had been reading and walked to where Danny and Audrey stood near the door. "Yeah, I do want to plant some roses. Maybe we could plant them around the structure you build outside, Danny? They'd be beautiful draping over side rails, if you end up building something like that." She closed her eyes, imagining it. "Gorgeous, in fact."

"That's a great idea," Audrey said. "When should we go?"

Danny dangled Jayden's car keys from a ring around his finger. "How about now?"

"All of us?" Ajei asked, excited.

"Yep, all of us," Danny said, picking up the little girl and carrying her outside as they all walked together to Jayden's truck and jumped inside. Audrey sat up front, next to Danny. Cori and Ajei sat in the back.

"I love Ithaca," Ajei said. "Can we stop for some ice cream, too?"

"Sure, why not?" Danny smiled, secretly pretending he and Audrey were an old married couple with their daughter riding in the backseat of their family car. "But first we need to drive around town and look at some outdoor structures. I have your dad's camera. We'll stop and take some pictures of anything we like."

"Yeh!" Ajei squealed. "This is going to be fun."

Danny drove slowly through the tree-lined streets of the upscale neighborhood of Cayuga Heights as they searched for something they liked. Audrey snapped some photographs as he drove. There were several beautiful designs amongst the sprawling backyards of the swank suburb, but one in particular—a rectangular gazebo with a shingled roof and lattice sides—caught their attention.

"Can you really build something like that?" Audrey asked as Danny pulled over and stopped along the curb.

"Sure, no problem." He put the truck in park and they all got out. "But that one looks to be about twelve by eight. I think ours should be bigger."

"How big?" Cori asked.

"Oh, I don't know, but probably about twice that size," he said. "Large enough for all the children and staff to fit inside while Audrey reads. Maybe twenty, or twenty-two, by fifteen feet would work."

Audrey smiled, thinking about Danny building such a fine structure. Not only was he intelligent, kind, handsome, and the man of her dreams, he was also a very skilled carpenter; a skill she greatly admired. She loved the feel of his strong, calloused hands. Shea could barely swing a hammer; something else that irritated her. "How long will it take you to build it, Danny?"

He thought for a few seconds. "Probably about two months, I guess. I could start working on it right away. It'll be up and ready for next summer." He winked and was pleased to see her cheeks grow pink.

"Do you think you'll be able to map out the location right away so I can plan the rose garden accordingly?" Cori asked. "If possible, I'd like to get the roses into the ground this fall."

"Yeah, no problem," Danny said. "Do you live close by, Cori?"

"Not really. I live in Albany, about three hours from here."

"Well if we get container plants instead of bare-root, you can plant them now before you leave. It won't take me too long to plan and clear the site for the gazebo."

"Are you sure?" Cori asked.

"Yeah, let's do it."

Cori smiled. "Thanks, Danny."

"You're welcome. Have you seen enough yet, Audrey?"

"Yes, I'm ready."

"Okay then, let's go," he clapped his hands.

"Can we get ice cream now?" Ajei asked, climbing back into the pickup.

Danny nodded. "There's an ice cream shop right in town next to the garden shop where we'll get the rose bushes."

Everyone was smiling as Danny turned the truck around and headed towards downtown Ithaca. Less than five minutes later, they were standing in line at Perry's Ice Cream Shop ready to place their orders. As Audrey continued to help Ajei decide what kind of ice cream she wanted, Danny and Cori, ice cream cones in hand, sat at an outdoor table together.

Cori thanked Danny for the roses again, and he was glad to see her warming to him. She'd never seemed really keen on him, but it was important to Danny now that Audrey's best friend liked him.

Danny glanced back around at Audrey and Ajei still standing at the counter. "Looks like they haven't even ordered yet and I'm almost finished." He popped the last chunk of his waffle cone into his mouth, swallowed politely and cleared his throat.

"Yeah, looks like it."

He waited a few seconds longer, secretly studying Cori's face, wondering if he could trust her. He didn't know that much about her, but Audrey liked her very much. She was probably trustworthy. "Cori, I'd like to talk to you about Audrey and I. That is, if you don't mind."

"Go ahead, shoot."

He smiled. "These last few weeks spent together with her have been the very best of my life, and I think she feels the same. I love her very much."

"I can tell," Cori said.

"And?"

"And what?"

"Do you agree that she feels the same about me? I thought the two of you may have talked about us. Don't women do that?"

Cori sighed and shook her head.

"Ohhh… that isn't exactly the response I was hoping for," Danny said.

"I'm sorry, Danny. It's really none of my business."

"I know, but I'd like your opinion. Audrey speaks very highly of you, so what you think is important to me. If you'd care to share it, that is."

Cori finished her ice cream and tucked her hands under her thighs to warm them while she spoke. "I'm concerned that it's all happening very fast. For both of you. I think you should both slow down, and see how you feel once you both return to your homes."

Danny nodded. "I understand, but I know my feelings will not change. To tell you the truth, I'm a little scared of losing her when she returns home."

That's an understatement. Cori nodded. "Maybe."

"Which is why I'm thinking about proposing to her before the end of the week."

"What?" Cori's mouth dropped open, and her eyes grew wide.

"Yeah, I know what you must be thinking. Especially after what you just said, but..." He reached into his front pocket and pulled out a shiny ring wrapped in cloth. "I drove home last weekend and picked up my mother's engagement ring. It's been in storage for years, in case I needed it. Now that I've found Audrey, I..."

"Danny, you can't."

His jaw dropped. "What? Why not?"

"I mean, you shouldn't. At least not before you talk to her first. Gauge her reaction about the possibility of marrying you."

"I already have. She feels the same."

Cori was furious. "She told you that?"

"Well not exactly, but she's said things that definitely imply that she'd love nothing more than to marry me."

"I think you need to talk to her some more about it first," Cori muttered, "but here they come."

Danny rewrapped the ring in the cloth and shoved it back into his pocket. "Thanks, I will."

"So, what flavor did you finally decide to get, Ajei?" Cori asked.

"Bubblegum!" She sunk her teeth into the pink ice cream cone and took a large bite.

"Be careful, you don't want to eat it too quickly. You'll get a headache," Audrey said. "Just lick it."

Danny smiled at Audrey's motherly advice and stood up. "Cori, why don't you and I walk over to the garden center and start picking out some plants while these ladies finish their ice cream?"

"Okay," Cori said. "If Audrey doesn't mind?"

"Not at all. Go on ahead, we'll join you as soon as we finish our ice cream."

After the bed of the truck was loaded up with twenty rose bushes, plant food, and mulch, they headed back to camp to arrive by lunch time.

"We can leave everything in the truck, Cori. Once you're ready to plant, I'll pull it up to the site and we can unload everything there," Danny said.

"Okay, that sounds great. Thanks again, Danny." Cori nodded and turned to the others. "Is everyone going to go get some lunch now?"

"In a minute," Danny said. "I want to drop by Uncle Jayden's cabin to drop off his camera first."

"I'll come with you," Audrey said. "I'd like to thank him."

"Okay, then. We'll catch up with you both a little later on," Cori said, as she and Ajei walked away.

As Danny and Audrey began walking towards Jayden's cabin, Danny whispered, "I'm dying to hold you."

"Me too," she said. "I'm not the least bit hungry for lunch."

"Good, me either. Let me run ahead and drop off the camera. I'll meet you in my cabin in five minutes."

"Sounds good. See you in a few."

When Audrey arrived at Danny's cabin, she looked around to make sure no one was watching and then let herself inside. While she waited, she grabbed a book off the kitchen table and sat down on the sofa to read.

Jayden looked up as Danny entered the cabin. "Hey, how'd you make out?"

"Pretty good. We found a gazebo we really liked. We took a few pictures of it along with a few others we saw." He handed his uncle the camera. "The last pictures are of the one we like."

"Okay, great. I'll get them developed right away. What about the roses?"

"Got them too. Twenty, in fact. I left them in the pick-up, by the way. After we decide where to build the gazebo, I'll rope off the perimeter so Cori can plant around it. I told her it would be ready later this week."

"That soon?"

"Yeah. I didn't realize that she lived so far away, so we got bushes in self-contained pots. They're fine to plant now. That way she doesn't need to drive back here in the fall."

Jayden nodded, not seeming particularly interested. He clearly trusted his nephew's opinion. As Danny turned to leave, he quickly said, "Hey, is Audrey still with you by any chance?"

Danny played it cool. "No. I think she went back to her cabin. Why?"

"I was hoping you could relay a message to her."

Danny stopped by the front door. "I'll probably see her over lunch in a little while, would that help?"

"Yeah, it'll save me a trip. Please tell her that her husband called about ten minutes ago. He wants her to call him back when she gets a chance. Nothing urgent, he said."

Danny froze. A wave of cold ran down his body, and he felt like his heart had stopped. It couldn't be...no. She was *his*. "Who...?" His voice cracked. *Dammit.* "Who called?"

Unaware of his nephew's heartbreak, Jayden had resumed studying some papers at his desk. "Huh? Oh, Shea, her husband. Just ten minutes ago."

"Shea?"

Jayden still didn't look up at his nephew. "Yeah, Shea. Tell her for me, would ya?"

Danny walked out of the cabin without a word. The sun seemed hotter than it was five minutes ago and he began to sweat. Inside, his mind was on fire. As he began walking slowly towards his cabin, his heartbreak turned to rage, and he began to run.

She lied to me!

Once he reached his cabin, he pushed open the door, stepped inside and slammed it behind him. Audrey looked up from her perch on the sofa, a shocked expression on her face. *As if she doesn't realize!*

Still incensed, Danny walked into the kitchen, took a seat at the table and began biting his fingernail. His hands were shaking. "You need to leave, Audrey. Your husband, Shea, called about fifteen minutes ago and wants you to call him back. Funny, all this time I thought you were unmarried. Silly me!"

"Danny, please, let me explain..." Audrey's voice was weak.

Silently, he began to recite the Lord's Prayer in his mind as she spoke, ignoring her excuses. Danny needed to pray for her, especially, and then himself. Oddly, he was suddenly very calm. "Is there anything you can say to change the fact that you are married, Audrey?" His voice was low.

She looked down at the floor and began to cry. "No."

"Then please leave me. I need to pray." Danny took a deep breath, turning from the tears streaking her cheeks. He would have wiped them away with tenderness, only ten minutes ago.

"No, I won't leave you! We need to talk about this."

"There's nothing to talk about, Audrey. My advice to you is to go home and confess to your priest, and then to your husband. You've committed a mortal sin. You know this, right?" She nodded and his heart began to break once more, as he dropped his head and began to pray.

"Danny, stop it! I'm going to divorce Shea so we can be together."

"That won't fix anything." He looked up. "Anyone who divorces his wife and marries another woman commits adultery, and the man who marries a divorced woman commits adultery. Luke 16 and 18."

"Danny, stop it! You're torturing yourself with scriptures written thousands of years ago by people who wanted nothing more than power and money."

"It's more than that, Audrey. To me, anyway."

Audrey looked deep into his eyes. "Your faith in God is important, but it's also important to hold onto your faith in our love. I know what I've done is wrong. And if I could take back time, I would tell you the truth right away."

"If you had, we never would have gotten together."

"Oh, Danny, please! Don't say that. God isn't a totalitarian. He loves us, always, no matter our sins. You know this. No maybes with God. He loves us, unconditionally. You don't have to forsake everything we feel for each other, Danny. Don't let your faith mess up our future. Forgive us, let me divorce Shea, and God will forgive us too!" She was shouting.

Danny stood up and calmly walked out of the cabin, but she irritatingly dogged his footsteps. Determined to get away from her, he walked to the shoreline and looked out over the lake. His guilt was like fuel to the fire of his anger—or was he angry because he couldn't face the weight of his guilt? Danny didn't even know. *Does it matter?* He'd betrayed everything he'd once stood for.

His insides dying slowly from the toxicity, needing no more than a spark to set it ablaze. The fire had burnt him out so badly there was nothing left but a shell of a man, an outline of the person he had been before coming to Camp Vision. He turned without anger to face her, yet exasperation was riding in his tone. "I feel God, Audrey, as keenly as the love I feel for you. Who's to say that isn't real? For if it's not, then what is? If we can't trust our senses, then the whole notion of reality is up for grabs. He is love. I feel His presence always. I hope you do, too." He walked closer to her, without touching her. "It's over between us, Audrey. Go back to your husband and beg him, and God, to forgive you."

"Oh, Danny, please don't walk away from me. I can't bear it!"

"My guilt is tearing away at my guts, Audrey! Yours should be, too. It could be a thousand years from now and I would still feel the same way about this. I can't melt its ugliness on my own, I can't even shift it. I need Him to show me that I can do better." He began to walk back in the direction of his cabin.

Audrey followed him again, stumbling as she ran. "Danny, we can seek His guidance together. Please don't throw away what we already have. I can say with a great amount of clarity that you may never find what we have, ever again."

He turned around to face her one last time. "That's the thing, Audrey. I've always had it. Ever since I was a little kid, and it kills me that I almost lost it here. I wanted to follow His ways from my earliest memories, nothing can make that untrue, but still I strayed. So, as difficult as it's going to be to forget about you and the love we made, I own my mistake, and accept that He will give me a second chance to do what I was born to do. I only hope that in time I can feel like I deserve it again."

Audrey collapsed to the ground, not caring who may see her, as the love of her life walked away from her, leaving her alone on the shore of the lake.

Never once looking back at her, Danny returned to his cabin to pack.

CHAPTER 26

GRACE
SATURDAY, SEPTEMBER 1, 2018

It was nearly midnight by the time Cori finished telling Grace everything she had either personally witnessed or that Audrey had shared with her about the summer of '69 and her love for Danny. Like Jack, Cori felt relieved that Grace finally knew the truth. She took another sip of her wine, sat back, and waited for Grace to speak.

"Did they ever figure out I was Danny's child?"

"Yes, almost immediately after you were born. Like you've noticed, you're the spitting image of him."

Grace looked down at the photograph of Danny again. "Yes, I guess I am."

"Even though we didn't have DNA testing available to us back then, they knew. Both of them."

Grace nodded. "And Danny never came after her? Not even to see me?"

"No. Your mother would have preferred him not to. She never even told him she was pregnant with his child before leaving the camp."

Grace stood up again. "Whatever happened to him? Do you know?"

"No," Cori said. "I'm not even sure if he's still alive."

Grace thought about how strange it felt, happening to her and not some stranger she had recently read about. It felt like an out-of-body experience. Very surreal. At least her mother loved her biological father and her conception wasn't the result of a one-night stand or something equally tawdry. "Thank you, Cori. I cannot tell you how much this means to me."

"You're welcome, honey. I've always thought you deserved to know, but your mother swore me to secrecy. My only regret now, is not tracking you down myself and telling you sooner." She sighed. "What are you going to do now that you know?"

"Right now, I'm going to head back to Trumansburg, to the cottage." Grace turned around and began walking towards the upstairs. She needed to get her suitcase.

"But you just got here. I thought you were going to be spending the night."

"I know, I did plan to stay, but now all I can think about is getting back to the cottage and talking to my brothers. I need to apologize to them."

"Are you sure?

"Yes. I want to see them and then get back home so I can begin searching for Danny Scarsi. Like you said, he may still be alive."

Cori spoke reluctantly "Danny's last name wasn't Scarsi, Grace."

Grace turned around to face her. "It wasn't?"

"No," she said, taking a seat next to the window. "I think you need to sit down again."

Grace looked closely at Cori, understanding for the first time how old she truly was. In the natural light her skin looked leathery, carved harshly by the sun. On the table next to her stood many framed photographs, including a black and white of her standing below the Camp Vision sign. Cori stood tall and proud standing there in her youth. Grace 's eyes begin to flick between

210

the two images, the current woman sitting before her and her youthful self in the photograph. *Time is a thief. It steals so much.*

She treaded lightly, understanding that perhaps Cori didn't want to see her leave so soon. "Cori, I'm so sorry I cannot stay longer, but I'll be back. We're not going to lose touch with one another again, I promise. But please, tell me Danny's last name so I can get on my way. I don't want to drive after dark."

Sensing Grace 's pity—something Cori clearly neither wanted nor deserved—she spoke somewhat abruptly this time. "Danny's last name was Pepitone, Grace."

"That's funny, we once had a priest in Cincinnatus by the name of Pepitone. He wasn't there very long, only briefly, when I was a child. Too bad, I remember liking him very much."

"Then you remember him?"

"Father Pepitone? Yes, of course. I liked him very much. Why?"

Cori stared at her for a little while longer, saying nothing.

"What is it, Cori? Aren't you feeling well?"

"Grace, please come sit next to me."

"Oh, Cori, I'm sorry. I really can't. I have to be leaving now before it starts raining. I hate driving in the rain even more than I hate driving in the dark." She turned to walk upstairs.

"Grace, please, wait! I need to tell you more..."

"What? Then tell me, please. I need to get going."

Cori drew a large breath. "Grace, Father Pepitone was your father. He was Danny."

Grace stopped dead in her tracks and, ever so slowly, turned her head around. *"What* did you say?"

"It's true, Grace. A few years after the summer he met your mother, Danny, who was nothing if not a wonderful man, returned to seminary school as he had planned to do before arriving at Camp Vision that year. He was so heartbroken, I remember it clearly, as was she, after they split up. His faith wouldn't allow him to agree to a divorce for your mother. He left a broken-hearted man, Grace. Eventually, though, I heard the following summer from Jayden, he returned to seminary school and was ordained soon after in Buffalo. After that, quite coincidentally, he was assigned to Our Lady of Perpetual Hope in Cincinnatus after Father Finnigan retired. Naturally, he had no way of knowing that was where all of you were living and attended church. Your mother never told him where she was from, either."

A high-pitched tone began to scream inside of Grace's head, and she suddenly felt nauseous. Her legs wobbled as she attempted to remain upright. Realizing she was about to faint, she backed herself up against a wall and allowed herself to sink slowly to the floor on bended knees.

Cori rushed to her side. "Just breathe with me, sweetheart. Like this."

Grace began to breathe along with Cori, in and out, in and out. Once her breathing was gaining control, she cried, "I can't believe this. Father Pepitone was my *father?"*

"Yes, Grace, he was. But you must understand, he was undecided about which direction to take his life. On the fence, as they say, between becoming a priest or not when he met your mother. I know for a fact that he had plans to marry her. He even showed me the ring. But once he discovered she was already married, he wouldn't—couldn't—allow her to divorce Shea. He truly was a lovely man, Grace, in every way. Just as he was when you met him as a little girl."

"Did Mom know he was thinking about becoming a priest when she met him?"

"No, she didn't. To her, he was simply a wonderful young man that she fell madly in love with."

"This is unbelievable. No wonder Jack and Matthew didn't want me to know about any of this." She dropped her head and started to cry.

Cori dropped her head to her chest, too. "Grace, there's more. But you need to rest a moment before I go on."

"What more can there possibly be? Isn't this enough?" She sobbed.

"I know this has to come as a huge shock to you. That's exactly why I think you should consider staying with me another night."

"No. Thank you," Grace said, wiping her tears. "I want to go home. I may not even bother stopping at the cottage now. I want to sleep in my own bed more than ever."

"You're thinking about driving all the way back to Philadelphia tonight? I'm not sure that's a good idea. Do you think you can even stand up?"

"Yeah," Grace said as she took to her feet. "My father was a priest. This is unbelievable."

"Yes, I suppose it is."

Grace looked into Cori's eyes. "I guess this explains why Mom suddenly stopped attending church with us."

"Yes. I'm afraid her faith had been hugely compromised due to these unfortunate circumstances. She blamed God for everything that happened."

Grace thought back to the time her mother had first refused to attend church any longer. "It was right after Jack came home from Vietnam, wasn't it? I think I remember it."

"Yes, that's right. You couldn't have been more than five or six at the time. I'm surprised you remember it."

Grace walked over to the sofa and took a seat. "It was Palm Sunday. Everyone, including Mom, was excited to meet the new priest that day during Mass. I remember it clearly. I also remember thinking how handsome he was when I finally caught a glimpse of him, standing at the top of the altar." She covered her face with both hands. "My God, and Mom didn't know it was going to be him there that day?"

"No, she had no idea. It turned out to be the biggest shock of her life, too. I don't know if you remember this, but she ended up spending a few days in the hospital after that." Cori took a seat next to her on the sofa.

"No, not really, I'm ashamed to admit."

"Don't. You have nothing to feel ashamed of. You were only a child. Besides, I'm sure your dad did everything he could to keep it from you. He was always so concerned about your happiness."

Grace began to cry again. "You mean my fake dad?"

"Grace, Shea loved you, which spoke volumes about his fine character, like you said earlier. He too was a wonderful man. Unfortunately, just not the man your mother really loved. She loved Danny, which Shea, sadly, was well aware of until the day he died. But even still, he loved you with all of his heart."

214

Grace cried uncontrollably and rested her head on Cori's shoulder. "Oh my God, I don't think my heart can bear to hear anymore," she sobbed. "Please don't tell me anything else. I can't stand to hear it!"

Cori sat in silence for several more minutes while Grace cried, resting her head on her shoulder. Once Grace finally stopped crying and sat up again, shoulders still shaking, Cori handed her the box of tissues resting on the coffee table.

"Thank you. I'm so glad you were the one to finally tell me all of this. I'm not sure Jack or Matthew would have been as gentle."

Cori cleared her throat. "Grace, like I said, there is more I think you need to know, but I think we should wait a few days. Would you please reconsider staying with me tonight? I'll worry about you driving away like this."

"You're probably right. I shouldn't drive," Grace finally admitted to herself. She could barely even see right now. "Thanks."

"No problem. I'll make us a pot of chamomile. It will help you relax."

"Thanks, Cori. That would be nice. It came as a big shock, is all. I actually knew my real father, but had no idea who he was at the time. It's totally surreal."

"I'm sure. I'll be right back with our tea."

Grace suddenly became acutely aware of every sound around her: one of the cats scurrying around the floor with a toy, Bailey licking his hind leg, tea beginning to boil on the stove, rain streaking against the living room windows. She thought about the anxiety and heartbreak she had felt for the last several weeks since receiving her DNA results. Her brothers' reaction, the sleepless nights and, finally, the shock of learning about her biological father. At least she finally had her answers.

Cori returned with their tea.

"Thank you," Grace said, as she sat up and took a sip of the hot tea. "This is delicious." She sat her tea cup on top of the coffee table, feeling her tension beginning to fade. "I'm feeling better already. Now, please tell me the rest of your story." She drew a deep breath and slowly exhaled, beginning to relax. "I'm ready to hear everything, Cori," Grace said. "What else is it that you wanted to tell me?"

"I've been sitting here thinking. And I feel that it would be better to wait until you've had a good night's rest before I tell you anymore."

"Oh, I don't know. I think I'm up for it now."

"Perhaps." Cori took a sip of her tea. "But I'm not sure *I* am. I'd like to finish our tea and go to bed. We can pick up where I left off tomorrow. Sound good?"

Grace was disappointed but, again, understood that Cori was an old woman who needed her rest. "Certainly, Cori. If that's what you'd like to do."

"I would."

CHAPTER 27

AUDREY
SATURDAY, AUGUST 30, 1969

On the last day of camp, after saying a long, tearful, and awful good-bye to Cori, Jayden, Sophia, and little Ajei, in that order—Danny had already headed out weeks earlier—Audrey got into her car and drove away from Camp Vision, tears blurring her view of the road. She didn't care. For the first time in her life, she thought it may be better to be dead; certainly, she would never get over the heartbreak of losing Danny. What she had done she could never un-do.

As she drove further away from the camp, Audrey pounded her fist on the dashboard and began to wail, trying to release her pain. "This isn't happening! Oh, Danny! Why can't you see how much I love you… how happy we'd be together!"

She pulled over onto the side of the road and turned off the car. She didn't know where to go because all she really wanted to do was turn around and find Danny standing on the front porch of his cabin, waiting for her as he had so many times before. Crawl into bed with him, one last time. Whisper in his ear, make sweet love to him, fall asleep in his arms and make him understand how much she loved him. How much she would always love him. She cried harder than she had ever before; until it felt as though her ribs would break under the pain of her sobs.

Looking back over her shoulder, far down the road, the 'Camp Vision' sign swayed gently in the breeze and it occurred to Audrey for the first time that she would never return. Never again would she read to the many children, never again would she see any of her new friends; maybe not even Cori, and worst of all, Camp Vision would always hold too many memories of Danny. Too many heartbreaks, too many lies and too many tears. She could never return.

Her eyes fell to her lap. She wanted to be in the lake again, in the desperate cold with Danny. Then at least she'd be with him again.

Maybe she'd swim, gliding dolphin-like around him for as long as she liked. It had been then, in those perfect moments back at camp, that she didn't bother thinking about what may happen. In the lake with Danny, where she could once again escape the dull drag of gravity, was where she wanted to be again. Maybe she'd sink beneath the water, and never come back up.

Audrey had felt as free as she had ever experienced in her thirty-seven years, being with Danny; nothing else would ever come close to what she had felt, loving him. She could die right now and she wouldn't care.

Audrey sat on the shoulder of the road for a very long time, crying, wiping her tears, and crying some more. Only two shorts months ago her life had been simple, uncluttered. But now it was completely different, complicated and painful. She felt as if her body was no longer large enough to hold all of her pain. Her heart ached for Danny's embrace. She wanted him to come back—from wherever he was right now, she didn't even know—and make everything like it had been before. Let him take her into his arms, hear him tell her he still loved her and that he always would. Despite everything, all would be okay, as long as they were always together.

But this was far from being true and it would never be okay again. Danny was lost to her memories, forever.

As she continued to cry, the sun broke through the clouds and shinned through the windshield. Audrey thought about her boys and even Shea, waiting for her at home. She had a family who loved her, after all. And although Shea wasn't Danny, and never would or could be, he loved her with all of his heart. Always had, perhaps always would. But his love would soon be tested, she knew, as she ran both of her shaking hands over the curve of her belly. Although she wasn't showing yet, she knew from experience that she was pregnant again. She also knew what she needed to do. This time, without fail, she would tell the truth. *No more cowardice!*

As soon as she was finished unpacking all of her things at home and the boys were outside doing something, anything, just as long as they couldn't overhear the horrible words that would come out of her mouth: the details of her betrayal to their father. *I will do it! As soon as I get home.*

Shea deserved to know the truth and Audrey knew it. Everything that happened between Danny and herself had been her fault. She would make amends in subtle ways, she promised God and herself as she drove. Her silent prayers would speak her heart and beg His forgiveness. And Shea's.

Audrey wiped away the tears from her face and made a silent vow never to shed another for what could have been. The fact that she loved Danny—and always would—would be buried along with her pain for the rest of her days. Now, if Shea would welcome her home and forgive her, she would learn how to live again.

CHAPTER 28

AUDREY
SUNDAY, MARCH 23, 1975

Six years later, in the early morning of Palm Sunday, 1975, Audrey stood over the stove frying bacon as Jack entered the kitchen. "Mom, that smells fantastic." His nostrils flared as he sniffed the air. "I missed the smell of your bacon more than anything while I was gone." He gave her a peck on the cheek and took a seat at the kitchen table.

She turned around and faced him. "You look good, Jack. Dad's old suit fits you pretty well."

Jack looked down at himself. "Yeah, I've filled out over the past two years, don't you think?"

Audrey thought about how he had left a boy and returned home a man from Vietnam. "You certainly have. I'm so happy you're home, safe and sound." She smiled and looked out the kitchen window. Five-year-old Grace sat on Shea's knee as he pointed towards the sky while he took another sip of whiskey from his flask. He had stopped hiding his drinking at home from her five years ago, when everything changed, and they settled into a melancholy existence together. One they both accepted too easily. Naturally, Shea had forgiven her. He loved her so, but still, she knew that being father to another man's child was something that took much patience and practice. It helped, she supposed, that Grace was such a lovely child.

"Looks like Dad is showing Gracie more birds." Audrey commented.

Jack turned his head around and stared out the window. "Yeah, so he is."

Audrey flipped a few more strips of bacon over in the pan. "Scrambled eggs okay, Jack?"

"Sure."

Matthew joined them, also wearing his Sunday best. "Do you need any help before I sit down, Mom?"

"Yeah, grab a large mixing bowl from the top shelf for me, will ya, Matty?"

Matthew grabbed the largest bowl, an old brown Pyrex that she typically used to mix together her famous chocolate cakes and Sunday morning pancakes, and sat it down on the counter beside her. "Anything else?"

"No, that's it, but let Dad and Gracie know we'll be ready to eat in about ten minutes."

Matthew opened the back door and stuck his head outside. It was a mild April morning, even the robins had returned to their backyard and the purple and yellow crocuses were popping up along the edges of the house. He yelled out to his dad, and received a wave in response.

Shea took another sip from his flask. "Okay, thanks," he said, turning his attention back to his daughter. "Come on Grace, time for us to get cleaned up for breakfast and then go to church."

"Mommy got me a new pink dress to wear today," Grace said. "Can I put it on now, Daddy?"

"In a little bit. You go on upstairs now and wash your face and hands. As soon as we finish eating our

221

breakfast, Mommy will help you get into your new dress."

"Yay!" Grace ran into the house and up the steps to the second floor. "I'll be right back, Mom!"

Jack laughed. "Mom? What happened to Mommy?"

Audrey smiled. "She calls me that once in a while. She's really growing up quickly--too quickly."

"Did she get the birthday card I sent her?" Jack asked.

"Yes," Shea said, closing the back door behind him. "She was so excited about that dollar-bill you included, she made me walk her down to Clyde's to buy candy the same day she received it." He took a seat at the table with his sons, shaking his head.

"Ha!" Jack said. "That's great. I'm glad it made her happy."

"It did indeed," Shea said, tucking his napkin under his chin as Audrey and Grace joined them at the table. "Let's pray."

After breakfast, as promised, Audrey helped Grace into her new dress and then slipped into hers. Also, pink, Audrey's dress was made from chiffon and lined with taffeta underneath the fully pleated skirt. The fitted bodice was gathered snuggly around her once again slender waist and topped with a standing collar decorated with a button-and-loop neck. The sleeves were gathered just below her elbows, and flowed when she walked.

"Spin around with me, Mommy," Grace said and Audrey complied. As they turned in circles, their skirts flew up and spun like tiny toy tops. "Let's do it again!"

"No," Audrey said. "That's enough now. We need to get going. Mass is about to begin; we don't want to be late."

Grace frowned.

"Come on, big girl. Let's spray on a little of our favorite perfume before we leave."

It worked. Grace giggled as Audrey sprayed her favorite scent, Desert Flower, on the inside of her daughter's little wrists and then her own. She then put on her favorite pair of gold hoop earrings and applied her lipstick as Grace sniffed her wrists again. "We're all set, big girl, let's go."

When the McKenzie family arrived at the church, it was already packed. "Figures," Matthew moaned. "Even Mr. Houck and his wife are here. They never come, except on holidays."

"Matty, be nice," Audrey said, as she dipped her fingers into a vessel of holy water, made the sign of the cross over her chest, and began walking down the aisle of the crowded church "Oh my," she sighed. Matty wasn't wrong; every pew was full. "Where are we going to sit, Shea?"

Shea scanned the many crowded rows. He spotted one near the back, wide enough for all five of them to fit "Follow me."

Jack whispered into Matthew's ear as they followed their father. "You're right. It's packed in here. Bunch of posers."

"Exactly," Matthew said. "Same thing happens on Easter and Christmas."

"Yeah, but there's a new priest expected today, right?"

"Yeah," Matthew said, taking his seat next to Audrey. "I'm sure that has a lot to do with it." Matthew scanned the church and spotted Sandy and her family right away, seated at the front of the church, and waved to her.

Grace sat between her mother and father on the end of the pew nearest the isle and Matthew and then Jack sat on the end, closest to the wall.

Grace and several other children began waving their palm branches above their heads as the organist pounded out a familiar tune. Someone dropped a hymn book in the very back of the church which landed on the hardwood floor with a *thud*. Most everyone followed the sound of the book crashing to the floor while simultaneously cranking their heads around in several directions, hoping to catch a glimpse of the new priest. With each word they sang, the anticipation grew, as it was customary for the priest to begin after the first hymn. But not until four agonizing verses of the song were sung did the organist abruptly stop playing and the singing finally cease.

The hush was palpable, all eyes on the rectory door to the right of the alter as it slowly opened. The priest who entered was young, probably no more than thirty. His priestly robes hung over his solid frame. His dark hair and eyes shined in the light of the candles around the altar, which made him appear exceptionally charming. Many women and teenage girls smiled a little wider. Some of the wives even elbowed their husbands as if to say, do you see how handsome he is?

Confidently, the smiling priest walked to the top of the alter, raised his outstretched arms to his parishioners and asked them to rise.

Instead, Audrey gasped loudly, and the people standing in front of her turned around and scowled. As the priest began to make the sign of the cross over his chest, she strained her eyes to get a better look at him.

When he spoke, "In the name of the Father, and of the Son, and of the Holy Spirit," she knew for sure. *It's Danny.*

"Amen," everyone replied, except one. Audrey sat frozen in her seat until Matthew noticed and helped her to her feet. He watched his mother slowly lift her head, open her eyes as wide as they would stretch, and stare directly into the face of their new priest. Audrey felt her face go pale.

The priest seeming to stare directly back at her, as if they were the only two people in the church. Finally, the priest shifted his eyes away from Audrey and onto the stained-glass replica of Jesus Christ at the back of the church. "May the Lord be with you," he said.

"And with you," the faithful replied.

As Danny continued speaking, panic rose in Audrey's chest, tightening, as if the muscles were trying to prevent her from breathing. When her breath finally did come, it was shallow and entirely too fast. Her thoughts were static, her legs wobbly, and nothing made sense. *It can't be him!* She looked up again, into his face. It was definitely him.

Everything began to swirl like the pink dresses had earlier but now, violently, like an F5 tornado; faster than a tsunami crashing to the shore of the mighty Pacific. One minute everything was fine and the next everything was moving. It would be funny if it weren't true, and she was only imagining it. But there he was, standing before her and her family as their new priest. "I can't," she sputtered.

"Mom, what is it?" Matthew asked from beside her, eyes gazing up worriedly at his mother.

It was too late, the mighty cyclone was all around her now, thrashing her around violently from the inside. Time passed both slowly and in a flash. Before Jack and Matthew knew what to expect, Audrey's eyes rolled back into her head and she collapsed to the floor. With the light in her eyes completely gone and the scattered debris of her heart all around her, she felt colder than she had ever felt before. Either the strong winds were sucking the heat from her body or she was bleeding out, she couldn't be sure. All she saw was blackness.

Shea and the boys huddled around her at the base of the pew. "Mom, can you hear me?" It was Matthew's voice. He gently slapped the side of her face. "Mom, wake up."

"Stay here with Grace, boys." It was Shea's voice now. Strong, confident, and very much in charge. Quickly, he lifted his wife into his arms and carried her outside while everyone in the back of the church and Father Pepitone watched on. Once outside, he rested her on soft grass, and she could smell the maple tree above her, just beginning to bud.

Audrey felt herself began to regain consciousness, and as feeling returned to her limbs, she opened her eyes. "I'm going to be sick." She leaned over to one side and, true to her word, began to vomit.

Shea rubbed her back and kept her hair away from her face. "It's okay, you're going to be fine. You just needed some air."

Audrey finished, lay back in the grass again and closed her eyes. Ten minutes ago, she hadn't a care in the world. Now she felt as if she was buried deep, with no way out. She was so weak. "It's him," she whispered.

Shea bent down and put his face closer to hers. "It's okay, Audrey. You fainted, just lay still for a little while."

"Where are the kids?"

"Still inside. I told them to wait there."

"G-good," she stuttered. "It's Danny, Shea."

Shea looked at her, his brow furrowed. "What are you talking about? Danny who?"

She looked up at him. "Danny. Grace's... father."

"Oh my God, woman. Even now you're thinking about him? At a time like this?" He pulled away from her.

"Shea, please, you must believe me. I don't understand it, but it's him. Danny. I know it."

Shea glanced over his shoulder at the marquee on the church lawn. He didn't need to read long. Written with black magnetic letters, at the top of the white sign were the words that none of them had previously noticed: Welcome Father Daniel Pepitone.

He stood up. "What in Christ's name is going on here?!"

"Take me home. I need to get out of here, Shea."

For an instant, he seemed to consider leaving her, but reluctantly, Shea extended his hand and helped her to her feet. "Can you walk?"

"Yes," Audrey nodded, and turned to walk back home.

"Wait here. I'm going to get Grace."

She called after him. "Why? The boys can..."

He waved his hand in the air, dismissing her as he continued inside the church to retrieve his only daughter.

CHAPTER 29

DANNY
SATURDAY, JUNE 21, 1969

Two days before Camp Vision opened inCa the summer of '69, Danny sat across from his uncle in the fine library of his home. They sat in two plush, comfortable chairs which must have cost a small fortune, Danny figured, rubbing his hands gingerly across the top of both arm rests. He recognized the expensive fabric immediately. Imported silk. *Perhaps all the way from Singapore.* The chair was constructed from white oak and trimmed with delicately-carved ivory, same as the *Cathedra Petri*, Thrown of Saint Peter, at the Vatican. Or so he had heard. He couldn't say for sure if this was actually true, having never been to Rome himself, much less the Vatican.

At least not yet. He was schedule to fly to Rome in ten days.

As regal as Danny felt, sitting in such a distinguished chair amongst his uncle's massive collection of hundreds, maybe thousands, of leather-bound books—first editions, no less—he couldn't help feeling depressed.

"Why so down, kid?" Uncle Jayden asked. "Aren't you excited about your trip to Rome?"

"Yeah... I'm very excited to see it."

"I see," Jayden said, unconvinced. "You're leaving in a couple of weeks, right?"

Danny began to bite his fingernails; a habit left over from childhood. Most times, like now, he wasn't even aware he was doing it. "Ten days. My flight leaves from Syracuse on July first."

Jayden Scarsi was a very wise man but even a ten-year-old, like little Ajei, could tell that something, something very big, was troubling his young nephew. "Do you mind if I smoke, Danny?"

"No."

"Good." Jayden opened the humidor resting on top of his desk and pulled out two Cubans. "Care to join me?"

"Yes, sir," Danny said, looking somewhat animated for the first time since joining his uncle in his library. He had never even thought about smoking a cigar before but suddenly found himself excited to try one. "I'd love to."

"Alright. Just don't tell your mother, the nag," Jayden joked as he sniped off one end of both cigars and handed one to his nephew. "Have you ever smoked a stogie before, Danny?" Danny hesitated briefly before admitting he had not. "Not a problem. Just do as I say."

Jayden pulled his trusty lighter from his shirt pocket. "First, you need to light it…like so." He held his cigar above the tip of the flame while simultaneously spinning it, ensuring he'd get an even burn. Once it began to burn with a bright orange glow he began to puff.

Seems easy enough, Danny thought, taking the lighter from his uncle's hand and lighting a flame under his cigar like his uncle had done. He then began to puff.

"Not yet," Jayden quickly corrected, "You need to have it properly lit first."

Beginning to understand that smoking a cigar wasn't as easy as he thought, Danny doused the lighter's flame and looked up at his uncle. "How do I know when *that* is?"

"When the tip of the cigar turns bright orange."

With a slight shake of his head, Danny tried again. This time waiting patiently until he noticed the correct color of the burn as his uncle had described. "Like this?"

"Yes, that's it. Now, go ahead and start puffing."

Danny took a long drag, inhaling the smoke deeply, which was immediately followed by very loud hacking and coughing. Feeling like a buffoon, he rested his cigar in the ashtray on the table between them, "Maybe this isn't for me..."

Jayden threw back his head and began to laugh. "Sorry, I forgot to tell you not to inhale right away."

"Thanks a lot," Danny managed to say between coughs which lasted for another two full minutes. "Nice to know," he added, once the hacking had finally stopped, his lungs aching.

"Here's what you do. Pick up your cigar again and pretend you're sucking something through a straw. Something small. Then fill your mouth with smoke and blow it out, four or five times, but don't inhale yet. Come on, do it with me."

Each man sat back in their chair and began to gently suck the end of their cigar until thick, white trails of smoke billowed across their faces and travelled upward, coating the ceiling. With both cigars now correctly lit, Jayden explained that it wasn't necessary to constantly puff on it. "Just a drag or two once every minute or so," he said.

Feeling much more relaxed, and enjoying the flavor of his very first cigar, Danny leaned back in his chair and smiled.

"That's better," Jayden said, noticing his expression. "Now you gonna tell me what's been bugging you."

Danny paused for a moment, but before he could speak his eyes began to fill with unexpected tears. Burning with embarrassment, he wiped them with the back of his hand—faking some smoke in his eyes—as quickly as he could and slumped deeper into his chair to further hide his face from his uncle.

"What is it, kid? Maybe I can help. Let it out."

Danny stared into his uncle's kind brown eyes and realized maybe he *could* help. "What the hell," Danny sat up straighter and began to explain the cause of his misery to his uncle as best he could. "You know I've been dreaming of the priesthood since I was a little kid," he began. "I really thought that once seminary was over, I'd be ready."

"Your mother mentioned something about more studies in Buffalo—is that the problem, Buffalo?

"No, not in the least bit. I like Buffalo. I actually find it a very exciting city."

"Then what is it, kid?"

Danny took another puff of his cigar and held his breath for a few seconds longer than the last time. Upon release of the warm smoke, he continued. "It's what comes next that's bothering me."

"That's it? Come on, kid. Spit it out," Jayden said, clearly growing impatient knowing that his nephew hadn't even begun to scratch the surface.

After I join, and the official ceremony… I will be sent to a parish in need, to begin my life of service to the people of God." Danny slumped back into his chair again. "I'm no longer certain this is what I want. I've suddenly began having so many other thoughts. Thoughts about falling in love, of romance, of having a family of my own consisting of many children, God willing.

Everything that I obviously cannot have if I enter the priesthood." Feeling exhausted, having bared his soul, Danny clasped his hands together and held them to his lips. "What do you think I should do, Uncle Jayden?"

"I can't answer that question for you, Danny. No one can. Only you can decide what's right for you. And with God's help, I'm certain that in time you will come to the right conclusion."

"Maybe, but I feel like it would be so *wrong* for me to attend the seminary in four short weeks if I'm already beginning to have doubts. And after Bishop Ricci has been so fantastic and accepting of me. The thought of wasting his time...I can't do that." Tears began to form in the corner of his eyes again, but this time he didn't try to conceal them from his uncle and allowed them to flow freely.

"You're right, Danny," Jayden said, making neither gesture nor comment about his nephew's tears. "It would be wrong."

Danny nodded; he knew what his uncle was saying was right.

"This is what I think you should do," Jayden continued. "Cancel your flight to Rome in the morning and come to Camp Vision and work for me this summer. I have plenty of odd jobs that need to be done around the place that someone with your carpentry skills could easily handle; painting, building a new deck off the back of the main dining hall, putting up some shelves in the library. Things like that. I'll set you up in a small cabin of your own so you can think, privately, when you're not busy working. And I will expect you to work every day, except on weekends. I would think that after spending two months in the countryside doing an honest day's work, you will have made up your mind regarding what's best for *you*. What do you say? You game?"

Danny stood up from the ornate chair and walked to the window. He opened the curtains and the full moon stared back at him. He dropped his head, "I'm so sorry…"

"Danny, don't be sorry. You have nothing to apologize to me. If you do not want to…"

"I wasn't speaking to you," Danny interrupted. *To God.* Jayden understood, and fell silent.

After a few moments of inner prayer, Danny turned away from the window and dropped the curtains. "I will work at your camp this summer. When should I be there?"

"Day after tomorrow, the 23rd. 7:00 a.m. sharp."

"Thanks. I won't be late."

CHAPTER 30

GRACE
SUNDAY, SEPTEMBER 2, 2018

The next morning, Cori was up early and downstairs preparing breakfast when Grace woke. She had tossed and turned all evening. Dreaming. Waking. Crying. Falling back to sleep just to repeat the same. Similar to the night before, she glanced at the clock on the wall: 5:14.

Grace considered rolling over and trying to fall back to sleep again, but the aroma of fresh coffee and bacon was too inviting. She sat up, stretched her arms above her head before getting up, throwing on a short, pale blue cotton robe, and walking into the bathroom. She splashed some cool water on her face and looked into the mirror. For the first time, she felt like she didn't know the woman staring back at her. *Father Pepitone?* It was still so very strange.

Grace brushed her teeth, remembering Easter Sunday 1975; the first Sunday her mother refused to attend Mass with the family. Understanding why now, thanks to Cori, she remembered something else she had forgotten. The following Sunday was the day that Father Pepitone introduced himself to her before Mass began. Her dad, she remembered, had left her alone in the pew for only a few minutes while he stepped outside. Jack and Matthew had not attended church that day, either, which she now considered strange.

While she had waited for her father to return, Father Pepitone had come and sat down beside her. She remembered liking him immediately. His eyes were kind and brown, like hers, and his smile was cheerful and very welcoming. He'd even smelled familiar to her, like cedar and bark.

"Irish Spring," Grace whispered, as she stepped into the shower. The same soap her mother always used.

"Hello, Grace," he said. "My name is Father Daniel Pepitone." He cupped her tiny hand between his larger, warmer ones and pressed a little wooden carving into her palm. "I'd like you to have this."

Grace opened her hand and examined the little item. "What is it?"

"It's a pelican. I carved it before you were even born. Do you like it?"

"Yeah, it's neat." She turned the pelican over a few times and examined it closely. "My dad teaches me about birds all the time, but I've never seen a pelican before."

"No, I don't suppose you would. Not around here, anyway. But it's a very special bird and I'd like you to have it. Will you keep it somewhere special to remind you of me?"

"Yeah, sure. I'll put it inside my dresser with my hair ribbons. Thanks."

"You're welcome." He stood up, put the palm of one hand on top of her head and made the sign of the cross over her with the other. "May God always be with you, Grace."

"And with you, Father," she said.

He chuckled and winked at her before walking away.

After her shower, Grace tried to remember more, and soon she was thinking about the week before that Easter. When she, Mom, and Dad had returned home from church that day, she was told to go outside. "Mom's not feeling well," Dad said. "Go play on the swing for a little while."

Excited that he hadn't mentioned anything about changing out of her new dress, her five-year-old self ran out the backdoor and into the yard. It was very warm and she amused herself for nearly an hour, watching her skirt fly up into the air when she swung over and over, higher and higher, from the single swing hanging from a limb of their maple tree. She played like this until she heard Matthew calling her name. "Grace, come on in. It's time for lunch."

Grace jumped from the swing and landed in the dirt below, staining her dress. Worried, she tried to brush off the dirt as best she could before she went inside the house, but she knew she hadn't done a very good job. Once inside, she was surprised when no one seemed to notice it—even though her dress was noticeably dirty and very wrinkled. "I'm going to go change," she said quickly, and ran upstairs.

At the top of the steps, she began tip-toeing past her parent's bedroom. The door was slightly ajar and Grace could see her mother lying on the bed from where she stood. Her father sat at the foot of the bed, staring out the window or something. Grace stopped in front of their door and watched them for a few seconds, before she felt it was safe to continue on to her bedroom, undetected.

After changing into her play clothes, she rolled the soiled, pink dress into a ball and shoved it under the mattress of her bed where she was certain no one would ever find it.

Jack and Matthew relaxed in the family canoe on the lake, appreciating a little early morning fishing together--one of their favorite pastimes.

"How much do you think Cori will tell Grace?" Jack asked, casting his line.

"Beats me. Why?"

Jack shrugged his shoulders. "I don't know, I just don't feel like talking with her about it. Ya know?"

"Yeah, I know."

As they continued casting, reeling in, and catching a fish or two, Matthew's mind returned to the same day Grace's had earlier, Palm Sunday 1975.

Shea and Audrey sat at the kitchen table discussing the day's events. Unbeknownst to them, Jack and Matthew sat on the back stoop of the house drinking a few beers, listening intently.

"Can we talk about this now?" Shea asked, his voice hushed. The brothers couldn't tell if their mother had agreed to talk or not, but the conversation continued. "How long have you known he was a priest?"

"I just found out today," she said.

"He wasn't a priest when you fucked him?" His voice was cutting and the boys recoiled.

"What did he just say?" Matthew whispered.

Jack put a finger to his lips. "Shhhh."

"I told you already. No! When I met him at camp, he told me he was simply a former college student and a carpenter."

Jack and Matthew stared at each other. "Camp?" Matthew whispered and again Jack signaled for him to be quiet.

"What's he doing here now?" Shea asked.

"I have no idea, Shea."

"Are you sure about that?!" He was angry now; the boys could tell. "How did he know to come here? To our church!"

Jack and Matthew heard a chair screech across the linoleum floor, followed by the sound of their mother walking away from the room. "Stop it!" She yelled. "You're hurting me!"

"You're not going anywhere, Audrey! Sit back down," Shea insisted. "I want to know how he ended up in Cincinnatus. Is he here to see Grace?"

"No!" She cried. "He doesn't even know she exists. I never told him I was pregnant."

"Are you sure?"

"Shea, if you keep asking me every question twice, I'm leaving."

"No, you're not!" The brothers could hear scuffling along the floor.

"Put me down!"

"Sure!" Shea said. Something toppled over and crashed to the floor, followed by the sickening sound of skin meeting skin. *Smack!*

"He hit her!" Matthew yelled. "I'm going in."

Jack put Matthew in a chokehold to keep him from rushing into the house after their father. "Shut up." He covered his mouth with his free hand. "They'll hear us."

"Now tell me again how it is that he doesn't know about Grace?" Shea demanded.

Audrey was crying now. "I never told him! He has no idea he's her father!"

Both boys sat leaning against the back door with their mouths hung open and their eyes wide. "What did she just say?" Matthew whispered.

Jack shook his head. "Unbelievable."

Shea spoke again. "There's no chance he's here to try and take her away?"

"No," Audrey said. "I honestly think it's all a giant coincidence that he ended up here."

"As a priest?"

Audrey put her head down on the table. When she finally spoke, it was difficult for the brothers to hear her. "I knew he had a very strong faith in God, but I had no idea he intended to become a priest. It explains everything."

"What's that supposed to mean?"

"I've told you everything I know, Shea. I'm going to bed now." The boys could hear her footsteps on the steps as she got up and left.

Shea sat quietly for a few seconds longer before standing. The boys could hear his footsteps, too, but were shocked when he suddenly pulled open the back door. They, along with several spent beer cans, fell onto the kitchen floor. "Get up and come inside, you two. We need to talk."

The boys sat across from their father at the kitchen table, their arms folded across their chests, their hearts beating madly. A bottle of Jack Daniels and single shot glass rested on the table next to Shea. It was 11:45 p.m.

"It's been quite a day," Shea began, pouring himself a shot. "Care to join me in a drink, boys?"

239

"Yes," Matthew said, immediately. Jack nodded yes as well.

Shea poured another shot and passed it to Matthew first who downed it in one gulp and then handed the empty glass back to his father. Jack followed suit. He took a careful sip first, and then swallowed the rest. When Jack was finished, Shea poured a second shot for himself and leaned back in his chair. "I guess you both heard your mother and I arguing."

They both nodded. "Grace isn't your daughter?" Matthew asked.

"Biologically, no, but in every other sense, yes. Very much so, in fact. I love that kid like crazy. I think you both know this."

"Yes," Jack said. "We know, Dad."

"Good. Let's see to it that that never changes. In addition, I do not want her to ever know anything about this. Do you both understand me?"

"Yes," they both said, in unison.

"I need you to both promise me, you'll never tell her about any of this. She's an innocent little girl. She doesn't need to know the ugly truth."

"I promise, I will never tell her," Matthew said.

"Me, too. I promise, Dad," Jack said.

"Alright, good." He cleared his throat. "What else did you hear?"

Jack turned his head and faced Matthew whose gaze remained fixed on Shea. "We heard everything," Matthew said.

"Then you also understand that Father Pepitone is Grace's biological father?"

"Yes."

"How did that happen?" Matthew asked.

"Normally, I wouldn't answer that question, Matthew, but this is an extraordinary situation. I know you both remember the summer Mom spent at that summer camp for blind children, correct?"

Again, Matthew and Jack nodded.

Shea let out a deep sigh before he continued. "Apparently, while there, your mother met a young man by the name of Danny Pepitone, and…" He choked back tears and turned his head away from his sons. "And they, well, you know."

"Yes, we understand. You don't need to tell us anymore, Dad. We get it," Jack said.

"So how is it he's our priest now?" Matthew asked.

Shea shook his head. "That's just it, we don't exactly know. According to your mother, he was simply a carpenter when she met him. Apparently, he later took the oath and here he is, our new priest."

"Unbelievable," Matthew said in disgust. "And now we're expected to sit in church every Sunday and try to forget that he's Grace's fucking father?"

Shea stared directly into Matthew's cold eyes. "I'm Grace's father. Don't you dare forget it."

"Yes, sir," Matthew said. "I'm sorry."

Shea downed his second shot and leaned back in his chair again. "I understand your concern about going to church, but we are a faithful Catholic family. For now, we continue to attend church every week despite the current priest situation. Understood?"

"Yes, sir," Jack said.

Matthew folded his arms across his chest. "I'm not sure I can do that, Dad. I'm afraid I might try to kill the guy."

Shea chuckled and shook his head again. "I admire your spunk, Matthew, but nobody is going to kill anyone. We continue to go to church as a family on Sunday mornings. Meanwhile, I intend to speak to Bishop Ricci about our situation. Perhaps Father Pepitone can be transferred elsewhere."

"I didn't tell you and Mom this yet," Jack said. "But I've been invited to attend Easter services next Sunday with my old friend Chris O'Donnell. You both remember him, right?"

Shea thought for a moment. "Yeah, wasn't he the kid whose family moved to Syracuse when you were both in junior high school?"

"Yeah, that's him. We ended up running into each other on the bus home yesterday. He was coming back from Vietnam, too. Army. Anyway, he invited me and Matthew, if he'd like, to join him and his family for Easter dinner and attend Mass with them in Syracuse. I was going to talk to everyone about it earlier today, but I can call him in the morning to cancel."

"No. Go ahead and go, both of you. That may be best. Give you both a little time to think about everything before returning to our church."

"Okay," Jack said. "We'll both go."

"Care for another shot before heading to bed, boys?"

"Yeah," Matthew said.

"I'll pass," Jack said. "Are we finished here?"

"Yeah, we're finished. Just don't forget your promise to me, Jack."

Jack stood up and pushed his chair back under the table. "I won't, Dad. I promise. I'm going to hit the sack."

"Goodnight," Shea said. "See you in the morning."

"Goodnight."

After Jack walked upstairs, Shea grabbed another glass from the cupboard and poured himself and Matthew another round. "To Grace," he said, lifting his shot glass and clinking it against Matthew's.

"To Grace," Matthew said, as he downed his shot with his father, swallowing his emotions. "You going to bed now too, Dad?"

Shea stood up and returned the bottle to the cabinet above the refrigerator. "Yeah, you?"

"I think I'm going to stretch out on the couch for the night, if that's okay."

"Suit yourself, goodnight."

"Goodnight."

It was 2:00 a.m. when Audrey woke and quickly got dressed in the bathroom, away from Shea's keen ears. She hadn't exactly planned it, but she couldn't rest any longer knowing that Danny slept only a few short blocks away. She couldn't wait until the light of day, she needed to see him now. Besides, it would be impossible to visit him once Shea was awake. If she was going to do it, now was her only chance.

Quietly she crept downstairs, barefoot, being careful to avoid the steps she knew would creak. Without a sound, she managed to slip into a pair of slippers at the bottom of the steps and cross the living room into the kitchen. Very slowly, she turned the knob of the back door and pushed it open, making her exit from the house undetected.

Or so she thought.

Once she reached the church, Audrey snuck around to the back where the rectory was located, and began throwing pebbles at an open window above her head. The back door opened a few seconds later and Father Pepitone step from the shadows and into the night.

"Who's there?"

"It's me, Danny. Audrey," she whispered. "I must speak to you. Please let me in."

He opened the back door a little wider and allowed her to step inside, closing the door behind them.

"What are you doing here, Audrey? It's the middle of the night."

"I'm aware of that. But what are *you* doing here? Since when have you been a priest?"

Danny walked to his desk and leaned up against it while he spoke. "I was ordained in Buffalo a few weeks ago. I had no idea you lived here. I intend to speak to Bishop Ricci in the morning to discuss a transfer. Don't worry, I'll probably be gone in a month."

She began to tear up. "I'm not certain I want you to leave. I still love..."

"Audrey, please, don't say things you will surely regret."

"I can't help it, I love you. I always have." Her tears were flowing fully now. "More than I have ever loved Shea. That's never changed."

Danny stepped towards her and gently wiped away her tears with the back of his calloused hand. Its familiar roughness flooded Audrey's mind with more memories and she began to cry harder. She had lost so much. He stood only a foot away from her now, gazing at her with his warm, tender eyes. To her surprise, he reached for her and began running his hand through her hair, gently, as if he couldn't quite believe she wasn't part of a forgotten dream. Then he kissed her. She wanted to keep kissing him, passionately, but he broke their brief embrace.

"Please, Danny, not again. Don't leave me," she begged. "My life isn't worth living without you."

Danny's mouth suddenly painted a soft, forgiving smile; a priestly smile, as he looked down at her. "Don't talk like that, Audrey. Every life is worth living, especially yours. Besides, you must know this can never happen between us again. It never should have happened in the first place." He returned to his desk.

All of her defenses were gone and she felt weak. Once again, she had felt his touch, tasted his flesh, and imagined his firm torso as she had once known it—above her, making love to her. Audrey began to shake, mourning the time she would never have back again, crying so hard, trying to release the tension of the long, five years since she'd seen him last. Completely broken, she slumped into one of the two chairs in front of his desk and grabbed a few tissues.

"I wish you nothing but happiness. I hope you know this, Audrey."

She felt her heart leap into her mouth as she began to speak. "I need to tell you something I've kept from you for far too long."

"Alright," he said, still leaning against his desk. "Go ahead. You can tell me anything."

Seeing that priestly look on his face, she got right to the point, wanting to hurt him as much as the smug look across his face hurt her now. "When I left Camp Vision, I was carrying your child, Danny."

He crinkled his forehead and stood up. "What?"

"You heard me. I was pregnant… with your child."

He bent over her. "You didn't…"

245

She cut him at the quick. "What, have an abortion? You're not the only one here who's Catholic!"

He stared back at her; his mouth open and his face registering total shock and disbelief. For once, he clearly couldn't think of a thing to say. His typical swagger gone, Danny retreated to behind his desk. "Are you sure the child is mine?"

"Yes, I'm sure. I've known since the day she was born. She has your eyes, the shape of your face, your coloring. Everything about her is you."

"A girl?"

Audrey wiped her face with a tissue. "Yes. She's five years old now."

"What's her name?

"Grace Ajei McKenzie. She was born on the first of April 1970, about seven and a half months after I left camp."

He smiled, and she knew he was thinking about Ajei Scarsi. "I would like to see her."

Audrey began to laugh. "You can't. My husband loves Grace very much and would never allow it. I'm very sorry."

Danny dropped his head. "You should have told me this years ago." His voice was nothing more than a whisper.

Matthew stretched his neck as far as he could to try and better when a hand slammed over his mouth and pulled him away from the window.

"Shhhh," Shea whispered, turning him around to face him. "Don't say a word." He released his hand from around Matthew's mouth once he saw the recognition in his son's eyes.

"What are you doing here, Dad?"

"I think you know." His voice was low and firm. "I will handle this. Go home. Get into your bed. I will bring your mother home. Do you understand me, Matthew? Go home. Now."

Matthew nodded. "You won't hurt her, right?"

Shea's eyes were narrowed to slits, and he looked angrier than Matthew had ever seen him before. "I'm not going to answer that question, Matthew. You must know me better than that."

"I'm sorry, Dad." Matthew whispered, walking in the direction of home.

"I'm going to kill you!" A voice screamed, and Audrey leapt out of Danny's embrace as Shea lunged forward. *How did he know I was here?*

"Shea, don't!" Audrey screamed.

Shea released his [fury on Danny; knocking him to the ground with one solid punch, striking a porcelain vase from the desk which crashed to the floor and broke into several pieces.

Danny quickly jumped to his feet and began trying to defend himself. Shea punched at him again, but this time Danny ducked, leaped forward, and tackled Shea to the floor. "Shea, stop! You have nothing to fear from me. I'm a priest."

Shea struggled beneath him and caught a glimpse of his face. His familiar smile, like Grace's, enraged him, and he exploded once more, breaking Danny's hold on him. He rolled away and stood up again. "I'm going to knock that fucking smile off of your face, you piece of shit!"

Shea lunged at Danny and clocked him square in his face and then in his gut, harder this time. Something cracked and Audrey screamed. Danny's lip was bleeding.

She bent over and hugged his midsection, blocking Shea. "Stop! You're going to kill him!"

"I intend to kill him, if it's the last thing I ever do!" Shea screamed, just as Bishop Ricci and Deacon Jenkins entered the room.

"What in God's name is happening here!"

Shea is panting, crouched; ready to keep fighting. Danny is moaning on the floor. The Bishop pulls Audrey off him and helps him onto his bed. Shea rose to his feet, but the Deacon held his arms up in front of him, stopping him from taking another step closer to any of them.

"Do I need to summon the police?" Bishop Ricci asked.

"No," Shea said, walking towards the door. "I'm finished with this guy. Audrey, let's go."

"I wasn't speaking to you." The Bishop turned his attention back to Danny. "Daniel, shall I call the police?"

Danny held his hand over his split lip, trying to stop the bleeding. Audrey handed him some of her tissues. "No. It's all been a big misunderstanding. No need to contact the police."

"You're sure?"

Danny nodded.

"Alright then, if that's your wish." The Bishop turned to Shea and Audrey. "Mr. and Mrs. McKenzie, you need to go home, right now."

Audrey looked at Danny one last time, longing clear in her eyes, before she turned towards the door, fresh tears dripping down her face. Once she reached the door, she didn't look back, neither at Danny nor Shea. Without a word, she entered the darkness and slowly began walking back home, away from Danny once again, for the rest of her life.

Shea followed behind her, head down, not saying a word.

Matthew was upstairs, shaking his brother in his bed. "Jack, wake up!"

Jack opened his eyes, shielded them with his hand from the bright light seeping in from the hallway. "What time is it?"

Matthew was trembling. "I don't know. Early. We need to talk."

Jack sat up. "What's happened?"

"You're not going to believe this shit... I think Dad may have gotten into a fight with Father Pepitone, probably beat the crap out of him, too."

"What! Where?"

"Inside the rectory. Mom snuck down there, and I followed her. Dad followed me, and told me to go home. When I left, I'm sure he was going to kill the guy."

"Are they still there?"

"I guess, but they'll probably be home any second." Making his word trues, they heard the sound of back door opening downstairs.

"Quick," Jack said. "Get into your bed and keep your mouth shut. We'll discuss this is the morning."

Shaken, Matthew crawled into the bed next to Jack's and fell asleep. He had heard enough for one night, perhaps a lifetime.

CHAPTER 31

GRACE
SUNDAY, SEPTEMBER 2, 2018

After breakfast, Grace and Cori decided to take Bailey for a walk down to Lincoln Park again. It was Sunday and Grace was scheduled to leave for Philadelphia the next day. She had set out to learn the truth about her biological father and she had, but before leaving town, she wanted to hear the rest of Cori's story regarding Danny Pepitone.

As the women stepped outside, the day was blustery and cold. They wore thick, wool sweaters and scarves, but still Grace shivered in the chill. Fallen leaves, strewn across the city sidewalk, crunched beneath their feet as they walked. The many front porches they passed were decorated with cornstalks, pumpkins, and a cornucopia of brightly-colored mums.

"I really do love fall," Grace said, remembering Matthew's view of the season. "It reminds me of number two pencils and school buses." She smiled. "It truly is beautiful here. I miss it sometimes."

"Maybe you'll move back one day. You never can be too sure about these things."

"Maybe," she shrugged. She asked Cori yet again to finish her tale, but the older woman merely smiled and asked that perhaps she could after they'd tired out the dog, and had a moment to sit in the park.

Grace reluctantly agreed. *One thing about old people,* she sighed to herself, *is that they're never in a hurry!*

Twenty minutes later, they sat on a park bench with Bailey resting on the grass near their feet, panting. Remembering her promise, Cori began telling Grace the rest of what she knew about Danny, Audrey, and Shea.

"It was Palm Sunday 1975 when Father Daniel Pepitone arrived in Cincinnatus at your church."

Grace nodded. "Yes, that's right."

"Well, later that night, your mother and father got into a heated argument. About Danny, naturally. Your mother told me all about it a few weeks later. Apparently, as they argued, your brothers were sitting on the stoop outside the kitchen door, listening."

"Yikes."

"Exactly. They overheard everything. Including the fact that you were Father Pepitone's daughter and that your mother had met him at Camp Vision. Shea was suspicious of his motivation for coming to Cincinnatus, your mother said. She did her best to convince him that it was nothing more than a coincidence because she had never divulged to Danny where you all lived. I believed her, but I'm not sure whether or not Shea did."

Grace wrinkled her forehead. "He was a priest at Camp Vision?"

"No, of course not. It wasn't until a few years later, after meeting your mother, that he became a priest."

Grace sighed. "That Palm Sunday must have been terrible for everyone."

"It was, and it got worse later that evening."

Grace closed her eyes and leaned back onto the bench. "Go on."

Cori told Grace of the fight in the rectory, and Grace listened in horror. "The next day," the older woman continued, "your Dad drove your Mom to Cortland

Hospital, where she was admitted to the psyche ward for a few days. I visited her there on the second day. She looked so weak, so unlike herself when I entered her room. I'll never forget it. She sat in a chair, all alone, staring at the white wall in front of her. I approached her slowly, and bent down on my knees to face her.

"She turned her head to face me, but I think it took her a few seconds to register who I was. 'I felt myself break,' she finally said, with no emotion. 'Like that vase falling off the desk and crashing to the floor, the one Shea knocked off of Danny's desk in the rectory. I felt myself shatter into a million pieces.' I pulled another chair next to hers and held her hand as she continued. 'The broken pieces of the vase lay on the floor, glittering in the lamp light on the desk. I kept glancing down at the beautiful, shattered pieces while the men continued to fight. So beautiful...' A single tear rolled down her cheek. 'Who knew breaking apart could look so wonderful, Cori. I knew there was no chance of putting it back together. I wasn't even willing to try. That's when I realized that I was like the vase. Broken.' She turned and faced the blank wall again. 'I'm done,' she whispered. 'I've reached the limit of what my heart can bear. I'm done trying to go on without him.'"

Grace was sobbing silently, and Cori put an arm around her shoulder. "Your mother loved Danny, Grace. It's a tragic shame that everything turned out the way it did. I hope you can forgive her for everything."

"I already have," Grace whispered, pulling a tissue from her bag.

"Eventually," Cori continued, "your mother recovered and was well enough to return home. But she was never the same after that. It was about two weeks later when Danny turned up missing."

"Missing? What do you mean?"

"To this day, no one knows for sure whatever happened to him."

"I don't understand."

Cori cleared her throat. "This part of the story, the last bit of information I have to share with you, is probably the main reason your brothers didn't want you to ever know anything about this, Grace. Are you certain you want to hear it?"

"Yes, of course I do. I have to know everything."

"Alright. Like I said, it was two, maybe three weeks after your mother returned home from the hospital that Father Pepitone, Danny, went missing. The last time anyone remembered seeing him was on the last Saturday in April that same year. According to the Deacon at your church, Father Pepitone left early that morning to take a walk along the river that ran through town."

"The Otselic River. I know it well," Grace said.

"Yes, that's it. A few people in town remembered seeing him, and he waved to them as he crossed the street to the river's edge. But the last person to see him alive was Shea, Grace. According to him, he was fly fishing in the river about three miles outside of town when Danny happened upon him. He told the investigators that they recognized each other immediately, but instead of walking to where your dad was fishing, Danny turned west and began walking along Route 26, towards Taylor Valley. By Monday, the local police couldn't find any trace of him, other than a piece of a leather camera strap they found along the bank of the river where your father was fishing. Deacon Jenkins later identified it as

253

belonging to Father Pepitone. From that moment, your father was under suspicion of murder."

"No, it's not possible. Dad couldn't even hurt a fly!" Grace said, naively certain she knew her dad better than anyone.

"I know. Everyone who knew him thought the same thing, but since there were witnesses who overheard him threaten to kill Father Pepitone only weeks before, he became a very viable suspect. Once the state police were called in..."

"The state police?" Grace's mouth dropped open.

"Yes. It was too big an investigation for the local sheriff and his deputies to handle alone. They needed help. Once the state police arrived, the town became split. Some people thought Shea had snapped and killed Father Pepitone, while others, myself included, believed in his innocence. Someone else must have been responsible for Danny's disappearance."

"Mom must have known that Dad was innocent."

Cori looked away. "No, Grace, she didn't think he was innocent. As a matter of fact, I'll never forget the fear in her eyes when she told me about the night Shea attacked Danny in the rectory."

"No! I won't believe it! What about my brothers? What do they think?"

"I don't know, Grace. I never asked them."

The wind picked up again and blew Grace's hair in front of her face. She brushed it back in frustration. "Was there a trial? Why don't I remember any of this?!"

"No trial. Since a body was never discovered, there wasn't sufficient evidence to charge anyone with a crime, including Shea. Eventually, people either let it go or moved away. By the time you were a teenager and your mother developed Alzheimer's, most everyone in town had forgotten all about it."

The wind began to blow harder. Leaves aflame with color swirled violently around their faces. Bailey huffed. "We better get going. Looks like another storm is coming," Cori said, looking east.

Grace stood but didn't respond, still thinking about her father murdering Danny. *No way!*

Once they arrived at Cori's door, the rain began to fall and they ducked inside the house as quickly as they could. "That was close," Cori said as she closed the door behind them. "Would you like another cup of coffee?"

"What?"

"Coffee. Would you like another cup?"

"Oh, I'm sorry, I was thinking about... everything."

Cori shook her head. "I can only imagine how you must be feeling. It's a lot to process."

"Yes," Grace said. "Actually, I think I'm going to pack up and get going. I'd really like to get back to the cottage. Maybe see my brothers."

"Of course, whatever you want to do."

"Thank you. For everything." Grace hugged her. "I can't tell you how much I appreciate you telling me the truth. It's why I decided to come home for the weekend."

"I've always felt you deserved to know who your real father was, Grace. Like I said, he was a lovely man."

"I wish I had known him, but I feel like I have, thanks to you."

Cori smiled a motherly smile and cupped Grace 's face between her hands. "Keep safe, kid."

"I will. Thanks again for everything, including the wonderful hospitality."

"It was my pleasure. I hope we can do it again sometime."

"Definitely." Bailey nudged his way between them. "We'll both be back."

Cori laughed. "Excellent, the kitties and I will be here."

Grace finished packing, put her phone in her bag, swung it over her shoulder and grabbed her suitcase.

After saying a heartfelt goodbye to Cori and her four cats, Grace set out towards Cincinnatus. Luckily, the rain had stopped by then, and the sun was trying to break loose from behind a stray cloud. She and Bailey walked outside and got into the car. Cori stood on the porch, waving goodbye.

When Grace drove past Lincoln Park on her way out of the city, she spotted a middle-aged couple walking hand in hand down the sidewalk, smiling and laughing. It had been fourteen months since her divorce and she hadn't even thought about dating again. Watching the couple, she hoped that someday someone could make her laugh like that again, too. Hopefully, he would be someone to share a bottle of wine with on the shore of the lake. Someone to hold at night. Someone to kiss. To love, and to be loved by. *A lot of hopes resting on an unknown man.* She began to laugh. "What do you think, Bailey? Possible?"

Bailey groaned and went to sleep. Once he began snoring, Grace turned west onto Interstate 90 and turned on the radio. She'd be in Cincinnatus soon enough and, hopefully, laughing once more. "One can dream," she whispered.

CHAPTER 32

AUDREY
SUNDAY, MARCH 23, 1975

After Shea and Audrey left the rectory, Bishop Ricci sat across from Danny at his desk while Deacon Jenkins grabbed a bag of frozen peas from the freezer for Father Pepitone's lip. "Here you are, Father," the Deacon said, handing him the frozen vegetables.

"Thanks." Danny held the bag to his lip.

"How're you feeling?" Bishop Ricci asked.

Danny winced as he rubbed his hand over his stomach and chest. "I think he broke a few ribs."

"Do you need me to call a doctor?"

"No, I'll be fine."

"I'll go get some elastic bandages to wrap you with, Father. We have some in the first aid room," Deacon Jenkins said, leaving the room.

After he left, Ricci leaned forward in his chair and rested his elbows on his knees. "So, what exactly happened here tonight?"

Danny glanced up at the ceiling. "It's a long story."

Before he could say anything more, the Deacon returned with the bandages and helped Danny wrap his ribcage. "How's that feel?" the Deacon asked, after he was satisfied with his doctoring.

"Terrible, but thank you," Danny said, laying back down on his bed.

"Deacon Jenkins, thank you for your assistance but that will be all for now. You may return to your bed," Ricci said.

"Thank you, Bishop. Father Pepitone, please do not hesitate to let me know if you need anything else." The Deacon then tipped his head at both of his superiors and left the room.

The Bishop spoke again. "So, what happened here, Daniel? Did you sleep with the McKenzie woman or something?" He was joking, but Danny winced.

He sighed. "Yes, I did."

"You've got to be kidding me, what in the hell were you thinking?"

"No, you misunderstand. It was six years ago, before I took my vows. Today, during Mass, was the first time I've seen her since then."

"What was she doing here tonight?"

Danny shook his head. "I really don't know. She just showed up, saying she needed to talk to me." .

"She came here with her husband?"

"No. He showed up about ten minutes after she arrived. He must have followed her here."

Ricci thought for a few minutes longer. He was a wise man, far too familiar with the many sins of the clergy. Still uncertain what he was dealing with, he pressed the young priest further. "I've known the McKenzie family for many years, probably twenty, and I've never known or heard of Sheamus raising a hand to anyone, much less a priest. There must be more to this story. I need you to tell me everything, Daniel."

Danny sat up a little straighter in his bed. "I understand, but this may come as a shock to you."

Bishop Ricci chuckled. "I've been doing this for thirty-seven years, Daniel. Nothing shocks me anymore."

Forgetting about his injured rib, Danny drew a deep breath. "Oh, that hurt," he said, holding his midsection. After a few seconds, the pressure eased and he regained his composure. "Audrey McKenzie and I met at Camp Vision in Trumansburg in the summer of '69." He began.

"Is there anything else I should know?" The Bishop finally asked after Danny finished explaining everything, from the moment he'd first met Audrey.

Danny paused a while longer, regaining his courage before answering the Bishop's question. "Yes. There's a child."

The Bishop gave him a sideways glance. "A child?"

"Yes. Apparently, Audrey was pregnant when she left camp that summer. Something else she never told me about, until tonight." He rubbed his sore jaw again.

The Bishop thought for a few seconds. "Do you mean the little girl, Grace, is yours?"

Danny shook his head. "Yes. That's what Audrey came here to tell me tonight, among other things."

The Bishop stood up. "I see. This is very unfortunate. And, I suppose, this would explain Shea's rage."

Again, Danny nodded. "Yes. That, and I was comforting Audrey with prayer when he walked into the rectory. He got the wrong idea and started swinging. Guy's got a hell of a right, too. I can tell you that much." He tried to smile, but it hurt too much.

"Alright then, let me rest on this for the night. In the morning, I will call for an episcopal conference with my peers to discuss the best course of action. Until then, do not attempt to contact any member of the McKenzie family, especially the woman. Is that clear, Father Pepitone?"

"Yes, Bishop Ricci, perfectly clear."

Early the next morning, the Bishop called the Cardinal and explained the situation.

"I see." Cardinal Mancini sighed over the line. "Before you call together the others for a conference, let me make a couple of calls myself, first. There are other methods at hand to take care of..." he paused. "...sticky situations like this one."

Bishop Ricci felt sick; he knew about Cardinal Antonio Mancini's shady connections. He liked Danny very much and didn't want him to be harmed in any way. "I'm not sure if that..."

"It's not up to you, Bishop. Do *not* do anything until you hear from me again," The Cardinal snapped, and hung up.

Returning the phone to its cradle, understanding there was nothing more he could do, Bishop Ricci bowed his head and began to pray. Seconds later, the phone began to ring again. Thinking it was the Cardinal calling him back, he lifted the phone to his ear right away. "Cardinal Mancini?"

"No," the caller said. "This is Shea McKenzie. I'd like to talk to you about what happened last night."

Bishop Ricci cleared his throat. "Of course, Sheamus. How are you feeling this morning?"

"Lousy."

"How may I help?"

"You can transfer Father Pepitone to another parish, immediately. That's how." Shea growled.

"I'm already working on it. I was just speaking to Cardinal Mancini about that exact thing moments ago."

"Good. What did he say?"

"He's working on it, Sheamus. But I need you to remain patient. These things don't happen overnight."

"Why not?"

"Sheamus, please. It takes time to find another church in need of a new priest. Meanwhile, Father Pepitone will not cause you or your family any harm. I promise you this."

"He better not, or…"

"Please let me stop you right there before you say something else you may regret. My advice to you is to reflect upon your life, Sheamus. This too shall pass."

Silence.

"Sheamus, are you there?"

"Yes, I was just thinking. I apologize for my behavior, but that guy and Audrey…"

"Yes, I know. He told me everything. Like I said, I will work with the Cardinal to get a transfer in place as soon as possible. Meanwhile, continue to pray. I will be doing the same, you can count on it."

"Thank you, Bishop. I will. Goodbye."

"Goodbye." Ricci hung up the phone and resumed with his prayers, beginning with those for Father Pepitone.

Two weeks later, Cardinal Mancini advised Bishop Ricci that an episcopal conference, a meeting between area bishops to air and discuss important issues, was not needed. Father Pepitone was to be transferred to another parish very soon. However, by the following week, nothing had been communicated regarding the details of this transfer, something that was troubling Bishop Ricci terribly. That morning, Danny had recovered well enough from his injuries and decided to take a hike along the

Otselic River. After being kept in the loop by the Bishop, and hearing the delays, he needed some fresh air.

It was early morning, the last Saturday in April. And although spring had come early to Cincinnatus, it was still very cool outside. As Danny walked along the bank of the river, he was grateful for the sight of wild flowers blossoming already. He spotted some blue phlox, chicken weed, multiflora roses and wild strawberries. All weeks ahead of schedule. He continued north, hoping to find some more uniquely New York state foliage, possibly even some wildlife. He pulled his tiny camera from his vest pocket and kept it at the ready; hanging snugly around his neck by a leather strap.

He wore a pair of faded blue jeans, a black shirt with white, priest's collar and a light-weight, navy blue down vest. On his feet, he wore his favorite pair of L.L. Bean brown duck boats. Had it not been for his recognizable white collar, he would have looked like any other man enjoying the wonders of nature along the river's edge on a pleasant, early spring morning.

As he continued walking, now about three miles outside of town, he stopped dead in his tracks when he suddenly spotted Shea ahead, wading knee deep in the river, fly fishing.

Shae turned his head in Danny's direction, a scowl growing upon his face. He dropped his fishing pole. Each man, with no one else around, stood facing one another as the wind began to howl.

CHAPTER 33

GRACE
SUNDAY, SEPTEMBER 2, 2018

Instead of reconnecting to Interstate 80, Grace drove the back roads connecting Cooperstown to Cincinnatus. She was very familiar with these particular New York state scenic routes, having driven them several times with Shea whenever he got an itch to visit the baseball-hall-of-fame again. He loved Cooperstown. She did, too.

Somewhere north of Norwich, she turned onto Route 23 which she knew dead ended at Cincinnatus, just over the Otselic River. The river was the lifeblood of Cincinnatus, at least for her and her family. They had all fished it, practically every weekend when she was growing up. Even Audrey tagged along and helped them pull trout and smallmouth bass from the river occasionally.

They'd carry home their day's catch in an old, red cooler. Shea would later clean and filet the fish out back under the large maple. Grace could be found close by, watching her father's every skilled move of his knife. Audrey would fry the fresh filets in butter and garlic and serve them on a bed of rice for supper.

As Grace continued to drive, she began wondering why she never went fishing anymore and resolved herself to start again, soon. She remembered her dad's favorite watering hole, too, and began wondering about Father Pepitone's disappearance as Cori had described it. *It couldn't have been Shea who killed him.* She was certain, but wondered what Matthew and Jack thought.

Grace decided to make a stop at the library in Cincinnatus first, to see if she could find any old newspaper articles regarding the priest's disappearance. *They must have something on file,* she thought. *And after that, I'll meet up with my brothers in town, I hope.*

Grace pulled up in front of the library in Cinncinatus at four o'clock.

Seated at a small table in front of a microfilm reader attached to an old school monitor—the small-town library still relied on outdated hardware—Grace began scanning the newspapers beginning in May 1975. Friday's edition, May 3, of *Cortland County Times* contained the first of two articles regarding the missing priest, Daniel Pepitone, along with a nice-sized picture of him:

> CINCINNATUS, New York: The New York State Police Department is seeking the public's assistance in ascertaining the whereabouts of 31-year-old male, Daniel Pepitone, reported missing within the confines of the town of Cincinnatus. It was reported to police that the missing man, a Catholic priest, was last seen leaving his residence (Our Lady of Perpetual Hope, Rectory) located at 2708 Lower Cincinnatus Rd, Cincinnatus, NY on Saturday, April 27, 1975 at approximately 8:15 a.m.

The missing is described as:

> A male of Italian descent, approximately 5'11" tall and 175 lbs.

> He was last seen wearing blue jeans, black shirt, white (priest) collar, navy blue down vest and boots.

Anyone with information in regards to this incident is asked to call the NYSPD's Crime Stoppers Hotline at 1-800-555-TIPS (8477). All calls are strictly confidential.

Grace stared at the picture of Father Pepitone for a while. He appeared exactly as she remembered him; a handsome face, nice smile, looking very kind. His nose, eyes and forehead similar to her own.

Scrolling further, she found the next article regarding his disappearance dated May 7, also appearing in the *Cortland County Times*:

> CINCINNATUS, New York: The New York State Police Department is seeking the public's assistance in ascertaining the whereabouts of 31-year-old male, Daniel Pepitone, reported missing within the confines of the town of Cincinnatus on April 27, 1975. The Catholic priest was last seen leaving his residence (Our Lady of Perpetual Hope, Rectory) located at 2708 Lower Cincinnatus Rd, Cincinnatus,

NY on Saturday, April 27, 1975 at approximately 8:15 a.m.

Four days later, when the state police arrived in Cincinnatus, they entered Father Pepitone's unlocked residence to find a Yankee hat on a cooler box and a barbecue chicken on top of the stove.

The authorities suspect foul play and have been treating the case as a homicide, with persons of interest in Cincinnatus being probed for clues.

A local man has been described as a person of interest. Detectives have also questioned the owner of a roadside ice cream parlor, close in vicinity to the location where a material clue, a piece of a personal item believing to have belonged to Father Pepitone, has been recovered. But with no clear evidence for Father Pepitone's disappearance, the investigation is ongoing in what has become the latest mystery to capture the small town's imagination.

Anyone with information in regards to this incident is asked to call the NYSPD's Crime Stoppers Hotline at 1-800-555-TIPS (8477). All calls are strictly confidential.

Grace reread each article twice. Even taking into consideration what Cori had told her earlier, she still didn't believe that Shea had killed Danny. She wondered about her mother, too, and whether she'd known the truth. With nothing more to read about the incident, she turned off the microfilm reader and returned the films to the desk. She needed to talk to her brothers. Grace called Jack, and he picked up right away.

"Hi, Grace."

"Hi. Are you mad at me?"

"Of course not. Where are you?" His voice crackled down the line.

"In Cincinnatus. Where are you?"

"Home."

"Great. Can I stop by and talk to you for a few minutes?" Grace twisted the phone cord around her finger.

"Sure. Come on up."

Grace was only a few minutes from Jack's home, and she drove through the open iron gates leading to their farmhouse soon after their call.

The private road was lined on both sides with a couple dozen starburst maple trees, burning with color; bright reds and oranges, as Jack had hoped they would the long ago fall day when he and Matthew planted them. The long road dead ended at a semi-circle in front of their farmhouse.

Jack stepped out onto the front porch as she pulled in. "Hi, Grace. Come on in."

Inside, Chelsea greeted her with a warm smile and big hug. "Hi, Grace. It's so nice to see you again. Are you hungry?"

"No, I just ate. But Bailey would probably appreciate a dog biscuit or two and some water."

"Coming right up," Chelsea said. Bailey followed her into the kitchen as she whistled at him.

"Let's have a seat in the parlor," Jack offered.

A wood fire was burning in the fireplace. The lighting in the room was low and soothing. In front of the hearth sat four, light-brown leather recliner chairs, arranged in a circle. In the center of the chairs stood a round, dark oak coffee table, an assortment of magazines resting on top: *Bark, Dogster, Modern Dog,* and *All Creatures.* "Some light reading for Chelsea?" Grace chuckled.

"Yep, same old Chelsea." Jack took a seat in one of the recliners as did Grace. "So how was your visit with Cori?"

"It was good, Jack. She told me everything I needed to know."

Bailey entered the room carrying a dog bone in his mouth, Chelsea behind him. "I'm going to go upstairs and catch up on some reading. Do either of you need anything?"

"No, honey. We're all set, go on ahead," Jack said.

Alone again, Jack crossed his legs and pulled his phone from his sweater pocket. "Would you mind if I gave Matthew a quick call and ask him to join us?"

"No. I guess I need to face him again sooner or later. He can be such an ass sometimes."

Jack smiled. "There's an open bottle of cab franc on the bar. Help yourself."

While Jack called Matthew, Grace took him up on his offer and poured herself a tall glass of wine. While her brothers talked, she stood next to the window and looked out at the back of their property. From where she stood, she could see the mountain ridge bordering Pitcher Springs State Forest, located only a few miles east of their hundred-acre farm.

"Matthew will be here shortly," Jack said. "Pour me a glass, too, would ya?"

Grace pulled a second wine glass down off the shelf above the bar, poured some wine for Jack and returned to her chair. She handed him a glass.

"Thanks." He took a sip. "This is good."

"Yes, it is," she said, "I hope it will help me sleep tonight. I haven't been able to lately. Not since…"

"You got here?"

"No, well, yes, that too. But I was going to say, not since I received my DNA results ten days ago."

"That recently, huh? You move quickly, Grace."

She smiled.

Five minutes later, Bailey let out a quick bark, announcing Matthew's arrival as Chelsea quietly let him in, directing him to the others.

"Great, you have the dog with you." Matthew muttered as he took a seat. "What are you drinking?" He asked, avoiding eye contact with Grace.

"Cab Franc. Help yourself, it's on the bar," Jack said.

After Matthew poured himself a healthy glass of wine, he rejoined his siblings by the fire. "So, what's new?" He asked, completely ignoring the tension in the room. The last time he'd spoken to them…it'd been less than friendly.

Grace had to laugh. "You are a son-of-a-bitch, Matthew, but I love ya."

"I love you, too, sis." He tipped his glass in her direction with a cheeky grin.

She took a deep breath. "Look, let's make this simple for all of us, okay? I'm exhausted and the two of you probably are too."

Jack said, "Okay, sounds good."

She continued. "Cori's the same. I've just come from her house in Albany. Although she stalled as much as she could, she eventually told me about Mom... and Father Pepitone. I know that he was my biological father and that he and Mom met the summer they both worked at Camp Vision, the year before I was born. I also know about Father Pepitone's mysterious disappearance. I just came from the library, as a matter of fact. Looking up old newspaper articles about it. There weren't many."

"No, there weren't. Thank God," Matthew said.

"What I don't know, probably same as the two of you, is whether or not Dad actually had anything to do with his disappearance. What do you guys think?" Grace asked in a rush. Better not to beat around the bush, not anymore.

There was a stunned silence, then Jack spoke first. "I don't really think he had it in him. I never have."

Several agonizing seconds passed. "Matthew?" Grace turned to her other brother, her fingers laced in her lap only to hide her trembling.

Matthew ran his hand through his hair. "I never told anyone this. Not even you, Jack. I'm sure Cori doesn't know this either, Grace. About the night Mom and Dad went down to the rectory after midnight to see Father Pepitone."

"She did," Grace said. "I know that Mom told Father Pepitone that night that I was his daughter, and that Dad beat him up pretty good. Even threatened to kill him."

Jack looked at her. "Dad did beat him up?"

"Yes, you didn't know this, Jack?" She asked, confused.

"No, how could I? I wasn't there."

"I was," Matthew said.

"But Dad found you at the window and told you to..." Jack stopped talking, thinking about it. He knew very well that Matthew rarely ever did what he was asked. "You didn't do it, did you? You didn't go back home."

"No. After I convinced him I had actually left the rectory, I waited until I heard him open the back door and then returned to the window. I heard everything, Mom crying and Dad pounding away on Father Pepitone, and then threatening to kill him. I guess the guy smiled at him or something, based on what Dad said to him; something about wiping the smug smile off of his face. I'll never forget it, guys. I've never heard Dad that angry before. That's when the Bishop and the Deacon walked into the room."

Grace nodded. "That's exactly how Mom explained it to Cori."

"Wow," Jack said. "I never knew any of this. No wonder you've always thought he killed him, Matthew." He drank the rest of his wine.

"You think he actually did, Matthew?" Grace's eyes were wide.

"Yeah, I do. I remember that day Dad went fishing, all alone, too. I remember telling him I'd grab my pole and tag along with him, but he insisted he wanted to go alone. Always struck me as kind of weird, you know? Dad rarely enjoyed fishing alone."

"Yes, but he did sometimes," Jack suggested. "You remember that, don't you, Grace?"

"Sort of, but I didn't spend as much time with Dad fishing like you and Matthew did. Regardless, no way did Dad kill anyone. Not possible."

Jack and Grace both looked at Matthew, who was deep in thought, staring at the fire. "I've held this inside for, what, forty-three years, I guess. Never thought I'd ever tell anyone. Not even Sandy." He looked away from the fire and stared into his siblings' eyes.

"What, Matthew? Tell us, please." Grace's voice was hushed.

"I need another glass of wine." Matthew got up and poured another drink for himself. "You guys need more?"

"Just bring the bottle," Jack sighed.

Returning to his chair, Matthew took another sip of his wine and stretched his neck. "I was still home that day, when Dad returned home from fishing. It was the same day that Father Pepitone was reported missing. I watched Dad from the kitchen window as he drove into the driveway, parked his truck, and went into the garage. I figured he was putting away his gear, like he always did. But twenty minutes later, when he still hadn't come into the house, I got curious about what was taking him so long." Jack and Grace exchanged a dreadful glance, but ignoring them, Matthew continued. "I decided to go check on him." He cleared his throat. "When I went into the garage, he was bent over the old sink, you remember the one, trying to wash blood from his good fishing jacket."

"Blood?" Jack asked.

"He was so drunk," Matthew continued. "Slurring his words and stumbling about. When I asked him where the blood came from, how it happened, he told me it was his. Said he was sitting in the field, next to the river, fileting his catch when he tripped and cut his hand. He tried to convince me that he had lost control of the knife."

"Did he have a cut on his hand?" Jack asked.

"Yeah, he did. But Jack, he never cleaned and fileted his catch at the river." Matthew shook his head. "Never."

"That's right. He never did," Grace realized. "I remember he always cleaned them out back, under the maple tree."

"And he hardly ever drank heavily while fishing, either. Honestly, I think it was the one thing he may have enjoyed more than drinking," Matthew said. "And when I asked him where the fish he had caught were, he told me he got so disgusted with the whole thing that he left them laying in the field. I always thought the whole thing sounded strange, but after the news of Father Pepitone's disappearance came out a few days later, I was convinced Dad had killed him."

"Oh my God," Grace moaned.

The three McKenzie children sat back in their chairs and stared into the fire. Grace uncertain how she should be feeling right now. *How could their kind, gentle man of a father possibly be a murderer?*

"One thing's for sure," Jack finally said, breaking the bitter silence. "This never leaves this room. Agreed?"

"Agreed," Matthew said. "We take this to our graves. For Dad's sake."

"Grace?" Jack asked. "Do you agree?"

"Yes of course, I agree. It never leaves this room, but I, for one, don't think he did it. Not Dad."

"But, Grace, he had blood…"

She stood up, abruptly cutting Matthew off in midsentence. "Listen, I love you Matthew, and I appreciate you sharing what you witnessed, but I won't believe Dad killed Father Pepitone. Can we please just agree to disagree?"

Matthew and Jack exchanged knowing glances. "Sure, sis, not a problem," Matthew said. "Let's just drop it."

Grace turned to leave the room, stopping once to address her brothers one last time. "You know, it's funny, but I think I love you guys more now than I ever have in the past." She shook her head. "And this whole thing has somehow brought me closer to Mom, too."

"Yeah," Jack said. "I think it has brought us all closer. I hated you not knowing the truth. I'm sorry, Grace."

"That's okay. I get it. I'm not sure I would have told you either, had the situation been reversed." She returned her wine glass to the bar. "I think I'm going to drive back to the cottage and close everything up."

"We already did," Jack said.

"Yeah, Sis. We've got you covered," Matthew said. For once, he didn't smile.

"Why don't you stay here tonight?" Jack asked.

Grace turned around and faced her brothers. The dimples in their chins, their beautiful blue eyes, their athletic bodies, their strength, so much like Dad. It felt good to feel love in her heart for them both again. She walked back to where they sat, gave each man a kiss on their cheek and turned once more towards the door. "Thanks, Jack. I think I will stay here for the night. I'm exhausted." She paused at the door. "I really love you guys."

"We love you, too, Grace. Always have," Matthew said.

"Thanks, Matty. Goodnight to you both."

CHAPTER 34

SHEA
MONDAY, DECEMBER 5, 1988

Two days before Audrey's sixty-eighth birthday, Shea sat next to her in her bed, holding her hand in his like he did every day. Although she no longer recognized him, he visited her at the nursing home regularly. Hoping for a miracle, every single day.

Today her breath was labored. She had a plastic tube in her nose, pumping supplemental oxygen into her lungs. Her eyes were closed. She had suffered a heart attack a week before and was slowing dying. Morphine dripped from an IV bag into her veins, giving her some relief from the pain.

"It won't be much longer now," the doctor said. "I'm very sorry."

Shea choked back tears and nodded. "Thank you." The doctor walked quietly from the room, leaving him alone with his grief and his dying wife.

As Shea watched Audrey's chest continue to rise and fall, his mind drifted back to better days. In particular, the first day they met on the ice. He remembered every detail, including what she wore: a red, wool coat and a black scarf with a matching hat and mittens. She had knitted them herself, he later learned. Her ice skates were khaki, as were her silk stockings which stretched across her beautiful legs. He remembered making her smile, and then even laugh as the day wore on.

While sharing a cup of hot cocoa together in the lounge, someone dropped a coin in the jukebox and *Hold Me Thrill Me Kiss Me* began to play, a song they each knew well. "Dance with me, Audrey," he had said. As they danced to the melody, cheek to cheek, he sang the words gently into her ear. She thought she might swoon, she said, and held him closer. That was when he knew she would always be his.

He stood beside her now, forty-six years later, as she lay dying, his hand gently rubbing the top of her head as he sang to her again, gently as a whisper:

"Hold me, hold me
And never let me go until you've told me, told me
What I want to know and then just hold me, hold me
Make me tell you I'm in love with you

Thrill me (thrill me), thrill me (thrill me)
Walk me down the lane where shadows
Will be (will be) will be (will be)
Hiding lovers just the same as we'll be, we'll be
When you make me tell you I love you

Kiss me (kiss me), kiss me (kiss me)
And when you do, I'll know that you
Will miss me (miss me), miss me (miss me)
If we ever say "Adieu", so kiss me, kiss me
Make me..."

Audrey suddenly opened her eyes. "Shea?" She murmured; her voice weak.

"Yes, darling, I'm here." Tears flooded his eyes. "I'm here, always right here." He squeezed her hand, ever so gently.

"I love you, Shea," she said, and then drew her last breath and closed her eyes, forever.

He bent over and cradled her in his arms and cried so loud he didn't recognize the sound of his own voice when he spoke. "Don't leave me, Audrey. Please don't go," he cried. But it was too late. She was already gone.

He lay with her for a very long time, before alerting the staff, reliving over and over again in his mind her dying words, comforting his broken heart: I love you, Shea. I love you, Shea. I love you, Shea...

CHAPTER 35

GRACE
MONDAY, SEPTEMBER 3, 2018

The next morning, Grace rose again very early, as she still couldn't sleep. After grabbing a cup of coffee, one she reheated in the microwave from yesterday's pot, she and Bailey were long gone before anyone else in the house woke. She didn't want to disturb them. Instead, she left a note on the kitchen thanking Jack and Chelsea, with an instruction to thank Matthew for her as well.

Due to two accidents and the never-ending construction occurring around the city of Binghamton, what would typically have been a five-hour drive took seven hours today. When she finally pulled into her driveway at home, feeling exhausted but very relieved to have arrived safely, she stepped out of her car and opened the back door for Bailey.

As happy to be home as she, Bailey rolled around in the grass in their front yard while she walked over to neighbor's house to collect her mail. Even though she was spent, Grace was convinced that she needed to take care of the last detail regarding her trip. She didn't want to be beholding to anyone for a second longer; not even Melissa for simply collecting mail from her doorstop.

After picking up her letters from her neighbor, and an unexpected Fed-Ex package, Grace poured herself a tall glass of wine and sat down on the sofa in her living room. It had been quite a week. Not only had she learned more about her mother and the identify of her biological father, she discovered that her Dad may have committed a mortal crime.

Grace sat in the quiet of her home for a few minutes longer, sipping her favorite dry red and considered the likelihood of Danny still being alive. Although what Matthew told her and Jack seemed unlikely, it was possible that Shea had been telling the truth about cleaning the fish in the field and cutting his hand.

The more she swirled the wine over her tongue, she considered it seemed more than likely that Danny Pepitone was dead, probably murdered by Shea. It seemed fruitless for her to even begin a formal search for him now. Unless, of course, he was alive and she could prove it, thereby erasing all suspicion from everyone's mind about Shea's guilt. That, if nothing else, would be worth her effort. Not to mention the added bonus of possibly meeting Father Pepitone in the flesh once again. As her natural father.

She considered that if Danny were still alive, he wouldn't be more than probably seventy-five or seventy-six. Still young enough to spend some time with her, get to know one another, God willing.

Pulling her laptop from the coffee table, she did a quick Google search for 'DNA testing to determine father of a child.' She clicked on a few sites, many entirely too technical for the late hour, until she finally found one with an explanation that was short, straightforward and easy to understand:

> *In a DNA paternity test, the analysis seeks matching fifteen specific allele number values between the alleged father and child. Because the child must receive one*

STR allele from his father at all locations (or loci), there should be matches for each marker. An alleged father can be excluded as the biological father with as little as one mismatch between the 15 DNA loci profiles. Therefore, all fifteen loci must match in order to determine paternal rights to a child."

"Huh," she said, closing her laptop. Bailey jumped up on the sofa, joining her. He rested his head in her lap. "Fifteen loci." Bailey looked up at her, his head turned slightly to one side. She smiled as he hung his tongue from his mouth a while longer as she continued stroking the top of his head. "Fifteen lovely loci," she whispered, before swallowing her last drop of wine.

Soon, her thoughts lingered on the handsome trooper who had pulled her over for speeding. Amused by her own curiosity, she grabbed her purse off of the floor and began fishing around inside until she located the ticket. As she hoped, it included the trooper's full name. "William Dukakis," she whispered. "Sounds Greek. Sexy." She smiled along with her daydream and then placed the ticket on top of the coffee table so she wouldn't forget to pay it in the morning.

Returning to her previous thoughts, she deciding the whole idea of Danny still being alive was ridiculous. He must be dead. Besides, as she knew, she was entirely too tired to be thinking about such heavy issues any longer. Hopefully, she would be able to finally get some quality sleep tonight. Maybe even forget about the terrible thoughts she had about Shea's possible guilt.

Completely exhausted, she walked into the kitchen to place her wine glass into the dishwasher. Resting on the window sill, above the sink, was the wood carving of the pelican that Father Pepitone had given her all those years ago. She picked it up, blew off a layer of dust, and turned it over. The date carved on the bottom of the bird's feet, 1969, now carried more meaning. Turning away from the sink, she dropped the pelican into the front pocket of her sweater, grabbed the bag of mail and FedEx package and turned off the lights. "Come on, Bailey. Let's go to bed."

Entering her bedroom, she dropped the bag of mail on top of her dresser and crawled into bed with the package. Bailey took his customary spot at the bottom of the bed near her feet. On the end table beside her, she placed the pelican.

Settling in, she tried to imagine what the FedEx package could possibly contain. Suddenly unsure, she turned the otherwise-innocent looking package over a few more times. Gently. The only address listed was of the FedEx location from where it had been shipped: Milan, Italy. She knew no one in Italy.

She thought about it for a while longer, not sure what to think until, finally, she ripped it open.

Carefully, she slid out the small box contained inside onto her lap. It was no larger than a deck of cards and made of supple, purple leather. *Very handsome.* She turned it over a few times, examining the gold etchings on all sides of the box. *Exquisite.* She looked inside the outer envelope, searching for a possible note or letter of explanation from the sender. There was neither.

Grace took a deep breath and popped open the little box. Inside, resting on top of a blanket of black satin, was an extraordinary necklace of very intricate design. She lifted the chain into her hand and watched in fascination as it cascaded—sparkling brightly—approximately ten inches in length from her fingertips. It appeared to be made from 24 karat gold. At the bottom of the necklace, swung a spectacular pendant, also gold. In her astonishment, she examined the pendant closely: a mother pelican feeding her baby chicks with her beak. On the back was the letter 'G', expertly engraved.

"For Grace," she whispered. "Shea never killed anyone," she gasped, covering her mouth with her hand. "I knew it! The old fool was so drunk, he really did cut himself with his own fishing knife!"

Bailey groaned and she smiled, ignoring him while she continued examining her gift. *It's from him, my 15 lovely loci!*

With her heart beginning to split apart, she thought about her two fathers, her wonderful mother and what could have been. Understanding the significance of the timely gift, she lifted the mother pelican and baby chicks to her face and gently caressed the side of her cheek with it, tears now rolling down her face.

Still clutching the precious gift in her hand, she pulled a pillow to her chest and breathed her last words for the night, "He's still alive." Then finally, after going too many nights without, Grace McKenzie Clark surrendered herself not only to sleep, but to her dreams.

Acknowledgements

First, I'd like to thank my son, Michael McCormick, for the gift of a DNA testing kit. This was my first step in learning the truth and, honestly, something I probably never would have bought for myself. Thank you, Michael. I love you.

Next, I'd like to thank my cousin, Jeff Nugent. He was the first person, outside of my immediate family, that I shared my DNA test results with. Jeff then shared a memory of his with me: Shortly after I was born, he asked his father, my uncle, a question. "Dad, isn't it funny, after all those boys (six) that Uncle Hoagy finally had a girl?" His father told him it wasn't funny at all. Rather, it was due to the fact that I wasn't his brother's real child.

Now I had a family member who had known for a very long time that I wasn't Hoagy's biological child. This led me to the next person I'd also like to thank: Bonnie Alvey, my ex sister-is-law and, more importantly, a person I've loved for a very long time. Bonnie, like Jeff, had known since I was a little girl that Dad wasn't my biological father. Something she learned directly from my mother's own lips. Thanks, Bon—especially for telling me that Mom really loved my biological father. This means more to me than you'll ever know.

Lastly, I'd like to thank my nephew, Scott Talbot, and his wonderful wife, Terrie Talbot, for unscrambling all of these random clues for me. Their involvement led me to the truth that had been hidden from me my entire life.

Dad & Me
July 1959

Biological Father
Circa 1940

ABOUT THE AUTHOR

Mary Mack was born in Cortland, New York and is the youngest of thirteen children but her parents' only child. As a young girl she often retreated to her bedroom to get lost between the pages of popular novels. By the age of thirteen she had already read hundreds, including her two favorites *GONE WITH THE WIND* (oh, that Scarlett!) and *PEYTON PLACE (how scandalous)*.

Married to a self-proclaimed historian for twelve charmed years, Mack does her best writing with her two lazy cats, Bella and Biscuit, resting by her side in her home located deep within the Pocono Mountains. Mack prefers writing about strong, independent women with a mission. Besides reading and writing, her favorite pastimes include interior decorating, attending movies and kayaking with her husband, visiting her extended family and friends, and sampling the many wonderful wines produced in the Finger Lakes Wine Region where she grew up.

This is Mack's fourth novel.

https://mm27274.wixsite.com/mysite

41631891R00175

Made in the USA
San Bernardino, CA
04 July 2019